"*More Bugs* is equal parts quirk
and almost absurdist story in th
with the defamiliarizing and stra
burn narrative. The characters
they navigate the uncomfortabl
ploring identity, sexuality, and
everything threatens to collaps
tendencies towards self destruction. Through complex and messy relationships, Reed shows how love can be developed as a form of reliance and survival. Meditative, philosophical, but also gloriously weird yet painfully familiar."

— Ai Jiang, Hugo, Nebula, and Bram Stoker Award nominee and author of *LINGHUN* and *I AM AI*

"After experiencing critical launch failure in New York, Amy returns to her sterile hometown expecting to pick at the husk of her stillborn chrysalis but soon finds herself tangled in knots of unbearably vague longing between her ex, her doppleganger, and a mysterious MILF who only wants to take care of her. *More Bugs* is a well observed and smartly droll novel about stagnation and growth, pleasure and self; about the trembling sensitivity of everyday alienation... and maybe some actual aliens too!"

— Jennifer Giesbrecht, author of *The Monster of Elendhaven*

"When newly single Amy returns to her hometown, she isn't expecting to become a casual babysitter for an attractive widow, nor does she expect to bump into her high school ex and his new girlfriend, but the destinies of all four are more closely interlinked than any of them realise. In *More Bugs*, Reed weaves supernatural elements with past trauma in a way that hurts and heals at the same time, and gives hilarious, poignant voice to all those awkward thoughts we're afraid to speak aloud at parties."

— Lindz McLeod, author of *Sunbathers* and *The Unlikely Pursuit of Mary Bennet*

"*I felt there was no 'here', here* narrates lovable failure Amy, who still has much to say about such herelessness. With a handful of characters, *More Bugs* portrays the alienation and agonies of returning to small town suburbia with a constant cynical love and wit, mixing observational comedy with a sprinkle of science fiction juice. Reed writes each of their cast — 'authentically human' and otherwise — with interiority and style, rendering the gulf between knowing each other a familiar blend of charm, hilarity, and pain."

— Freya Campbell, author of *Winter, The Tower,* and *Good Writers Are Perverts*

"Aliens do unquestionably exist in this world — as revealed a little less than two thirds of the way into the novel — and this revelation does lead to a few shocking, surreal, and even erotic moments of body horror. But *More Bugs* never stops being first and foremost a slow-paced, melancholic, existentialist character study about what it means to feel alienated as a human being, and how important it is that we reach out to one another even though true understanding may remain forever beyond our grasp. Reed leaves many questions unanswered and mysterious, and keeps the focus on the relationships [...] You don't have to be a hero, *More Bugs* suggests, or perhaps to be a persevering monster is its own kind of heroism. Either way, sometimes compassion for the alien is more important than vanquishing it. Sometimes your life feels like a series of dead ends, and that's okay; the only thing for it is to pick yourself back up and try again. There's no shame in that."

— Briar Ripley Page, author of *The False Sister* and *Corrupted Vessels*

"A book-length compulsion to pull off the scab and look underneath. What an expectationfuck of a novel and I say that in the most affectionate sense! I truly loved how this book took you down a familiar route (disillusioned college girl comes back home to the 'burbs to Figure It All Out) and then just turned all of that right on its head — and then turned it back again. This is a relentless probe into the rhythm of metamorphosis and coming-out (AKA revealing to your surroundings and community that they have assumed a default about you that is not true). A delicate examination of the constant dance of calibration and recalibration we are performing with ourselves and those around us, to maintain some tentative equilibrium. *More Bugs* posits the question: need someone be inherently harmful just because they are not at all who or what you assumed them to be?

Combining the charming, brainy neuroticism of an 00s-era Zach

Braff with tits (I think Amy wouldn't get mad at me for that description!); things that go bump in suburbia; extraterrestrial!!!!; aching post–coming-of-age bisexuality; and some truly beautiful, winding prose; Reed contrasts themes of dreary familiarity with the delicious urge to scratch off the wound and expose all the writhing unknowables. Sometimes, comfort and understanding really do come from where you would least expect it... Like great books do, *More Bugs* leaves its hero Amy, and us, with more questions than answers."

— Ryszard Merey of tRaum Books

Published by Knight Errant Press CIC
Falkirk, Scotland
www.knighterrantpress.com

Design and typesetting by Nathaniel Kunitsky

ISBN (paperback): 978-1-916665-03-3
eISBN (ebook): 978-1-916665-04-0

Printed and bound by Ashford Colour Press Ltd, Gosport, Hampshire, PO13 0FW

Knight Errant Press acknowledges support for this title from individually generous contributors, Jamie Graham and Ian W.

MORE BUGS

by Em Reed

Knight Errant Press

2024

Chapter One

Somewhere along the highway, the interchangeable strip malls had, against their very nature, become specific — places I'd been. The jolt of dread this recognition gave me felt strong enough to send an SOS beacon up and out from the top of my head, wishing that, if there was a line that could be drawn from my location to the weightless dome of a UFO, anywhere in the known universe, it would receive my distress signal, draw closer, land on the roof of this bus.

My own vessel status: diverted, possibly lost. No point sending a search party. Two days earlier, my glamorous city girlfriend had, just before I also understood it, determined that the only future our relationship addressed was the future of my ability to afford rent.

That part of my life had abruptly broken away, and without the cash flow to propel me towards a lease of my own, whatever would be the new part couldn't start. It was a post-collegiate failure so typical it could only already feel like a farce; in short, a perfect time for the rubbery, b-movie aliens to arrive. However they came, friendly, unfriendly, or merely annoyed, materialising a crystal spike through my skull for my impertinence, it would be some kind of alternative — instantly changing everything about my life that needed to be changed. It was always *possible,* I often thought to comfort myself, despite it not being probable enough to bother glancing up.

While the bus pulled into my hometown's only station, I avoided searching for familiar faces. The YoutubetoMp3 rip of *Big Black – Atomizer (Full Album)* I'd loaded onto my overstuffed phone at short notice looped and raged to the bitter end of the journey, holding off the finality of getting packed into the family hatchback, as long as I could pretend I was going somewhere else. Still, in the small crowd where people were outnumbered by parked cars, I noticed my mom immediately. Through the darkened glass of the bus windows I averted my eyes, interpreting the glimpse I got of her face, implications splaying out like pain impulses around a pinprick. Her mouth was in a firm line, pulled a bit to the side and sloping downwards, and she was wearing huge sunglasses that completely concealed her eyes and eyebrows.

I knew she hated that my desperate and low-budget return from New York had brought her here, but part of her had to be pleased with the news, too. Weeks ago, during my second-most-recent call home, she had managed to work out of me that 'things were not good' on the employment front with the smug sadism of her instinct being, of course, correct. She would still treat it like something my irresponsibility was inflicting on her, but I could manage some counter-satisfaction in how the bus station made an appropriate stage for my arrival as a scandal and a failure.

Mom had built herself a life where bus stations figured rarely, much less getting on one. The last time she had been here, she'd hitched a ride with a woman from her church group to collect the family car my father left behind when boarding a departing bus, some private conviction demanding an unsanctioned sabbatical. I wondered if, pulling away, he had seen the same view as mine in reverse, then realised, feeling embarrassed, like when a word rhymes in your head but not spoken aloud, that he would have been facing in the opposite direction.

I sank low in the seat, signalling to the other passengers that they could go ahead of me. When there was no one left to file out I stood up, taking off my headphones and shutting off the last rattle of spiky static. I pulled my two gigantic bags down from where they were wedged in the overhead rack, both times riding the top heaviness down to hurl them onto the floor. Outside, my mother was waiting almost exactly opposite where the bus door opened, her arms still folded, her car keys still in one hand. After opening her arms to take me in a perfunctory hug, she popped the trunk and took one bag from me.

"So, that's it with Josie?" she asked.

I tried not to pull a face.

"Yes, I told you."

"You should have let me know sooner, sweetie. I only just had time to put sheets on your bed."

"Sorry. It was pretty sudden." I wrenched open one of the car's side doors and threw my own bag in before walking around to the shotgun seat. She got in the driver's seat and started the car, craning her neck around as she backed out of the parking lot and turned onto the highway.

"Takeaway for next time: you should have a plan besides splitting rent with someone." I made a vague hum of acknowledgment, trying not to sound annoyed, but she still sighed, as if that was as good as talking back to her. She'd performed her emotional duties, plus a nugget of constructive criticism, what more could a daughter want? From her position it was loving care, but it landed on me like a scolding. Pushing back, rather than trying to end the conversation as soon as possible, was a capacity that had, over many years, been rendered futile. I was used to people taking my silence with offence, like I had a choice, paradoxical willfulness over paralysis, when the feeling was the opposite. I knew how to talk, internally my voice overflowed and never shut up. But when it hit resistance, it felt like this: I could have a whole bicycle assembled in my mind, with no idea how to push forward on the pedal.

"It's fine, it's tough out there," my mother said, frowning, after pulling off an exit and passing through a few four way stops. The landscape outside the car window grew more intimate, cul-de-sacs and curving streets leading deeper into suburban developments, boxy houses, no sidewalks. "You don't have to get it perfect on your first try."

"I know," I said.

"The twins finished up their semester but went right into summer classes, so you'll have the house to yourself."

"Great."

At the foot of our driveway she reached up to hit the automatic garage door switch. The incline of the driveway pressed me softly into my seat, a sensation from my childhood sneaking back up on me, before the car lurched to a stop, the garage door rattling shut behind us. My mom grabbed one bag out of the trunk for me, and I hoisted them over either shoulder to carry them inside.

"Are you hungry?"

"I think I'm just going to nap, I'm tired."

The kitchen was tinted bluish by evening light coming in through the back windows. Outside, you could see our backyard, uniformly maintained by some local, industrious teenager, except for a dried out and flattened patch of dirt where dad used to garden that grass refused to grow back over. I glanced at the fridge on my way past. Printer paper photos of the twins showed them advancing in age, taken at some honours award ceremony or research trip;

but the picture of me, held down with a round black magnet, was the same as it had been for years. It had been displayed with pride of place when I came home from college one winter break, a snapshot I had put on Facebook without a thought. In it, I was pulling a goofy wave at a low-resolution webcam, posing with a friend who had been cropped out, wearing a blouse and circle skirt. My hair was long and layered, kicking up at the ends, smoothed under a ruched velvet headband.

In front of the photo now, wearing a leather jacket, men's jeans and boots, it foregrounded the awkwardness of how I must look to my mom. Home had not really changed, for better or worse, so long as this cherished icon of subtle disapproval was still on display.

In the room at the top of the stairs, my old room, the air felt dense and warm from how long it had stood uninhabited, the way direct sunlight eternally beat on it during the afternoon and evening. I threw my bags on the floor, pulled out of my boots and lay on top of the covers in my clothes, regarding myself in the narrow, twin-size coffin of my childhood bed.

Already the series of decisions that brought me here felt like they'd been made in a different universe, under alternate laws of physics. Claustrophobia set in, the old certainty of being isolated, stuck, under constant surveillance as the hegemony of the family car set hard, practical boundaries. In walking distance there was what, an elementary school? A single gas station, the sorry outpost I had worked at through high school. What was the plan? To go back to hauling around leaking, human-sized trash bags, scrubbing toilets, and getting berated by women for putting mustard on their turkey sandwiches, but not enough, while right next to a bin of mustard packets, there? Where could I go, with any dignity, by myself?

I hadn't put up much of a fight when Josie broke up with me, and now I was starting to regret it. Josie lived with roommates for the countercultural liveliness of it even though her parents were 'cool' and had a 'huge place' themselves. The story of how her mom and dad met, described as a *You've Got Mail* situation but for midtown artist spaces, and *she* was the bigger one, actually, was a regular routine at dinners I nodded through without having seen the film. Josie found me appealingly provincial and 'real' when I talked about church camp or fair food, but the shine started to wear off when, months turning into a year, then two, I had failed to spin this into a consistent work portfolio, much less a personal narrative that would snag me a fawning up-and-coming feature.

The particular argument that broke us up hadn't seemed like an emergency; I had been facetiously asserting the month when you died implied more concrete personality traits than the one you were born in, but, in hindsight, I guess it isn't the sort of thing which could be planned so far in advance that it was useful to mine for some universal readymade of self-knowledge. She started getting annoyed, asked if this was some roundabout way to call one of her pals, particularly into predestination, stupid, which was too true by that point to convincingly deny.

She settled on saying, "That's mean," and my response jutted out like a foot kicked during a reflex test: "Oh, poor Josie, I'm mean!" This was maybe unsportsmanlike. What I meant was that her problem, non-unanimous acceptance of her friend's ordering principle of choice, felt tiny and irritating next to my own: all evening I had been running down my remaining contract work, and the search for more consisted of begging favours from her party acquaintances who mostly looked like they were only just holding back from calling me *rumspringa girl*. It began to seem like we were headed for 'a break', a standard relationship juncture, never a good sign, but always an indicator that there were several months left to while away, so the final split was logical and mutual rather than raw. In this case, how calmly I seemed to take this ended up being what pissed her off most. She asked, then insisted, I leave.

The conversation hung in my mind as the splitting point, where I could have been some sort of better, nicer person, someone who would still be tucked away in *my* corner of *our* apartment, but looping back around to the beginning of our relationship, how she'd sometimes looked at me with gut-dropping irritation from the start, was an insight that cut through the Gordian Knot; it was pointless.

The way Josie had frowned at me, telling me I had to go, like I was the one forcing her hand, was the last in a series of ways she had made me feel stressed and cornered, because she was someone who had invested a lot of their self image in being remarkably open and generous. She seemed to get an erotic thrill out of every event where she had to make a big show of introducing me to another group of people who already knew each other. When I mentioned on one of our first dates that I didn't really talk to any of my exes, (mainly to avoid having to describe them, a series of grotesque, self-effacing experiences that made people who hadn't grown up in small towns regard me as slightly dim or some sort of masochist), she immediately saw this as a Goofus-style character flaw to vigorously disavow.

"No way! I'm still friends with all of my exes. I mean,

it's fine because we just talk it out. And it's not like I can burn bridges, right?" She laughed. "If they're not at the next artists' book fair, they'll be at the next gallery opening, or reading group meeting. You know how it is."

I did not, really, know how it was. I could parcel off sections of my life to regard like specimens behind glass a few months later. Moving in with a girlfriend in New York and making my best effort to mix with a big city art crowd would be another episode to seal off. I wasn't the hero, more like whatever mutant freak was defeated on a weekly kid's TV show, never to be seen again, except I had to keep going as a valiant, persevering monster. My life looped into a chain of these embarrassments, indignities and failures — still unclear if they would add up to anything. I had put myself in a situation where quickly ingratiating myself into some order, a workplace or friend group, was key. There was a humiliating and endless to-do list of things I had neglected or screwed up: I should have pushed harder and made myself more memorable when I got some contract work with that one magazine that would have surely led somewhere, I shouldn't have gotten so sulky about how it seemed like everyone who was going to be successful already knew each other and would hold me at a suspicious arm's length anyways, I shouldn't have taken it so personally when people made their disinterest obvious as soon as I had to explain where the college I'd gone to actually was.

Listening to something abrasive enough to turn off the noise of anyone around me while glaring out the bus window had made it easy to push away any tender feelings and contemplate the situation, already receding into the distance, with detachment. The alternative, among the chatter, would have been a bus cry, to let the panic and insecurity — of being unlovable, of having screwed up so badly a person who beamed out nothing but kindness was, apparently, no longer able to tolerate my anxious sullenness, of always coming back to being a burden on my mother, of feeling fundamentally cut off from a place where I had expected to finally feel any sort of agency, but maybe hadn't at all, et cetera — all burble up.

What would happen to me? A long silence.

What *could* happen to me? Not much. That was much more horrible to contemplate.

I dutifully got up, lowered the blinds to dim the room and closed the door as far as it would go, though the latch never properly shut. I pulled the sheets on my bed down and wrapped myself in them, then laid my face on a dusty-smelling throw pillow and planned to let myself cry, quiet enough that from outside the room it would seem like I was napping. I waited, and nothing happened. The room around me was both strange and like an eternal part of myself I had returned to. What brought me closest to tears was how much nicer the mattress was than any I had spent significant time sleeping on over the past five years. When my mom came to check on me, with the same irritating gesture as always, pushing the misaligned door in enough to look at me before half-heartedly knocking, I pretended to be asleep.

I audited myself again, mind and body. As if I had crossed over to a strange type of survival mode, all emotional frivolity stripped, I didn't feel like crying. Had something changed?

♦♦♦

I woke up hungry, but when I dug through my bag to find the chocolate bar I'd left unfinished during the bus ride, a trail of ants was swarming it. Grimacing, I held the wrapper with the very tips of my fingers as I ran downstairs and dropped it into the trash can, which had a finicky, automatic lid. I brushed my hands together over the opening until it whirred shut like a strange, animal mouth, leaving a crawling sensation on my hands. In the city I left half-finished snacks in my bag or on my desk all the time. Even then, I'd never attracted bugs like this. The kitchen was scrupulously gleaming around me. Maybe it wasn't so hard, since my mother had been living mostly alone, but it made me anxious to contemplate the force put in to keep it this clean.

The ants hadn't put me off breakfast. In fact, my stomach felt urgently empty again as soon as the chocolate bar disappeared into the trash. I scanned the cupboards in an overslept stupor, and my desperation for at least coffee knocked loose an early memory of my father. It wasn't one I could trace to a photograph or home video; real, I sensed, even though it felt like a dream I just woke up from. We were outside, an autumn evening, enjoying a cold dark sky above. It was some kind of camping trip, maybe, or a church event. He was drinking from a styrofoam cup. He noticed me looking up at him and handed me the cup.

"Amy, want to try it? Careful, it's strong."

I took the cup, and, sensing the maturity the situation called for, resisted the urge to sink my bumpy, emerging permanent teeth into the squeaky texture of the foam. When I tilted it, the mostly cold liquid at the bottom of the cup hit me all at once. I screwed up my face and shoved the cup back at him.

"You'll like it someday."

It took a decade but he had been correct; I swapped to coffee out of teenage weight anxiety about the free fountain soda at my high school job, and eventually it took a bucket-like travel cup to keep me awake through an average college seminar. Recently, the cups marked the edgy, anxious passing of time. I'd have one in the morning, while sizing up the increasingly arcane and unlikely job applications I had to fill out that day, and another whenever I finished, mentally exhausted but determined to try to wring something out of my waking hours that didn't feel like it vanished into the giant void that lapped threateningly up against the base of financial feasibility, success, existence.

Well, no more of that. I'd fallen in. I could at least have a few days of doing and thinking absolutely fucking nothing.

I kept rooting through jars and boxes next to where the yellow enamel kettle sat on the stove. Assorted tea bags, mostly herbal. My mother somehow managed to propel herself out of bed, early at that, and maybe even go for a jog without any sort of caffeine, another detail to append to the tally of features I clearly hadn't inherited. At the very bottom of a jar I found a handful of packets of instant coffee, crumpled and softened from being rummaged through by guests, examined, and never taken. I took two and emptied them into a large mug. My mother returned to the house through the front door as I flicked open the spout of the kettle and filled it at the sink.

"You just got up?"

"Yeah," I said, fiddling with a stovetop light until it clicked. She tried not to express approval or disapproval at this, and failed. My mom shifted on her feet, the soles of her running shoes squishing against the floor tile, and unhooked a workout monitor from her wrist. She was taking deep, steadying breaths and wearing shorts, a loose t-shirt, and a band holding back her hair.

"I'll take a shower if you're still getting breakfast, then."

"Sounds good."

She went upstairs without any further curiosity on what I planned to do, not yet, and I stared at my phone on the counter in front of me as I waited for the water to boil. When the hollow sound of bubbles collecting inside the kettle broke through the fugue of scrolling further and further down Twitter, I switched the burner off. I had been skimming, seeing if Josie or any of her acquaintances I'd made tenuous impressions on at parties, gallery openings or talks had a sense that I was missing from their lives. Even once it was clear none of these people would ever wonder where I was, I kept going, looking for a sign that they were doing anything interesting, that excited me or made me jealous, still nothing. I locked my phone and poured hot water into the mug, found the spoons that had been moved to a different drawer than I remembered, and stirred until the clumps of instant coffee were mostly liquid.

There would be no gallery openings or book talks here, unless it was the public broadcasting station's annual artisans' fundraising telethon and/or bible study. But people still had parties, even cookouts, and at 11 AM the desire to get myself punitively drunk insisted on itself like the rapid drum machine beat still in my ears from yesterday. I could scale the cliff I knew well, becoming charismatic, laughing, easy (*like swimming, like sex*), and then fall off, going sullen, feeling doomed. Of course I ruined the vibe, but sometimes I treated it as a noble endeavour, being true to my frowning, buzzkill self. It was a fair price to pay for the weird clarity immense, still sadness left me alone with, peeled off from everyone and everything.

My mom turned down a single small cup of wine at Christmas, she went for the white grape juice at communion. I was afraid to see what would happen if I indulged my desperation tactics at home. My hands started to feel cold, so I wrapped them around the mug and looked at the black screen of my phone.

I hadn't used Facebook for a while, but locked away in my old account would be any remaining local contacts I had. I re-downloaded the app, and when it fully loaded, it unnervingly remembered how to log me in. Enough for now. I took an experimental sip of the instant coffee, which was stomach-roiling, only vaguely similar to what it claimed to be, primarily in appearance. I poured it down the sink and rinsed the mug.

While I stood at the sink, my mom came downstairs dressed in one of those stretchy floral blouses and teal capri pants.

"Did you find something to eat?"

"Not yet, I just made coffee." She looked confused so I clarified. "There's some instant packets in one of those jars." Then she frowned, like they weren't meant for me.

"Well, if you want me to take you around to the Target later to get some of your own stuff…" She trailed off.

"Yeah, in a bit." I said. "I'll take a shower now."

I didn't want to resign myself to fully unpacking and only unzipped the part of the suitcase where I had stuffed what bits of my own toiletries were worth saving. I used some of my mom's shampoo and shower gel, and wrapped myself in a fresh, thick towel. Then, back in my bedroom, I dawdled, crouching by the bookcase at the foot of my bed, one of three in the room. I flipped through a book of clothing patterns I had purchased for some reason, and wondered who I was when I had, apparently, briefly considered myself someone who would make her own clothes. I pressed my fingers down certain spines, mass market art books about Dalí and Mucha alongside standoffish modernist tomes that had once held some far off promise of culture when I unearthed them at the used bookstore, and turned out to sometimes be the only great bricks of privacy I had to sink into, experimenting with indulging my own sense of an 'internal life'. My priorities were so different now, or rather, I had been able to dig deeper into what interested me, like a termite. Sometimes I wondered if I would ever chew all the way through, eventually come out the other side with something worth communicating, or if I'd keep tunnelling forever. My clumsy attempts to break out hadn't been warmly received anywhere so far. I heard the door creak open behind me.

"Sometime soon?" My mom asked. I stood up, leaving the book in my hand on the floor.

"I'm getting dressed, I'll be down in five," I said.

The clothes I brought home felt like a costume. If someone recognised me, tried to talk to me, I could maybe pretend to be a completely different person. All black was a bit rugged for Target, but it was also all I wore anymore. Would I have to change the way I dressed, on top of everything?

Downstairs, my mom was already in sunglasses, with a large tote bag over her shoulder. She didn't comment on my clothes. When we got in the car, she dropped the bag onto the centre console.

"How much do you have left in your bank account?" She asked, pulling out of the driveway. I shifted in the passenger seat.

"I dunno, sixty bucks?" The exact amount was forty

seven dollars and twelve cents, I knew because I had looked at the bank app on my phone first thing upon waking up. At the approximate figure, my mom's eyes widened slightly, but she stuck with the same line of argument.

"Okay, I think it sets a good precedent to cover your own food then." She must have sensed my wince. "Not all of it. I'm not going to let you starve, of course."

"Yeah, of course." I said. "I'm just a little stressed out."

"You have nothing to worry about." She said it like she was trying to hypnotise me into believing it.

♦♦♦

I had forgotten how open and flat parking lots were, where wind and sun could pursue you uniquely unfettered. Patches of green lawn in the parking islands with scrawny, leafless trees shooting up from them almost glowed. The light allowed no subtlety, everything cast hard shadows, radiated heat. There was nowhere to hide. This was why mom wore sunglasses everywhere.

She found a parking spot not far from the entrance but with no anchoring landmarks to remember it by. We walked towards the store, politely waiting for all the family vans pulling in and backing out. Inside, she rattled a large shopping cart away from the long line of fellows it was nestled into. I didn't even bother getting a basket. A sweet sterile smell, mostly cleaning products, but also new plastic and cardboard packaging, enveloped us as we stepped through the automatic doors. Carts glided, spaced out and swerving gently on the shiny floor, like wide ocean liners. I went to the grocery aisles while my mother split off to the stationery section, to stock up on envelopes for the next church card drive.

I looked down the aisles until I spotted bags of coffee grounds. My learned intellectual awareness of how capitalism worked, how it only appeared to offer freedom through an abundance of superficial variety, crumbled into disorientation in the face of this basic retail strategy, which put a massive grid of flavours and varieties before me. While I read and re-read the packages of coffee, I heard a high, excited laugh, and turned my attention towards it. At the other end of the aisle a guy with darkish hair wearing a camo-patterned windbreaker and khakis was carrying a shopping basket. It looked heavy, stacked with random boxes and oddly shaped items. I glanced past him, looking for the source of the laugh, which sounded like a woman's. As he lingered in my peripheral, I recognised him. I immediately looked away and grabbed the bag of coffee directly across from me.

He was shopping, with the woman. I tried to watch him out of the corner of my eye still, as I faced straight ahead. He was talking to her about what was on the end cap of the aisle. I looped around to the adjacent aisle, mostly condiments, to see if I could get a look. No, she must have turned into the aisle I just left.

Externally, I tried to appear to shop for groceries as usual. The shelf in front of me had a bounty of mayonnaise subtypes to consider: chipotle mayo sauce (*that was Martin*), reduced fat chipotle mayo sauce (*probably the worst person to run into but also the one I had the most morbid interest in*), Hellman's Mayonnaise, Hellman's Reduced Fat Mayonnaise, Hellman's All-Natural Mayonnaise (*of course, we would just avoid each other*), garlic mayonnaise dip, pesto mayonnaise dip (*if he would even recognise me like this, probably not*).

"It'll be fine. I can pitch in too since I've gotten more

hours at work now, so why don't we make the place less..." The voice paused, she was thinking.

It was a voice that could only be paired to that high, free laugh I'd heard. I turned to sneak a glance down the aisle again, and Martin was standing there, ignoring what she was saying and looking straight at me, the overburdened basket swinging comically at his side. I stared for too long, registering his definite recognition. My changed appearance no longer felt like a disguise. It drew attention to me, as if I had been shopping in a neon green feather boa. Of course, Martin basically looked the same.

"Hey," I said, taking one of the idiotic sauces off the shelf, like I fully intended to buy it. He nodded, maybe smiling, and muttered some sort of friendly acknowledgement. I hadn't considered how, maybe, he worried that if we ever met again I'd be angry. The possibility flashed in my mind like an anime title card: a musical sting, white text on a black background, "Confrontation at Target!"

Needing to look away, for lack of any idea of what else to do, my eyes strayed to the girl now standing next to him, who was looking back at me with startled curiosity. I realised why the laugh had caught my attention. It sounded like my own, but the weird, alienating version of it, when I heard myself slipping into customer service mode or in a recording played through a tinny phone speaker.

The girl Martin was shopping with was a redhead like me, her hair cut into a more relaxed version of the bob I wore in high school; where it puffed out like a mushroom on me, it hung down to delicately brush her shoulders. She'd dyed it a slightly unnatural, glowing orange, but towards the roots it was the same shade as my own. She wore heavy eye liner like I had then too, though it was more competently applied than what I had roughly smudged onto my eyelids, hoping it would somehow make my unhappy, intense gaze look right. She retained my perky high school tits, which, to my chagrin, had conspired to make almost any top 'cleavage baring'. If I more closely studied her other physical features, and referred to any general heuristic of what was possible in reality, I'd have to conclude that she was obviously a different person. I emphasised this to myself; in response to the immediate sense that I was facing some kind of alien impostor or fantastical double. I wanted to be objective, realistic, not paranoid. But I couldn't deny the feeling of having been body-snatched, that Martin had crystallised the way it seemed I could have turned out, maybe, and continued to date it.

It? It felt wrong to have these thoughts about a woman I hadn't even spoken to yet. This sort of unflattering spontaneous dislike (which obviously said more about me than her — what did I even know about her, after all?) was one reason I didn't stay in contact with my exes. The rap sheet scrolled by in my head again, all the things I should have done to avoid coming home, and, by extension, whatever was about to happen.

"I didn't know you were back in town," Martin said. He took a few seconds to formulate a best guess as I tried to construct my own excuse. "Sisters graduating?" It was thoughtful of him to offer an out, even though he didn't produce it enthusiastically.

"I'm just around for a bit." I tried to leave a confident, measured pause, but didn't hold out long before making a panicked leap into the conversational lull. "You know."

"Oh, right. Amy, this is Mollie." Martin said. I must have been staring at her.

"Martin and Mollie," I said. Alliterative names! How could I resist? *Cute, they're destined to be together forever,* I sneered to myself.

When I'd last seen Martin I would have found this funny enough to say out loud. Even before things started to go south with Josie, I'd felt in a funk, like I'd been muting myself around people in general, in a way I had only ever done on phone calls with my mother. I cringed, kept mental logs of every time my voice went pitched up and palliating, a dead giveaway I thought I'd left behind in customer service.

"Anyways, how have you been?" I tried to smile, but my face felt strained. The actual expression it produced was more likely off-putting.

"Normal. Steady job, can't complain." Martin leaned, shifting the shopping basket. "We're getting some odds and ends for the house. My house, I mean. I've had it for a few months, and Mollie moved in recently."

"That's nice," I said. The idea of owning a house was, naturally, completely alien to me.

"How weird," he said. He looked down at my boots and seemed happy for some reason, maybe for the same reason people laughed at frightening or intense experiences.

"Totally weird," I agreed.

My mother spotted us then, surprised but pleased to see me speaking with Martin. Her presence elongated the conversation, and I wondered how Mollie must look, to her. Maybe like the picture she kept on the fridge, even though I no longer looked anything like it. While my mother was 'catching up', my eyes narrowed and my hands started to feel a bit sweaty, clinging to the single bag of coffee and what, on inspection, was a squeeze bottle of 'cheddar bacon mayo dip'. Why did she care what Martin was up to? Was she hoping the rules were that you get re-virgined if you're on mature speaking terms with your high school ex?

Somehow, she had filled her cart, so as we left the store, my mom sorted herself into one of the wider checkout bays. Kindred antisocial spirits still, Martin and I opted for the self-checkout. I chatted with Mollie as he scanned their basket of cosy knickknacks, trying to tamp down any whiff of hostility towards her in my tone and body language. A mantra repeated whenever there was a gap in my thoughts: *I am being insanely friendly. I am attentive to every line.* Mollie worked at a frozen yoghurt place now and all the girls there were totally nice. She moved here, not too long ago, you know? Low cost of living, lots of nature nearby. Sure, that's convincing. I nodded. Whenever she turned away, distracted by something in the store or checking how much of the basket Martin had gotten through, I tried to study her from different angles, comparing them to impressions I could call up of candid photos of myself. The makeup and blunt bangs reshaped her face, but she really fucking looked like me.

"Martin," she said suddenly, when she noticed him fiddling with the card reader.

"What."

"Pay for her stuff! It's only two things."

"Oh, I don't need you to."

"It's fine." She took the two items straight from my hands. "It's faster. Your mom's already done."

"Thanks," I said. Martin folded his arms, trying to figure out how to cancel out of the transaction and make the self-checkout scan another item. "That's really generous of you."

"It's mayonnaise and a bag of coffee," Martin said.

In the parking lot, my mom gave us some space. "I'll pull up with the car," she said, leaving me at the curb, one hand tethering the cart full of plastic bags so it didn't coast away.

"You'll be around for a bit, then?" Mollie asked.

"Yeah," I said.

"We should hang out, or something." She looked expectantly at Martin, who was flicking through messages on his phone.

"Sure," he said. "Is your phone number the same?"

"Uh, no." I took his phone, carefully avoiding touching his hand. It was a larger, heavier model than my own, a real cutting-edge slab of a thing. I had to hold it with one hand and hook my elbow around the cart handle to type in my number with the other, the entire time worrying about dropping it face-down onto the concrete, and then considering what would happen if I did. Martin was taking a risk and he seemed to know it, staying in touch with me simply to defuse an awkward moment at Target. Martin's life, from what I could tell, now consisted of a semi-respectable job, a mortgage, a younger, cuter girlfriend. Permitting someone who could embarrass him into this careful structure was reckless, and I toyed with the idea of making that clear to him, then hit 'save contact'.

"There." I handed the phone back and realised Martin hadn't yet made a move to introduce me, which meant that Mollie probably had some idea of who I was, and, unless Martin had gotten really good at bluffing, this explained why she treated me a bit pitiably.

"Great," she chirped. Martin slid the phone back into his pocket. They both waited with me until my mom pulled up and then made in the direction of Martin's car, indistinguishable among all the others.

"That was nice," my mother commented on the way home. "I didn't know you still talked to Martin." I was willing to let her think we'd been privately friendly all along. When we got home, I left the mayonnaise in one of the shopping bags clustered across the kitchen floor, but rooted around for the coffee.

The coffee maker was at the very back of the cupboard; I had to excavate a whole history of abandoned kitchen appliances to get it out. When I opened the top, there was darkish residue all through the funnel and the coffee pot had hard water stains at the bottom, so I washed them in the sink, trying to get the water as hot and soapy as it would go. At first, my mother watched with snide, amused interest, but eventually got bored and went upstairs.

I dried off the parts as much as I could with a fist full of paper towels and plugged the cord into the wall behind the counter. The pot, speckled with droplets, hissed a bit as I set it in place. I popped in the funnel.

"Shit." I hadn't bought any filters. In desperation, I stuck a paper towel into the base of the funnel, then put a few spoonfuls of the coffee grounds on top. "It'll work, maybe," I said aloud, like a charm. I used the pot to fill the tank with water from the sink. The smallest amount of water that would trigger the mechanism was two cups, and I was, by then, too frazzled to object to being classified as lonely, even by a coffee maker. The water settled in the tank and, after a suspenseful moment, the appliance clicked alive.

As it sucked and spat the water, I checked my phone. There was one text from Martin, just *Hey*. I added the number to contacts, not planning to make any immediate response. As I did, another message arrived, from a different unknown number.

it's mollie!!

I added her to contacts and replied with an emoji I thought came across as random and kind of funny, the woman making a circle with her arms. She responded within a few seconds: *lol.*

The coffee maker was rattling, sputtering the last bit of what I had brewed at high cost of dignity and ingenuity into the pot. I grabbed the mug I had rinsed out before from the cabinet and waited for the machine to go silent before pouring myself a cup. As it cooled, I surveyed the pantry and made myself a massive bowl of my mom's frosted wheat cereal. I let the bottoms get soggy before eating them, crunching through the thin layer of hard sugar, cold comfort across the tops. My phone sat next to the bowl with the screen facing up, but it stayed dark, and I thought about Mollie and Martin, in one of the houses nearby, garage, plastic siding, off-white walls, unpacking new tissue box covers and toilet brushes and hand-held vacuums, now with me in the back of their minds. When I finally sipped the coffee it had cooled too much and felt tepid and musty in my mouth.

Chapter Two

The opportunities, in this zip code, for someone like me, seemed the same, if not even narrower than when I left for college. Despite this, it only took about a week before my mom seemed to view letting me come home as an overly permissive indulgence, even while I experienced it as a humiliation I was only barely coping with.

One evening she thawed some frozen chicken breasts and grilled them in a pan, then sliced them over a tossed salad, only just enough for both of us. My laptop was perched on the couch arm rest, playing George Kuchar's *Weather Diary 1* in a windowed VLC player. His camcorder gazed up at the round, reddish glow of a streetlight, with the sound low enough that I could still hear the news my mom was only half paying attention to. When the program switched over to a commercial she spoke up like an idea had just occurred to her. Her voice laid over the jingle for a local grocery chain, which hadn't changed while I was away.

"By the way." She drew out a pause, waiting for me to respond. Whatever she was about to say, she had been stewing in it all day, or longer. "One of the mothers down the way could use a babysitter over the summer."

"Ah," I replied, trying not to sound particularly eager or distasteful towards this information. Obviously, she wanted me to do it, and it could be a better option than applying to the few jobs within reach. But dealing with children intimidated me. I didn't have intuitive warmth for them, or much in the way of negotiation skills. I'd risk revealing a new set of inadequacies when I was already at a low point, especially if it involved some prim helicopter mom sizing me up. I felt categorically not the type of person for this job. But what kind of job, especially within my diminished remit, was I the type of person for?

"She's got two children, her name is Jessica Wain. It's the house at the very end, the one with the brick accents."

"Uh huh."

"Her husband passed away, that's why she needs the help over the summer. They got a big insurance settlement because it was some kind of accident, but it's gotten to the point where she needs to go back to work. She's doing admin work at one of those law offices in town, you know, the one with all those billboards."

This was the typical irrelevant info my mother took a nosy, suggestive interest in. "That's too bad, about the dad I mean," I said. She shrugged. Right, life goes on. "How old are the kids?"

"The little girl is five, and her brother is nine. He's almost old enough to take care of himself most of the day but he's been having emotional problems. You know, no father."

"I'll think about it," I said. I reached across to take her bowl, so I could go put both in the sink. She picked it up, lifting it away from me even though there wasn't anything else in it.

"I'd really prefer it if you go over. Introduce yourself, at least."

"What, now?" She pushed the bowl into my hands.

"Well, sometime this evening."

It was 6 PM, but the sun stayed out so long it didn't feel

late in the day at all. Before leaving I asked: "Can you at least call to tell her I'm coming or something?" and my mom nodded to get me out the door, but, in the end, did not.

I tried to remember the details of the house; only one was on our side of the road, on the corner and with some brickwork, but my deductions didn't fill me with confidence. The oblong, panopticon loop of the development made any searching or hesitation feel like creeping around. Once an older woman I'd never seen before had peeked out of her curtains to glare at me holding up my first camera phone, trying to fit the secondhand bike I was straddling in the tiny, pixelated frame. I evaluated my own behaviour with that level of maximum distrust: *what are you doing out here, looking at houses, thinking about ringing a doorbell?* I approached the door and pressed the narrow, smooth button, taking a deep breath to tamp down my heartbeat.

The door opened. I could hear the sound of a television and one child narrating some sort of game from inside. The woman who answered the door had one elbow pulled in tight to her side, still holding the handle. Her hair was pulled into a loose ponytail, gone limp and frizzy by this time of day. She smiled at me, looking over my entire modest length with no recognition.

"Hi," she said.

Pinned down, struggling to justify why I was standing on a doorstep like some bizarre idiot/pervert, I was buzzing, hyperaware, under her friendly but evaluating look. She was the closest thing Central Pennsylvania had so far produced to a softly gleaming, blonde Kim Novak, and I was Scottie, dumb, easy, named for a dog. There it was: raw desire's hooks set in me. Right away, this pathetic, immediate attraction became the most exciting thing I could have access to, in a twenty mile radius at least. I would take the job, if she would have me.

"I'm here," I said, coming up with nothing else.

"Yes, sorry, for what?" She tilted her head. The pressure towards conversation knocked me loose, the lowest sufficient terms for the situation supplied themselves.

"My mom should have called. Mrs. Schumaker." I said it easily, smiling back. It was the correct thing to say, but I hadn't really wanted to have to say it. As casually as it came out — I felt embarrassed. *She* was a mother too, and not that much older than me. People my age already were mothers, very regularly, and it drew attention to how different we were to refer to my own.

"Oh, for the babysitting."

"Yes, the babysitting!" Amazing. She looked even happier to have a reason to pull the door all the way open and invite me in. Rather than being illuminated by the light from outside passing through, the house seemed to glow with its own activity. The child I heard, the girl, was half-watching a nature program on the television, improvising her own subplots with a pair of stuffed animals clutched in each hand. The boy, with prominent, knobbly knees was slouched low in a fraying, upholstered armchair, absorbed in a game on his tablet.

"Cecil, Susie, say hello!" She called. The girl looked over.

"Who is that?" Her voice shot up around the question mark, like I was a pile of unidentifiable gunk on the sidewalk she'd stepped in. The boy narrowed his eyes behind his glasses.

"Hello."

"She's going to be around during the day, when I have to work." I stood at her side, trying to look friendly with a small, goofy wave. The whole conversation was moving extremely fast. I was already the babysitter, before sitting down to negotiate, though part of me knew I should be grateful she didn't see me as too much of a weirdo, a threat to her darling children. The kids were uninterested and turned back to what they had been doing.

She turned to me again, with a more apologetic grin. I was already sharpening my attentiveness, trying to draw out a dictionary of subtle and deep emotional profundity I could use to decode her.

"They're not super sociable."

"I understand, really. That works for me."

"That's true, your mother said so." She looked at me again, taking in my appearance more closely in the context of her kitchen, still not seeming, like I had worried, concerned or disappointed at what she saw. "Can I make you a coffee?" She asked. "Or I have tea, if it's a bit late in the day for that."

"Coffee's great." Instead of pulling out an appliance, she heated some water in a kettle to pour into a glass French press that was still drying on the counter next to the sink. She gestured to the kitchen table and I took a seat there, fiddling with the tassels of a fabric placemat until she brought two mugs of coffee over.

"Night owl?" she asked.

"Well, if I was watching the kids I'd try to be responsible." I curved my fingers around the mug, a smooth enamel one with a faded Garfield comic on the side. I tried to lace them together in a way that hid my ragged cuticles when I noticed she glanced down at the cup, waiting for me to take a sip. "But normally, yeah, kind of."

"I was too, way back when," she admitted. "It was an adjustment."

We sat companionably for a few minutes. I didn't feel like I had to talk, or that I couldn't. When Jessica would turn to check on the kids, or just look out the back window of the kitchen, I took the chance to study her more closely. She had a long, mature-looking face, eyes softened with workday exhaustion but still able to call up parental authority, if she had to. Above them, her eyebrows were hyper expressive, born to animate good humour, surprise, worry, empathy. They were so unlike mine, which sat flat like lazy caterpillars, hardly able to budge, giving me a constant resting bitch face. Jessica picked up her mug, a plain but cheerful yellow one, blew across the surface, then drank some. She pressed her lips together like she was getting away with something when anything satisfied or amused her.

"I have to leave for work around eight. I know, not fun. But it would be nice if you could be here at 7:45 or so?"

"That's not too bad. I'll manage." I lifted my own mug and had to disguise that the coffee still felt scalding hot to me. "And do you get home around 5:30?"

"Most days, yeah. Is forty dollars a day alright? I know it's not great, but I can pay in cash. You can do what you like most of the time, and help yourself to any of the food, of course." She shifted on the chair, looking anxious, which made me feel closer in station to her. "I feel a little embarrassed. But I just need to get back to having a good record at a decent job."

"Oh yeah, no, it's better than nothing," I said. The figure approximately matched what a professor had once furnished me with to live in his house and make sure his cat was fed and entertained while he attended a panel at a glitzy European art conference. It was true, based on the quick calculations I made in my mind, that she was offering well below minimum wage. But the bullshit of dealing with managers who could always produce another toilet to be scrubbed or a tendentious argument for not sitting down, of having to wait for the pay slip to arrive weeks later, plus the whole indignity of having to submit a resume for their judgement in the first place seemed worth taking the cut — until I built up enough to go somewhere else, at least. When I worked at the gas station I stole time leaning on the counter or sitting on the bags of ice in the walk-in freezer, usually considering when exactly in the shift I'd be willing to start paying $7.25 to not have to be there for another hour. Stuck doing that kind of math again, I'd have no escape on the horizon.

"I'll get you an amazing Christmas present once they're back at school," Jessica said, leaning back in her chair and taking another sip of the coffee. I tested mine, but the mug was still hot enough to sting my fingertips. Still being here at Christmas had not been something I wanted or even allowed myself to consider; now, all of a sudden, I had to.

"I might be around just for the summer," I said.

"Doing grad school?" She asked. I laughed at that.

"No. Just don't want to stay any longer than I have to, you know? I've kind of done everything here."

"Born for other things." She flexed her fingers around the mug. "We only moved here around two years ago, but I get it."

"Why'd you move?"

"My husband was a private pilot, so we lived near the city. But with the money from the settlement to live on, it was pretty unsustainable, right? Downsizing a bit gave me some more time with them."

"Oh, shit, I'm sorry." I lowered my voice. Depending on how strict the rules on swearing (quietly, in an adjacent room) or how sore the memories of her husband were, I began to worry I had already screwed up. Real grief was something I felt unequipped for, my own losses besides a few grandparents being indefinitely suspended, never resolving like the certainty of death, being cleanly no longer of this world. When other people brought it up, my instinct was to either escape as gracefully as I could or try to spin the best out of the situation, given its inevitability.

"No, don't worry. You fill out enough forms and it's just another thing that happened in your life, you know."

I didn't. A partner dying in a plane crash, much less one they were piloting, seemed like such a bizarre scenario that it would tear through my life, I wouldn't think of anything else.

"The Cessna just vanished, over open ocean," she added. "He was returning from dropping off passengers so no one else was hurt but… the plane was small and the range where it could have fallen was so huge. They didn't even expect to find anything."

"Oh my god," I said.

She glanced over her shoulder. Cecil was still sprawled on the armchair in the living room, holding the tablet directly over his face with propped up elbows. "Susie doesn't really remember, but Cecil took in everything. How can you not soften it when you say it to a child, right? It wasn't found so… that's where his head goes."

In the other room, Cecil was absorbed in poking at his game, but pointedly squinted over at me when he sensed this turn in the conversation. Jessica lowered her voice and leaned across the table to whisper. I felt too close to her face and turned away slightly, like I needed to angle my ear towards her.

"So his thing, lately, is that the aeroplane was taken by aliens. Like, a UFO or something."

I kept my gaze straight ahead at the pantry, a clock on the wall, even though I was suddenly afraid she was pulling my leg. But, I considered, kids also believe really weird things. I hadn't mentioned any of them to my own mother, like my belief that my stuffed toys were sentient and cried out when neglected, or that my thoughts, especially visualising something bad, could make things happen. Like a mediaeval peasant, I sometimes returned to the old superstitions whenever times got tough. Maybe Jessica was a better mother, to know this about her child.

"I'm just telling you because he might want to talk about it, or he'll say things about seeing lights at night, stuff like that."

"How do you handle it?"

She shrugged, leaning back in the chair. "I listen, I gently change the subject, I don't know. I'm just glad he wants to talk about something. I don't want to make him feel more anxious by scolding him about it. He takes that really hard."

"Right," I said. "Because it's really about his dad."

"Yeah." She smiled, relaxing. "Susie is Susie, just keep her busy so she doesn't get into things she shouldn't."

Next, I was shown around: the large, open kitchen all the houses on the street had, living room, guest bathroom, upstairs bathroom, the kids' rooms. Jessica showed me where the spare key was, extra toilet paper and paper towels, and the medicine cabinet, just in case. In the pantry, she indicated which snacks were favoured more by Cecil or Susie and some things that were handy for making quick lunches.

Compared to living with only my mother, this house felt cluttered, comforting and overstimulating all at once, even though the floor plan was identical. I almost felt like a teenager again as we walked past the door I knew led to the basement. My father had soundproofed and lined ours like a Faraday cage, part of his slow build to full-on crank that ran parallel to my childhood. If something, like an abduction or out of body experience had clued him into psychic transmissions and elegant coincidences all around him, I wish I'd known then how those who've experienced it draw towards each other with an eerie synchronicity that excludes others, as if they're marked by invisible tattoos under their skin. My desire to somehow play along, my eagerness and suggestibility, because I wanted to please, probably repulsed him. Mom, of course, silently bore his eccentric hobby, even when it passed well beyond that point. But I tried to show sincere interest, reading his notes and handwritten, tabulated results on the kitchen counter as if I could grasp some shining, impressive insight from them. In my fantasies it would feel like reaching into a stream and pulling out a fat fish. Maybe then I would be special too, and prove my own supernatural intuition.

I'd ponder what to say when he would come clomping up the wooden steps, usually with one of the twins while I studied the cards left alongside his notes with neat symbols in their centres: circle, plus, star. I'd stand them up, one corner on the counter and the diagonal opposite pressed into my fingertip, then try to flip them up to stand on top of my knuckles. My attempt to spontaneously develop some sort of telekinetic force field that would attract my father's interest never succeeded. I was the remainder, left mostly for my mom to deal with.

I realised, standing in front of Jessica's pantry, that I was coming off a little distracted.

"Are you sure you don't want anything to eat?" Jessica asked. My stomach, unused to salads, felt worse than empty. It wouldn't have surprised me if Jessica could hear it growl.

"A snack would be good," I admitted. She slipped me a packet of cheese crackers shaped like whales, almost mischievously, even though she was the one who had the right to hand it to me.

"That's about it, I think." She called over to the children. "Cecil, Susie, say bye to Miss Schumaker before she has to go!" I winced mid-wave at the kids. Her insistence on using my last name made me sound like a substitute teacher. Cecil and Susie regarded me warily, and were right to. "She'll be back tomorrow."

"Okay," Cecil said, no sentiment wasted.

"Bye Miss!" Susie said, exercising her capacity to scream. Jessica tutted at this and led me back towards the front door.

"It's getting dark out. You probably want to go home. But I'll see you tomorrow?"

"Yeah," I paused, looking at her. The soft light from the kitchen that diffused into the hallway suited her. "I'm not great with kids, so I'm sorry if anything goes wrong. My mom put me up to this since I had to move back home suddenly."

"You don't think you're good with kids?" Jessica asked.

"Not that anything bad's ever happened. I've never felt any indication that I would be good," I corrected myself.

"Well, I'm not hiring for NASA. You're easy to talk to. You come across as straightforward and friendly."

"Okay, no one has ever said that about me, to my knowledge." My hand was still clamped around the packet of cheese crackers. I felt bug-eyed, shuffling on the spot and trying not to crumple them too loudly, searching for an opening to leave. Our conversation took on the appearance of ease, once I pushed through my initial nerves. I was surprising myself. The ease could always be punctured like a balloon, the colourful shell whipping away and jolting me with the sense that I was navigating the situation by the seat of my pants.

"I'm sure they've thought it, or said it to other people."

"That makes me feel worse!" My exclamation made her laugh. I had gone from awed and embarrassed in her presence to at least being able to act like I wasn't, and naturally, pleasantly, at that.

"Well, see you tomorrow," she said, opening the door. "Out you go."

I let myself grin. "See you."

The door closed behind me. I half-expected to turn around and see her watching after me, but that was it, I was sent on my way, with everything changed. My life had already taken on a character completely detached from how it was when I had been in the middle of things, when I had been under the impression that I was where I was supposed to be.

♦♦♦

The first few nights in my childhood bed I slept like a TV set being turned off and on again. That night, I dreamed. I realised I was dreaming immediately, and inside the dream I thought to myself, *oh great.*

I was sitting on the cinder block steps that went down to the poured cement bed of our back porch, next to Martin, under a full moon. It was dark, and deeper in summer, dream air thick and warm, but no fireflies. In the strange way dreams smudge time, we were still kids and in love and also adults who regarded each other awkwardly.

Dreams don't have the resolution of skin-on-skin. Next to my leg, Martin's knee hovered like a warm ball of pleasure and queasiness. Cut to the point. When he turned to me and kissed me and lowered me onto my back on the cement of the porch it felt like a bed, obviously a fantasy of not having to furtively grope each other in a car parked in a quiet back road. Maybe, if we'd had a shot like that — you know, the kind of things a sudden dream about an ex always makes you think.

Once I was flat on my back, Mollie was there too, lying perpendicular to me, her face next to mine. As I pulled away to get a better look at her, she pressed her lips into a cute frown. Mollie was herself, but even at close proximity she could also be me from back in high school, and both possibilities seemed to look at me with disappointment, like I was a failed doppelgänger that couldn't actually take either place. I put my mouth on hers and ran my hand down her neck and towards her chest. I was outside of myself, above the whole scene, a high thin cloud passing over the moon. Then I was awake.

Waking so abruptly left me with a melancholic nostalgia that manifested as physical dread. I rooted around in the sheets for my phone and discovered it was fifteen minutes until my alarm would go off. Indulging the feeling that there was something good and golden in the past, or worse, and more desperate, that if only it was a bit different it would have been golden, was something I had come home knowing I would need to avoid. In retaliation, I directed myself to recall something that'd make me want to hide my face in embarrassment, even though I was alone and the house was quiet. I would think the worst of the past. Like a little punishment imposed on myself, a memory from high school, from just before Martin and I started dating, eagerly resurfaced.

Two girls I had been briefly friendly with (as always, better friends with each other than with me) were cooing and chuckling over a magazine splayed out on their desks. When I tried to get a look, they covered the pages.

"What is it?" I asked.

"She's too uptight," one of them said. The other giggled, then asked, "Oh, you like Martin, right? That runner? What's his birthday?"

"I don't know," I lied, poorly. "February 23rd or something."

"A Pisces." The girl peeked under her hands at whatever was on the magazine page. "He likes to do it in the doggy position, because it makes him feel secure." They both laughed at this, but to me it was a totally obscene thing to contemplate. My completely flowered mind was so turned around that I imagined Martin naked and crawling around on all fours, at my feet. My face must have been glowing, even better for them to laugh at than the cheesiness of the astrological diagnosis itself. I hadn't carried on a conversation longer than three lines with Martin at that point, but it still felt like I had done something awful to him by not dispelling the image before it even popped into my mind.

I lay in bed, letting myself get mortified over my naiveté from almost 10 years ago. But the warm, fluttery feeling over the top of my stomach stuck around, my heart rate ran hot. I lifted up the waistband of my underwear with my fore- and middle finger and poked around. Dreams, even with their psychologically ambivalent character, tended to get me more physically aroused than real life.

Since then my fantasies had developed into a way to cope with the repeated indignities and stymied feeling of everyday life. I became a committedly polymorphous pervert, by now one of the few things that could be considered a principle I ordered my life around. For a moment, I could think a woman sitting across from me on the train had great tits and imagine sticking my face straight in them. I could look at a guy's calves or ass pressing against his pants and imagine how they'd give under my hand — and nothing in the world would happen. I could fantasise about dragging the sketchy character who came into the convenience store at around 10 PM to order two hamburgers with mustard in a kind of bitchy, controlling way into the back office based only on his grimy and flushed resemblance to an actor I liked. The door to this freedom opened when I realised, a dam of some kind of separate impatience I didn't even know I had built up buckling when Martin shoved his hand down the front of my pants in the far end of the high school parking lot, that of course things I did with another person signified something different, that it had some sort of social-emotional purpose but ultimately didn't substitute for my internal operations — what I could do by and to myself.

To feel shame again — over a dream! — felt like regressing. Like old times, I anxiously got myself off, watching the door, stuffing the side of my hand in my mouth, not even to muffle any sounds but because I wanted something to press against, to get warm from my own breath.

Afterwards, I lay still, embarrassment out of mind at the very least. I could almost drift back to sleep. Then the alarm blared right next to my face.

Under the even pressure and consistent warmth of the shower in my mom's bathroom, I started thinking about my new job that had come almost suspiciously easy. She was so effortless, Jessica, I mean, that she must have been putting it on thick being so nice to me. My mother had probably cornered her at some cookout or garage sale when the seeds of this arrangement had been planted. After exhausting the topic of her wonderful twin daughters, there was always plenty to say about me, the other one, who had studied art in college and had gone to the city trying to scrape together some sort of cultural career, who had a girlfriend, no, not that there's anything wrong with that, I knew plenty of lesbians in college (I played sports!) and they were all very normal, but she's been dressing down so often too, and if only she had a better attitude — I could see my mother standing in front of a potato salad or punch bowl just barely stopping herself from wondering aloud where her happy, bright little girl had gone. The drain had a few long hairs stuck around it. The colour of my own but not mine. The most exciting and consequential perspective on my life was starting to be how people talked about me in my absence.

Maybe Jessica felt that her kids would benefit from exposure to someone vaguely 'alternative'. She seemed to consider suburban Pennsylvania as an obvious cultural black hole; she'd agreed it was boring. So, I could be bravely piloting a sort of de-sexed, family friendly rent-a-Kathy-Acker-alike outreach program, as someone who could only just pull off the androgynous dishevelment, not the sex appeal or tips for fitness nuts. My new, lucrative economic niche (sub minimum wage)! Or maybe she secretly thought her daughter was gay.

I turned the water off, dried my hair, dressed myself as I usually did, only faintly considering trying on a few pieces of what remained, in the very bottoms of drawers, of my high school wardrobe. There was no time for the agony. Downstairs, I skipped coffee, thinking I could make some at Jessica's, and ate a bowl of my own cereal, plain and store-brand.

♦♦♦

When I rang the doorbell, the inside of the house was dim and quieter than it had been the evening before.

"Great, you're here," Jessica said, opening the door wide to look at me on the step below her. If I was at eye level with her, I thought, I'd be thinking about kissing her on the mouth, which I realised wasn't completely *not* thinking about it. I stepped up and walked past her into the house and she closed the door behind me. "How are you?"

"A little anxious," I said. "But I slept okay."

"That's good." There was a pot still half-filled with coffee on the counter. She noticed me looking at it. "Would you like some?"

"Yeah, I didn't have time before I left."

Jessica went to the cabinet where her odd assortment of mugs were kept. She pulled out an unwieldy one with a novelty handle shaped like a cow.

"I understand if you pass on this one."

"No, it's fine!"

She filled the mug and handed it to me. We stood around the kitchen island as the sound of one of the kids rolling out of bed, opening and closing drawers, softly went on above us. I traced my finger around the lumpy outline of the cow.

"I was a little anxious last night, too," she said. "Usually school keeps them occupied enough, and last summer I was able to stay home. I feel like they're growing up, and coping better, but leaving them completely alone still felt like a bad idea, you know?"

Theoretically, I could try to give them a little structure, provide companionship in a basic sense, but I didn't have any plans about the loftier issues Jessica seemed to think my presence would address, being a sort of orienting beacon of productivity, maturity and resilience. It was above my pay grade and experience.

"No pressure," she said, responding to my awkward silence. She pointed at the mug. "Cecil loves that one, you know."

There was a sound like something tumbling down the steps, though it didn't seem to bother Jessica. Susie bounded into the room.

"Summer!" She shouted. I thought, what an incredible, unbelievable amount of energy.

"Hey honey," Jessica said brightly. "I'm leaving for work soon. Do you remember the lady I introduced you to last night?" I pointed at myself derisively in response to being called a lady. The girl looked at me with either obliviousness or indifference.

"Hi," she said. As driven as an office drone clocking into work, she walked over to a little cabinet in the living room and started selecting dolls from it. Jessica shrugged and laughed.

"She can be very focused." She raised her voice gently,

calling to Susie. "Remember to eat some breakfast. The babysitter can make you cereal, or oatmeal, or a bagel, okay? Is your brother up?"

"Cecil's lazy," Susie said.

"He can sleep in on the first day of summer, I guess," Jessica said. She stood up, grabbed a practical handbag off the kitchen table and the keys to the car from a small wicker basket, then checked the tiny silver watch clasped to her wrist. She walked over to the stairs. Her voice reverberated against the high, empty walls around the staircase. "Cecil, I'm heading to work, honey. The babysitter can help you get breakfast, okay? Don't sleep too late." She smiled at me, crossing the kitchen to leave for the garage. "Oh, my number! Here." Jessica reached out a hand and I gave her my phone. She typed in a number, and after she left I texted *Hello* to it with a little party popper.

Hello she sent back, a few minutes later, next to the smiling emoji with little hands at its cheeks.

Susie was absorbed in playing with her dolls, lining them up, sorting them, arranging them into little dramas, overall seeming very busy. At a lull in the action, I convinced her to come over and eat a bowl of Apple Jacks, then turned the TV on in the background while she got back to work. I scanned the channels, since I hadn't lived anywhere with a TV for ages. It was as dull as ever, the same sort of things I remembered quizzically skimming on days I was home sick.

Cecil came downstairs around 11 AM. He looked bleary and irritated, with slight shadows under his eyes. Since he had hardly glanced up from his game last night, I assumed he had pulled a trick I often did as a kid, sneaking some strictly controlled personal device into his room to play games or chat with friends until practically passing out with it in his hands.

"Hey bud, want something to eat?" I tried.

"I can get it myself," he said.

"That's cool." I watched as he went on his toes to slide a cereal box off the pantry shelf, then took a bowl from the cabinets across the kitchen and poured in Fruit Pebbles until there was a slight mound peeking over the rim. He got out a nearly full jug of milk from the fridge, and, tipping it towards the bowl, overshot his mark for the first few splashes. He glanced up at me and I politely looked away as he circled around the counter to get some paper towels from under the sink. I felt the couch cushions shift slightly as he sat on the opposite end from me and started eating.

"Why don't you keep it on the same channel," he said, annoyed.

"You can pick. I'm just browsing." I handed him the remote and he typed in some numbers with his thumb automatically. The TV switched to a channel where a group of guys with really corny goatees were carrying around equipment designed for antagonising ghosts. I tried to follow his investment in the show, which was rapt, and only occasionally checked my phone.

"Do you think ghosts are real?" I asked. Cecil scoffed but didn't look away from the TV.

"No way. This show is just funny." The guys on the TV were crawling through the air ducts of an abandoned insane asylum in night vision. "But the detectors and stuff are cool, you know? Like I didn't know they made stuff that could sense those kinds of things."

"Totally," I said.

"Totally," Susie parroted, making one of the dolls toss its hair.

My phone's screen flashed and I looked at it with a level of agitation even the kids could detect. It could have been the dreaded notification from Josie or one of her friends, a *where are you?* now almost as daunting as the ongoing radio silence. It could be something from Martin or Mollie. What if one or both of them invites me to something? What if one or both of them were suddenly curious, or confrontational?

I checked the message. It was just Jessica. *Everything OK?*

Leaning onto the couch's arm rest, I balanced my chin on my fist thoughtfully. Cecil was scooping the last bits of very soggy cereal out of a low pool of greyish milk, Susie had changed her primary activity to systematically pulling each book out of the small bookcase on top of the cabinet she'd gotten the dolls from, looking at the first page, and letting it fall to the floor, apparently dissatisfied. On TV, a new show was starting, about how aliens communicated with ancient civilizations. Cecil hopped up to dump his bowl into the sink and return to the couch while the introduction went on. I read the message again and waited a bit.

Of course, it was normal, but responding immediately would be strange, showing I wasn't busy enough or too desperate to project perfection. I bounced the message box around with my fingers, pulling it down and then letting it spring back up because the message history was still less than the length of the screen. I looked at the beaming face emoji she had sent me along with *Hello* above the most recent message, and let myself read into her excess attention, feeling a bit giddy.

All good. I sent back, with a thumbs up.

Successfully preparing a few grilled cheese sandwiches for lunch made me feel overconfident, insanely proficient in my ability to care for children, but I knew I was playing on easy mode. Being stuck at home all day was still a novelty, things to do around the house hadn't gotten intractably boring, and I was still a new, unknown presence. The kids were scoping me out, trying to understand my precise location between adult and peer.

When Jessica returned home, I watched the tortoise clip holding back most of her hair sink down the nape of her neck and bob with her head as she checked to make sure everything was still in order. After releasing a theatrical sigh she offered me a portion of dinner, which was going to be a reheated pasta casserole. Sitting opposite her at the small square kitchen table, kids eating on either side, made me feel intimidated and shy, so I declined. She put a hand on my arm, meaningless, but it lit me like a match touching a candle.

"It went okay, though, really? You're not running off because it was awful?" She had been just as anxious as me, nervous energy still banging around from rushing home and finding everything basically fine.

"No, the kids are great," I said.

At home, I put my own dinner together out of leftovers from the fridge without complaint. I went up to my room and poked around, running my finger down spines of the books I had lined up so long ago, like wards in the bookshelves at the head and foot of my bed. I opened a few, but mostly let myself sink into my own feelings, enjoying solitude coupled with eagerness for seeing someone again, always the best when it first unexpectedly emerged. I even felt tentative gratitude for the structure my return home had taken on, during weekdays at least. I would wake up, watch Jessica's kids, come home. Maybe work up the nerve to stay for dinner. The benign anticipation let me fall into an easy and dreamless sleep.

Chapter Three

On Friday, Jessica called me in the evening, after I'd gone home. Of course, I missed it. My phone was always set to silent, not even vibrate, because I was so unaccustomed to anyone calling me. So when I saw the missed call notification with her name, not a random number or 'unknown', I panicked. My mother glanced away from the baking competition show she'd been watching when I stood up suddenly, frowning and raising her eyebrows.

"Sorry, just have to call someone." I paced out of the room, looking down at the phone screen.

In my bedroom, I leaned on the flimsy door with the non-functioning latch. Outside, the sun was setting and low light still came in through my windows, so I didn't bother turning the lights on. I stared at the notification, a greyish-white box holding her name glowing out at me, and considered how to initiate my side of the call.

Phone calls made me anxious, with their silent delay that the other person could completely vanish into. It wasn't a normal lull in a conversation, a gap I still rushed to fill, where the other person was still there, providing some kind of response with their presence. And, unlike the brainy abstraction of text-based communication that appealed to me, you also had to act in real time, stepping forward into total darkness. Jessica was a little older, she might not have understood this. I estimated she had eight to ten years on me, probably someone with a seamless, natural irl presence that incorporated her body, her face, her voice, rather than forging it over tortuously deployed forum posts, status messages and texts, like I had.

Or, I observed my heart rate, my knees pressing together, alternately, she just made me feel shy.

In either case, punishment-based motivation was a reliable way to work myself up to action, so I started on myself: I had to treat this like a job if I ever wanted to leave, right? And it would be a new and particularly awful character flaw to let someone down on something as important as childcare, right? I looked at the notification again. A small caption showed that the missed call had happened 12 minutes ago. I held my breath and hit 'call back', prepared to wait out the droning tone, but I hardly had to.

"Hey, Amy, sorry for calling when you're relaxing on a Friday," Jessica said playfully on the other end of the line. I'm sure it sounded like I was gasping my way into the next words.

"No, it's fine! I'm sorry I missed your call. Is something up?"

She lowered her voice, and I became cognisant that I was holding its source up next to my ear, that the phone was going warm and slightly greasy from being rested flush against my cheek.

"Yeah, I was wondering if you wanted to pop out, just really quick. I can come by and pick you up."

"Sure," I paused, realising I had curved up that 'sure' like a long question mark. "What for?"

"The kids are winding down for the evening, so I can leave them alone for a bit. I just wanted to check in with you, about how things are going. And I didn't want you to feel… well, whenever Cecil gets the sense that I'm having a serious conversation with someone, he waits at the top of the stairs to eavesdrop." She laughed, the way people do to dispel the tension around something, a sad fact that was no one's fault. "He's probably doing it now."

I knew where Cecil was standing. It was the same place I had perched, not even shifting on my feet for fear it would make the house creak, listening to my mother making one-sided calls with whatever family she could get in touch with, and, rarely, my father. What I could hear circled around the same few sentiments. It was shameful, it was embarrassing, it was unreasonable, what he was doing.

"I just want to hear how the first week went," Jessica said, keeping her voice low, in a total murmur. "And, you know, feel free to be honest because the kids won't be listening in." She sensed my long pause. "I'll pick you up."

"Oh, okay," I stammered at first, then lowered my voice too. "Can you park at the end of the street and I'll be there in 15 minutes?"

"Why?"

"I just don't want my mom to be nosy about it. Seeing your car or whatever. I'll just say I'm going for a walk."

"Sure," she said. "I remember how it was. I'm not that old."

I met her at the corner of our development like a kid catching the bus. The half-dark of evening made me shiver with delight at doing something unusual and slightly illicit already. I opened the side door of the car and smiled. Under the yellow interior lights Jessica looked extra exhausted but still glad to see me. We didn't say anything significant as the ride swallowed up the distance I used to walk after school and on weekends in minutes. The umbrella of fluorescent lights hanging over the gas pumps was familiar, even though the logo for the store and its colour scheme had changed several times since I worked there. Jessica pulled into one of the parking spaces along the front of the store.

"Sorry it's not super fancy, but it's the nearest place to sit and talk. Unless you want Taco Bell?"

I told her, "I used to work here, during high school."

"We can go then, if it's bad memories."

"No, I'm pretty sure no one would recognise me," I said. "If they're even still here."

"Really?" She opened the door on her side, grabbing her bag from the centre console before sliding out to rest her shoes on the dull asphalt.

"I was more girly in high school," I got out of the car and glanced across at her to see her reaction, if she pulled any sort of face from imagining this. "Plus I'm not wearing the uniform." I levered my whole shoulder to close the car door, and the sound echoed across the empty lot.

Even though the ads, the uniforms, the designs of the bucket-like styrofoam cups had all been superficially shuffled, the bones of the place were the same. A cooler of sandwiches, soda fountain, coffee thermoses, two aisles of chips and candy pointing back towards the single, miserable bathroom, all still intact. Candy bars lined the front of the register, rows and rows of cigs behind. There wasn't a formal seating area, just some tiny booths screwed into the wall near the bathrooms. But Jessica was right, this was, by my estimation, the nearest place to sit and have a private conversation that wasn't outdoors, an empty lot or a parked car. At the register, Jessica ordered two burgers for herself from a frowning, middle aged woman, and asked if I wanted anything. I said no, distracted from trying to recognise the cashier. She wasn't familiar, but I also couldn't rule out that I had traded off a shift to her once, the other type of person who worked here, besides miserable teenagers from the nearby suburbs, but I don't think I could have identified anyone in particular out of either group.

The woman was the only one working the counter, though I knew that meant someone was in the back stocking the fridge and freezer, cut off in that surreal cold still air, muffled from the rest of the noise of the job. I could almost miss it. The cloying, pink smell of the same mop bucket solution recalled the tactile sensations of this work, things I thought I forgot the moment I walked out the door for the last time. After a few minutes the burgers were passed to Jessica wrapped in tinfoil, and she offered again to get me something. When I actually paid attention to myself I did feel a little hungry. I avoided any of the food prepared behind the counter and grabbed a bag of Doritos.

We slid into one of the little booths and she opened up both hamburgers, letting them stand in the centre of their foil wrappers as she carefully flattened the edges out with the tips of her fingers. I pulled open the bag of Doritos and tried to muffle the awful sound they made in my mouth as I waited for her to decide how to begin.

"What was it like to work here?" Jessica asked. She lifted the top buns off the burger. They still had the same strange, lumpy shape, felt eternal, like cockroaches. These may have even been the same ones I'd rewarm in the microwave and then put back on the steam table on an opening shift. Jessica fiddled with a packet of mustard then squeezed half of it over each patty.

"It was miserable, it sucked," I said. "The garbage cans outside were the worst. People filled them with the most random shit and it sat out in the sun for hours, so they stank. And they leaked."

"Well, I hope the kids aren't that bad." She put the tops back on the burgers. Her elbows rested on the table and she lifted the first burger to her mouth, framing her tits against the scuffed reddish particle board surface of the booth's table and curved seat.

"No, of course not," I said. I looked away as she ate, watching cars streak by towards the highway. "It's been fine so far, they just kind of do their own thing."

"That's good to hear," she said between mouthfuls. "Cecil's teachers say he can be difficult sometimes, but school is a higher-pressure situation, I guess."

"Yeah, I let them do what they feel like, and make sure they eat."

"Try to get them outside a little too, if you haven't."

"Oh yeah, of course."

She finished the first burger as I went on crunching the chips.

"Light dinner?" She looked up at me like she didn't understand what I was asking. "I mean, why get two burgers?"

"Leftovers didn't go as far as I thought. And a bit of a craving, too," she said. "If you know some awful secret about how they're made, don't tell me." I sighed portentously, I couldn't help it, but she didn't seem bothered, digging into the second burger. Part of me thought, this must be the stomach of someone who has given birth twice, but on the other hand, going for an evening snack run together, away from her home and children, made her seem like someone I could run into, have a great conversation, go out for a spontaneous date with, back in the city. I had let men older than her buy me drinks without thinking twice, or even once, about their family life.

I tried it out. An INXS song was playing over the frail speaker system, and I hammily mouthed along to one of the lyrics. *What do you think? Can't think at all.* I felt like such a stud when she chuckled through a mouthful of spongy burger bun at me.

When she had finished both burgers, Jessica crumpled the foil up into tight balls. I offered her a few of the chips left at the bottom of my bag, and she pinched out two with the very tips of her fingers. Her deportment turned more serious when we emptied the bag between us.

"I should be straightforward, since I made such a fuss about privacy," she said. "I want you to feel comfortable being totally candid about Cecil saying anything weird or, like, distressing to you. About his father or anything else. Or the whole UFO thing. Trust me, nothing will shock me. I think I've heard it all by now."

I made a show of looking like I was thinking for a while, even though I knew I didn't really have anything so strange to report. Broaching the subject had left her a bit nervous, and I wanted to put her at ease.

"He likes watching shows about that kind of stuff on TV, but no, nothing in particular."

She sighed and shifted in the booth, slumping down in it a bit, extending her legs out straight. I eyed them weaving past my own in the space underneath the narrow booth.

"I don't know if that's good or bad. He's shy, he's probably still on his best behaviour and wants you to like him. But I want him to be able to talk to someone about it, you know? Especially if he's convincing himself that his father was taken by aliens or whatever else, I want to be able... I don't know. I feel like I should be able to do something."

I looked off to the side and acted like I wasn't sure what

she meant. When my father had vanished, perhaps not as dramatically, but from my point of view with equal finality, my feelings were that I didn't want to talk about it and couldn't bear to hear about it. Another feeling emerged as any potential resolution was postponed and then forgotten; with everyone around me acting normally, I sometimes wanted to scream: "Is anyone aware that my father is missing, that he one day just up and left entirely?" But both feelings manifested as total silence on my part.

"I think you have to trust that he's adjusting, figuring out how to feel in his head. You just have to be there to hear what he says when he's ready to say it. Or well, both of us, now."

"That's kind of wise," she said.

"I was just going by what I wished I had when my dad, you know."

"Oh, I'm sorry."

"No, he's not dead, or at least I don't think so. He just like, walked out and refused to come home or talk about it with any of us. And my mom was so pissed off, so it was like, I couldn't say I missed him, I wasn't supposed to bring it up at all. It was complicated." The awkward, stilted summary came out of me even as I wanted it to stop. Each sentence was excessive, not quite accurate, but also inadequate. How could I explain, when I didn't fully understand it myself? I felt a lump forming in my throat to accompany the mental block. "I'm sorry."

"It's ok." Jessica stared at me with compassion, a move that usually made me feel like a rodent getting eyed up by an apex predator. She pulled a handful of napkins from the napkin dispenser and passed them to me, and I pressed the filmy layers against my eye line. It was preemptive after all; even though I felt awful they only came back with a bit of grease and grit on them. "What was he like, if you want to talk about it?"

I laughed. "I mean, he was crazy. He worked at an electronics testing lab, like, making sure TV designs were sturdy enough or whatever. But he also started to have this weird fixation on finding physical explanations for supernatural stuff. Like, before he left there would be times where he did tests on my sisters? ESP type stuff, because they were twins. It was like a game to them, they liked it, so I wondered if he'd ever thought there was anything special about me, too. If he did, he took a pretty hands-off approach to it." I wished I could stick my head in the freezer, cool down my face, which felt soft and flushed. I looked out over the parking lot, receding further away on the other side of the plate glass window, dark now, with only a faint blue tinge at the horizon. Beyond excavating the sob story of my father again, I wanted to say that ever since I came back, I also felt like some tinhat hiding in their basement. Every place or association that pulled me into a memory was like continuous encounters, little grey faces at every window, skinny arms pulling me into an indistinct, glowing corridor, but wasn't that too weird? Couldn't I just be happy to be home? It made it all fresh again: why did he have to go? Why then? Why alone? In my high school computer lab, I'd branched out down I-83 and beyond, gathering city names from satellite maps to assemble a list of hot spots after hours of Google scouring alien and psychic activity across the United States. I wanted to see if I could reverse-engineer the location my father departed for, a place where the solution to literally everything could bloom with the nakedness of a flower, where the positive space of observed but unexplained phenomena and the negative space at the edges of known mathematics, chemistry and physics could meet and shake hands.

Area 51 or Roswell were too obvious. Dad always had a sense of discernment, and chasing after the greater meaning of it all was equally fleeing from the stifling repetition that got in the way — maintaining a suburban house, desk job, wife and daughters. When I daydreamed about trekking out to find him, I also hoped he wouldn't make a homebody like me go out to the great, mysterious deserts of the west, or beyond, to Silicon Valley. Even if he'd only gone as far as Pittsburgh, a metropolis where he could make regular excursions out to Kecksburg, a six hour bus ride away, it may as well have been anywhere. Finding him seemed, then and now, as likely as waking up on a different planet.

"It's whatever. Sorry. You probably didn't want to hear all that."

"I asked," she said. Her bluntness was pleasant and she didn't just dissolve into the soupy coos of 'what's wrong?' that made me panic. "I guess I just wanted to understand how kids see parents that aren't there anymore."

"I think it'll be fine, with Cecil," I said. I looked across the table at the side of her face. She was staring over the racks of candy, frowning, deep in thought. "You're his mother, after all." When I said it, she looked at me for a moment as if she wasn't sure what I meant.

♦♦♦

On Saturday, my mother informed me, as I rolled myself over in bed, that she was going to meet friends for lunch then spend the entire afternoon at a church crafting circle. Jessica didn't need me either, so, freed from childcare duties I had the house to myself. How did I deal with the boredom before, when I lived here, besides frowning at a laptop screen? Sifting through my desktop folders would be a tour of aborted job applications and failed projects. Instead, when I finally got out of bed, I crouched next to one of my half-unpacked bags, rummaging for one of the books I had managed to bring back with me, a slim volume of art criticism. I lay on the floor, paging through it and trying to make myself read, even keeping a ball point pen to hand as if I had an idea of what I'd do with any notes I'd take, but mostly clicking it as I went. Eventually, I was flat on my back with the book resting pages down over my boobs, staring at the ceiling. I had only underlined one passage: "It is possible for someone to be highly intelligent, and yet have no information. This condition — usually associated with youth or prolonged adolescence — results often in *boredom* —"[1]

Subsequent paragraphs constructed an argument for *boredom* as the base from which all transgressive culture emerged. It was a nice thought, had made my heart jump with affinity and even jot an exclamation point in the margin. Reading it had felt hopeful, like there was a narrative arc to my terminal dissatisfaction, but now, only a few minutes later, totally unable to concentrate on the same words I had just found so compelling, I wasn't sure if I found it true. Was it possible to fail at boredom? Could you lose information once you had it? Maybe I needed the data of skin on skin, getting swallowed up by a room of Cy Twombly canvases for the first time, getting fucking drunk. But what had I done with that information when I escaped the ring fence of the picturesque family home for the first time? I had ended up bored again, then retreated back here.

I felt the thrum that so often ran through the bodies of

the bored and suburban returning. The familiarity of this urge could almost lure me into sighing nostalgia, as much as the overabundance of direct sunlight in summer, bruised strawberries in softened green paperboard crates, the smell of manure and road tar and cut grass, corny wooden cut-out lawn decorations. I hated it. The hopelessness of my situation had closed the horizon so much that this idea was tantalising again: I wanted to buy something, or at least go look at objects I theoretically could want, or buy. I didn't have much money, though Jessica had paid me in cash — fresh, sticky 20s — as we left the convenience store. I had accepted them as calmly as I could manage, even while my heart pounded over what felt like a portentous and even suggestive transaction carried out in a parked car. Now the bills were burning a hole in my pocket, the same way I almost automatically bought an iPod with my first high school paycheck.

I looked at my phone and opened up a text window, Martin's message still hanging there.

hey I sent across, vocabulary of the completely caddish. *are you around?*

I ended up waiting a while. It felt like a long time because I didn't move or try to figure out anything different to do, beyond worrying about his response. We had been kind of awful to each other, hadn't we? Was he only being nice to me at Target under the scrutiny of his new girlfriend and my mom? Of course, I feared this all the time, that after any normal social interaction I would later find out my behaviour had been so inappropriate, so unnerving, that I was totally mistaken to think it had gone fine, but—

Grey dots peeked over the bottom of the message screen. Four minutes had passed. I groaned into the empty house and watched them start and stop several times before a message appeared.

I'll have some time in a bit

A shorter pause.

Why?

my moms out all day and I forgot I need something at target

How nostalgic

Almost immediately followed by: *1230 ok?*

see you then

I checked the time, only an hour, all of an hour.

♦♦♦

An hour later, Martin's car stopped at the bottom of the driveway. I sat and waited for him on the front step, looking like a kid who'd locked myself out. As I walked towards the car, Martin got out of the driver's side to greet me, wearing a Best Buy polo and khakis.

"This has got to be a joke," I said.

"I'm on my lunch break," he replied. "So hurry up."

While I had left town and drastically expanded my intellectual horizons, Martin had gotten a job at the first retail location that would have him and bore down until he was practically shoved into a suddenly vacant shift leader role. The key, from his perspective, had been to stick around. In a place like this you'll be the last one standing of the people who were there when you were hired sooner than you think.

"That's great for you," I said. The benefits of sticking around was something I'd failed to account for. I could tell, from his tense, frustrated attitude, that it hadn't necessarily been easy, but it had at least been the tool he instinctively reached for, and he found some sort of success with it.

Inside the store, it annoyed me to realise that my mood had improved, how easy and unchanging I was.

"What did you need, anyways?" Martin asked.

"Some art stuff," I said, off the top of my head.

"Doesn't your mom have a ton?"

"Like she'd let me use it." It was a stupid thing to call someone over for, to pretend I needed it urgently. My lack of effort to come up with a convincing need was a message in itself, I hoped. "And I use different stuff, anyways."

"Just be quick." In the stationery aisle I grabbed a pack of glue sticks, a small pair of scissors and a sketchbook with slippery, shitty paper. Then I took the long way around the store, through the electronic section to the long rack of magazines, crouching to get a good look at the cheap ones, and opted for a gun catalogue, something for housewives and an unscrupulous celebrity tabloid.

"I'm going to start getting into collage," I announced, and looked over my shoulder at Martin, a few paces away, studying the DVDs on the aisle's endcap. He picked up a recent release and flipped it over, and I tried to decide what felt different about him. His face had gotten softer, his body more squareish than gangly now. He hadn't, to put it in a crass way, filled out or gotten more muscular, but just, with the added weight of routine stresses and a non-teenaged metabolism, became more solid. I thought he probably felt warm. He looked over the top of the DVD case at me. I tried a smile, it came out more like a wince and landed unimpressively.

"You do collage?" he asked.

"I didn't do much at school, I mean. I did video art

stuff, but that's kind of out of my budget for now. And what would you even film around here."

"Video art?"

"Yeah, you know. Like some of the weirder stuff you're into but also even weirder."

Martin at least smiled at this and put the DVD of *The Revenant* back on the shelf. He consulted store shelves with the lazy curiosity of someone who would indiscriminately download everything they managed to still remember when they got home.

Before I'd gotten into video work, I had been deep into Lee Lozano and Adrian Piper style shit. One semester I showed up to crit with a punch bowl full of plastic toy capsules I'd found a trash bag of at a thrift store. I sat on one stool, sat the bowl on another, and said anyone who gave me three dollars was free to open one and read the slip of paper inside, which would have one search from my recent history written on it. I explained that this was a performance-based project, interfering with and exposing Google's proprietary 'ownership' of my online activity. I'd prepared a t-shirt as well, painting the lucrative demographic categories Google thought I belonged to across my chest: female, 18-23, some college education, recommended for advertisers of cosmetics and pregnancy tests. The whole piece was working with layers of transparency and opacity, like a striptease: the promised experience was some genuine exposure, but in all likelihood you would get a few coy, incomplete glances. Taking control meant hiding myself, in the gap between the lucrative social functions my demographics represented and an incomprehensible, piecemeal 'product'.

Exerting all my will on extractive charisma, I only managed to cajole the professor into pulling his wallet from his back pocket. It was a stupid stunt to attempt anyways, on campus hardly any of the students carried around cash.

"This is for real," I said. "You're really giving me three dollars." He was grimacing.

"Yes, I'll let you know if I get sanctioned on any teacher-student regulations over this."

I offered the punch bowl and he took a translucent capsule with a red lid. When he popped it open, he read the tiny scribble on the rolled strip of printer paper aloud to the class.

"Peruse definition."

It was one of the more boring possibilities, though the good ones also weren't that good. The three dollars being a clear ripoff for this bit of non-information let everyone laugh at last, though I knew they wanted to before. What I was selling only really made sense in a set or series, a classic art world hustle. My recent history, presented chronologically, for example: new york hostel new york self storage train from new york bus from new york bus ticket coupon code — was something I would not have been able to perch cockily on a high metal stool and dispense to a crowd of peers and competitors.

"I get you're going for something conceptual, but it's kind of aloof, like it doesn't give the viewer anything about larger issues, or about yourself," the professor said after the punchline faded. It really pissed me off that day, the exhortation to give, to make some sort of positive claim, or hand over a part of myself. What was wrong with just provoking? Or refusing? To affirm anything had seemed basically insane to me. I was over beauty. Sentiment was just everything I found annoying or false about the world, heightened to fetish roleplay.

After that, I didn't do any more 'performance' or 'conceptual' stuff. Instead I insisted on myself by monopolising as much of the department's AV equipment as I could. This was what I held in my heart as my main motivation for working in video: long, textural, abstract shots, opaque fuck yous. Sometimes I worried I was moving backwards. Lozano's erotic, tripped-out wave paintings came before she started blowing up her own interpersonal relationships and wielding jars of money as her practice. Now I was starting to feel like her best work was reported in a salacious NYT so-sad burnout girl profile — that she'd once smashed a plate at an art world dinner party and screamed, "I'm bored!"

I looked at the magazines stacked over my knees, surprised by how absolute my own cynicism had gotten. I had journeyed out in the pursuit of art, or, more simply, for the love of it, after all. Guns, housewifery and the most exploitative and banal aspects of pop culture were all that was on offer here. Giving up on my art of huge ideas had been a tactical retreat, but I was also trying to recapture the pleasure of watching Tarkovsky's long shots of seaweed, of water dripping, and mud, my face propped on an arm rest, aware of Martin's steady attention above me as I lay across his lap, the ridged texture of the corduroy couch in his dad's basement imprinting into my cheek; the childish faith in something else out there.

"It's weird, to think of you doing stuff like that. I figured since you always got such good grades, you'd end up like, an English teacher or something," Martin said, after looking at me like I was acting clueless, somehow.

"I could never be a teacher," I said, hoisting myself back up with the selection of magazines. "Two kids freaks me out enough already." As we went back through the store, towards the checkouts, I considered what Martin's statement revealed: a) that he didn't really associate artistic expression with being smart, which, fair, and / or b) that he found me making art to be some kind of waste of intelligence, a poor investment of my capacities, which he still held in some sort of regard. So far it kind of had been.

Failing to conquer my malaise with a handful of mediocre art supplies, I looped back to get a bag of sour skittles and a pack of bobby pins, partially since my hair was beginning to get fluffy, but I also craved scraping clumps of earwax out of my ears, a bad habit I gained from observing my father and knew disgusted my mom. I scanned everything at the self-checkout, confident until I reached around to my back pocket and noticed a peeled label stuck to the machine that said 'card payment only'.

I hadn't checked my bank account in a few days. I had to bluff proficiency, throw myself forward like a gymnast, to regain some ground. Martin stood next to me as I swiped my bank card, and after a few seconds of suspense, the card still hadn't read, so I said, buckling under the pressure, "Oh, please, god!" Then it went through.

When we got back in the car, Martin had gone from looking irate and put-upon to almost laughing.

"What's so funny?" I said.

"'Oh, please, god!' I forgot you always did that. Even at the slightest thing, you sound like someone's lowering you into a shark tank or something." This was familiar, how he acted when he was genuinely charmed with something I did, but it still surprised me. I smiled through the feeling, despite myself.

"I was pleading for my life in there, like in *Sonatine,* right?"

"What?"

"The shark tank thing. It's from that gangster movie we watched together that one time, isn't it?"

"They just use a crane to lower a guy into some water until he drowns. It's not really that kind of movie. Didn't you fall asleep during that one?"

"Oh." I sat back in the car seat. I let us joke at my own expense to change the arc of my anxious composure into something endearing. It didn't always work that well. Seeing me briefly off-balance had always made Martin friendlier, and I was an old hand at breaking his cold, sullen annoyance. I had probably been dozing through the movie, like Martin said. But I remember trying to make sense of the ending, too. As the credits rolled I had an uncomfortable feeling, at the time rare between us, that he had experienced something profound and totally private from the film that I couldn't even begin to get at, resulting in a disappointed silence.

"Are you doing anything this afternoon?" He asked after we'd pulled out of the parking lot. I glanced at my phone again.

"No, not at all."

"I have to get back, but Mollie's afternoon shift got called off so she needs me to pick her up. Do you want to come around to the house? If you're just going to be alone all afternoon."

"Why are you inviting me to things now?" I said, acting distracted, like I was watching the road signs. Our breakup, from the outside, looked like sudden total indifference, but I figured the chances of Martin just maturely moving on, and having a response of sincere, healthy, adult friendship towards me were zero to negligible. He occupied himself with navigating the series of turns that would get us to a gas station on the other side of the road.

"I dunno. You just seem like you could use some people to hang out with."

"Jesus Christ." I glanced at him, then rested my arm against the window and watched the cars inching up behind each other, waiting, signalling, a nightmare of communication via heavy machinery. I chafed at any change of plan that affected my strategic retreat from a social situation, but his offer was also more interesting than going straight home, and I wanted to show my willingness to play along, even if there was a bit of cruelty mixed into it. "Try saying that again without grinning so much."

"Seriously? Have you talked to anyone else from our class, since graduating?" I didn't answer. We both stewed, me at the blatant implication that he found my nonexistent social status either entertaining or pitiful, and Martin regretting that he telegraphed this too strongly.

High school had been a practically continuous reinforcement that I was undesirable on almost every level. I was a loner, tangential to a few tightly knit groups, considered kind of gross in my inability to socialise or dress attractively. I was short, round-shouldered and unathletic. The way my body grew out, rounded hips, soft pouch of stomach, excessive breasts, made me feel a begrudging kinship with the dairy cows grazing in the fields around town. They had novel fluctuations of hormones pumping through them too, dutifully producing the portions of milk that came with every cafeteria meal, sometimes in experimental flavours like root beer or creamsicle. I was the perfect sort of girlfriend for Martin to have at the time because he wasn't a great fit anywhere either. He committed his free period to the cross country team but was hardly a star, even in that understated, geeky sport; he also wasn't academically focused or career-minded enough to have anything in common with honour roll nerds.

I had an overwhelming curiosity about what sex was exactly. It seemed like a massive mystery that only grew as I looked up lists of contraceptives and how to use them online, or scanned blogs and advice columns for issues of sexual dysfunction I could only contemplate as a tourist. Porn didn't really tempt me, it felt too expedient, like it would give the game away all at once in a shoddy explanation. I wanted to defer the end of the mystery as long as I could, and then worried it would never come regardless of what I wanted to do or actually did.

With Martin I could try whatever the confined opportunities for privacy we had let us get away with. It facilitated classic teenaged horniness, sure, but something else motivated my pursuit, the idea that I could collect this knowledge directly, as information, with my body. Certain acts were still worth bothering with (blow jobs, for example, kind of sucked) beyond realising they left me feeling bored. Pressing on, I assumed it would all add up to some massive insight. I had stopped believing in an answer ages ago, but still wondered when I would stop feeling clueless.

I felt the car sway as Martin turned into the parking lot of the gas station at last. I shut my eyes. It wasn't the same car he had in high school, of course. This car was sensible but a bit spendy, sleek and black with leather seats and subtle blue accent lights on the automatic locks and window switches. The inside was bare of any other incidental items hinting at hobbies or after-work activities, except a bottled Frappuccino in the centre console, warm and growing a skin from sitting in the hot car all morning. I assumed it was Mollie's. Like how Mollie dressed, her slight out-of-sync naiveté, it felt like an emissary from a time too fresh and unpleasant to be nostalgic, the flat, slightly rancid sweetness of them a beacon of coerced mid-aughts optimism. I'd last had one maybe on a youth group trip at 14 years old. The total expurgation of non-artificial smells inside the car implied Martin made regular use of a car wash loyalty card. His car in high school had been a junker of a 1995 Neon, green outside, paint flaking away from road salt corrosion, fuzzy and brownish inside. It must have had its own terroir that could be detected on us by smell, organic must of exhale and deteriorating seat foam. We thought we were getting away with something, in hindsight it must have been obvious to everyone, even our parents.

Martin spoke into the long, ruminative silence that served as my answer.

"I wouldn't have gone out of my way to find out if you were home or anything, but since we ran into each other..." He yanked the key out of the ignition. I opened my eyes and caught him looking at me, slouched in the shotgun seat and leaning on my own fist, like an old painting of a poet. We both looked away, shifting our comportment as little as possible in the process. "We got along before, for a while anyways. I guess I thought cutting each other out like that, when it was so much to do with the circumstances back then, it was childish, right?"

This was the most satisfactory resolution I could hope for: he would say that he just didn't care, because he had become the bigger person. He was a fancy car owner, paying down a house, new cohabiting partner, hitting all the normal life benchmarks that articles on Bloomberg continuously griped about our age bracket's inability or disinterest to meet. High school era battles coming back and trying to strike from below would barely scuff him. He was a cliff face now. In fact, it was embarrassing that I cared, that I still felt nervous about those things, and he wanted me to know that he was aware of this *while* expertly navigating around it.

"Yeah, we both had so much going on, we just needed a break," I agreed. My fall-back and basest strategy for negotiating relationships.

Martin exited the car and from inside I heard the deep clunk of the gas valve opening, the nozzle being inserted. I caught a whiff of the pure, astringent gasoline smell unique to large gas stations like this one, gross but enjoyable. There was the sound of the gas flowing into the tank until it jerked to a stop; Martin, like my father, jiggled it around a bit to see how much more could come out before tripping the auto-stop again. He paid at the card reader without going inside and re-entered the car.

"I want to show you I don't have any hard feelings. It's whatever. And Mollie is a lot like you. She's newish here, kind of introverted."

"She has no friends besides you," I suggested.

"See, very similar."

We drove to the frozen yoghurt place where Mollie worked, and after a minute or two she came out the front door in a lime green apron, grinning, making a show of turning back to the building and waving. She jogged over to the car and raised her eyebrows at seeing me in the front seat. Her apron was embroidered with her name and FROG-GURT, which was the name of the store, with a helpful clarification that this stood for 'fully rely on God', rather than representing anything about the ingredients. She walked around to the back seat without saying anything.

"Hey babe," Martin said. "Amy needed me to drive her to Target. Everything okay?"

Mollie sighed, still holding onto a stiff smile. "It's fine, apparently they cut some hours last week, I should have noticed," she replied. "Are you dropping Amy off?"

"I was just going to hang out," I cut in. "At the house I mean. Martin suggested it. Unless you don't feel like it." I wanted to give her an out, which she'd maybe extend to me. The situation was probably more awkward and annoying for her, but her response was instantaneous, generous.

"No, that's fine!"

Martin's house was different from the ones in my development. It was narrower, better placed in relation to the nearest area that could be called 'town', but still fairly remote, despite being on a busy road. White plastic siding covered all four sides, the shutters were blue. Martin parked the car on the driveway and let us in through the front door.

Inside, knickknacks selected by Mollie stuck out against untouched white walls and faux hardwood flooring. She dropped her own set of keys from her apron pocket into a wooden bowl on a narrow table near the door and kicked off her sneakers, which sat in a scuffed corner. If the interior had any sort of intentional style, it was trying to be an Ikea display without enough warm lighting or budget. Mollie pivoted on her toes, sliding her socks over the perfectly smooth wood pattern laminate, smelling of hypersweet Bath and Body something as she untied the back of the apron, lifting it over her head.

"Back in a sec," she said, going up the stairs. A bathroom light and fan clicked on, and a faucet started running. Martin walked me through to the back of the house, pointing out the kitchen and downstairs bathroom.

The house had the sense of sitting still, dark and completely quiet while no one was there, and I was glad they didn't have a dog, probably put off by Martin's father's attachment to a bounding, piece-of-shit boxer that would relentlessly jump on me whenever I came over until Martin kicked it into the backyard. It had none of the redeeming personality other people detected in or, failing that, projected onto their pets. Martin's father seemed satisfied to treat it like an appendage he could use to impose on others, to fill the house with chaotic, unpredictable energy even when he wasn't in his typical state of being mildly day-drunk.

"That's a really high fence," I observed, looking out at the backyard through the sliding door leading out of the kitchen while we waited for Mollie to come back downstairs. The fence was the smooth white plastic kind, staggered so that nothing was visible through the slats. Some of the dirt in a far corner of the yard was unsettled, like he had tried starting a garden at one point but gave up.

"It's for privacy, I guess." His mouth had a little pressed down smile to it.

"Oh, gross." Our constant fooling around in his car, pulled down random side streets or undisturbed stretches of road after school, was a matter of expedience, of not having any reliable right to privacy in either of our homes, or so I had thought. He laughed with grim surprise, a sad undertone to it that made me think my assumption may have been off. Or maybe he just found it embarrassing, me scrutinising the sexual practices of his current relationship. Inside his home, I could feel out the climbing holds of his interior, run my fingers along the walls to push into cracks, all more intimately.

If inviting me here was just a gesture of friendship, I was being abnormal, scrambling for ways to know how to get one over on him, while constantly suspecting him of jockeying for petty superiority over me. It wasn't like me to be provocative, I preferred to roll over unless it really counted. But I needed to test if this stability and accomplishment was real, in the sense that it actually satisfied him. I had loved him because he was a portal — of anger, of dissatisfaction — opening glimpses to somewhere else through the films he found online and how he got to go to Washington DC to stay with his mom on holidays. When I told him I wanted to study art in college, he couldn't tell where I'd gotten the idea. He held it over my head. Pursue art? Sight unseen! Had I even been inside an art museum in my life?

That had stung. The edge of cruelty he took on when my aspirations came up made me feel embarrassed even now. Now it was dulled, disarmed — I had managed to escape for a few years, after all — like a knife rolled up in layers and layers of cloth, concealed and waiting.

Mollie's bouncing gait came down the steps, she was wearing pajama pants with a sweatshirt that cut off to hang just above her hips. If she didn't seem so resolutely heterosexual, I would have thought she was really trying to come on to me.

"Alright, I have to go," Martin said. He slid his arm around Mollie's waist and pulled her in for a kiss, much more graceful than the way he'd often clubbed me with an awkward arm around the shoulders years ago. I pretended to be distracted by something in the backyard, but felt his eyes in my peripheral vision as he pulled away. "See you."

"Yeah, see you later," I said. Mollie waited, looking at

me, trying to get a sense if I was the type to propose what we'd do immediately. There was the sound of the front door closing and Martin's car starting.

A doppelgänger is usually only glimpsed, a vague and unsettling omen, but now I had been forced into typical friendly conversation with her, twice, and following this we were ambiguously 'hanging out'. The briefness of an encounter allows whatever is seen to be written off as a trick of the eye, its significance more psychological than comprehensively 'real'. Seeing Mollie across several different contexts, in different outfits and lighting, and working myself up to studying her for longer periods of time didn't reassure me that we *looked* different. Conversely, it also convinced me that she wasn't attempting to be 'like' me either. She was a completely standard sort of different person; the more I observed how her moods moved across her face, her mannerisms, the more sure of this I was. There was no malice and no attempt to supplant me in how she acted. If it bothered her that her boyfriend's ex had re-entered the picture, I couldn't detect any obvious tells. It would be absurd to get upset anyways, no girl like her had ever seen me as a threat.

"Want to watch a movie?" she asked at last.

"Sure, you choose." I smiled, relieved, sensing a slight kindred spirit in her choosing a low-impact, semi-social activity. She grinned back at me, like I would have, feeling someone was being friendly to me, desperate to keep it going.

Chapter Four

I hadn't fully adjusted to how strange it was, without intention or the typical lead-up to parenthood, to find myself regularly responsible for children. There was a firm delineation between us, I was not only legally a not-child, but an authority figure now. To be called 'Ms. Amy' didn't make me feel old, not exactly, but like I was being yanked along without my entire will, into the land of the superego — the one who denies, rather than someone still sorting out my own life.

By the middle of the second week, the kids had given me full, indifferent reign over the TV, which was a break from my mom cutting in with her opinion on whatever was on. I could watch melodramatic reality shows, gory sci-fi reruns, things that would make me squirm to openly show interest in around her. The kids didn't care. Cecil was usually absorbed in a Minecraft project on his tablet while Susie rigorously arranged her collection of variously new and *n*th-hand Barbie dolls on the floor.

Some of the dolls had gruesome disfigurements. She had balled together bits of tin foil to furnish several with hook hands, or grafted popsicle sticks to the more significant losses with thick layers of tape, others were left with raw-rubbed nubs. Their little dramas were also far from sugar-and-spice; there were always potions, disguises, reasons for the dolls to be undressed and re-dressed, put under marker and safety scissors. I assumed Jessica was fine with it, since few of the dolls were spared from this condition; it had long been their lot.

Something frustrating happened. Cecil pushed his tablet away from him over the carpet, then reached out a finger to press the lock button. He sat for a moment in thought, looked at me, then crossed the room with deliberate strides to the bookshelf. Unlike Susie, he didn't rummage, chucking half of the shelves' contents to the floor in the process. The single book he pulled from the shelf was several inches thick, with gold text on a spiral galaxy background proclaiming "Secrets of the Universe". He sat on the couch next to me and opened it to a page where some CGI aliens had been superimposed into a photo of JFK giving a speech. The heading of the page read, in shouting capitals: TIME TRAVEL — ALREADY POSSIBLE? I tried to skim over his shoulder. The content combined scientifically plausible explanations of wormholes, relativity and so on, with more fantastical extrapolations about what far-flung advanced societies out in the infinite universe could already do upon harnessing such phenomena. He turned the page and the topic abruptly changed to "THE HUMAN BODY INSIDE A BLACK HOLE". Cecil spoke up, noticing my attention.

"My teacher gave me The Lion, the Witch and the Wardrobe books to read because she says there's a lot of them to keep me occupied. But they're kind of kiddie?" He treated it as a slightly provocative statement, prodding me to see how 'cool' I was with more adult-minded, realistic and grounded topics to him.

"Those were awful," I agreed. "Child abuse to make anyone read those." Even my childish sense of injustice had hated that the story so cleanly sorted kids into categories of twee suck-up and problem child. I fantasised about being the one that had sold out their family to the ice milf, except I'd get to live with her forever, possibly marry her.

Cecil snorted. "Yeah, who cares about frickin talking animals these days." He was satisfied to get away with being a little mischievous. "I really like reading about quantum theory and time travel and stuff or just like, how much stuff might be out there, in space. Which is a lot."

"That's cool," I said. He seemed happy, and went back to reading. I thought of a future where he made the logical leap to flight tracking sites, slipped on the hard, slick rim of the basin that careens down to new world order conspiracy nuts and hardcore OSINT doomsday preppers. My dad had toed the periphery, often going out into the backyard with a pair of binoculars when there was the sound of aircraft overhead in the evening, and the drone of late-night AM radio would click on in my parents' bedroom when he couldn't sleep.

Both still had some innocence to them, in my mind. A nine year old would reach for the tools available to him, which, in his books about the mysteries of the cosmos, were wormholes, time travel, alien abduction. I thought of Jung's self-conscious apologia for his interest, like my father, in flying objects, unexplained coincidence, psychic intuition between twins or people at least very similar, under the correctly felt inference that he was straying too far from the humanistic science that had reared him. He seemed to express the sinking feeling when you catch yourself succumbing to magical thinking, but can't stop it either: *something is being seen, but it isn't known what.*

Everything in front of me had been charged, lately, with this ominous significance, or maybe I was just living in my head even more since coming home, pattern-hunting. I looked at Cecil, thoughtfully flipping through increasingly spectacular and dubious possibilities, seeking the answer that would click everything into place. Maybe we should keep an eye on each other.

Despite indulging in some trash TV about a condition called 'sexsomnia' and preparing some microwaved mini pizzas for lunch that went over well, by the afternoon I was systematically checking all routes towards potential novelty on my phone. As days in Jessica's home became only a mildly uneasy norm, and my duties became more routine, I still avoided checking Facebook, the platform defined by lingering, inappropriate connections to past lives. It felt like spying, to observe what high school or college ex classmates were presenting themselves as doing (yoga, marriage, dog fostering, career advancement, divorce), but now it all felt too close, as if to look would be potentially to be drawn in, to see something happening down the street from me now, or to myself.

I opened it. Just one thing. Whatever would show up at the top. Mollie was asking if anyone wanted to come by and pick up a floor lamp she and Martin decided they didn't want. The lamp looked guilty, cornered in the photo, like an abandoned animal. I looked out the window.

"It's nice out," I said. "We should go outside."

Cecil looked up from the book, then flopped it face down over the couch's arm rest, thinking.

"I sup-pose," he said, in the pseudo-sophisticated manner of a child who reads a lot of books where characters say things like that. I tried not to show too much of a reaction to it. I had been like that when I was his age too, and didn't know I was doing it. "Just don't try to make me do any sports." I shook my head. He looked back at the book, checking that he hadn't creased any of the pages, but also trying to buy some time, mentally accounting for every possible negative scenario. "Or exercise," he added at last.

"Wouldn't dream of it. I promise."

Outside, we all stood in the front lawn, with no particular direction in mind to head in. I realised, of course, that the kids would turn to me, so I tried to think. There were fewer empty lots than I remembered, from my early childhood summers playing outdoors, usually by myself, scaling piles of displaced dirt mounded next to construction sites, or sliding down the packed soil ramps to play house in dug out basements.

"Where do you usually go?" I asked. Cecil, without hesitation, rolled his eyes.

"This was your idea!"

"I know. I know some places, I'm just curious."

"Well," he started, after a pause, "there's the field with the cows nearby, where weird stuff happened."

"Weird stuff?"

"My school bus goes by it. I saw it when I was riding the bus, really early in the morning, there was a cow lying on the ground, getting dragged away by a machine."

He seemed very concerned about this, with the sort of intense solemnity only children can manage. I thought, it's a bit gruesome for a kid, maybe, but yeah, they probably do need some sort of equipment to drag dead cows away. I looked at Susie to see if she had any reaction to this story, but she seemed bored without something to occupy her hands.

"Susie, do you want to go back in the house and get one doll to take along?" I offered. She nodded and I let her back in the front door. The moment we were alone Cecil continued.

"It was really mutilated. I didn't want to say it while Susie was here because she's little. And it was the day after I saw red lights at night, when I went down to the kitchen to get water."

"Red lights?" I asked. Susie burst back through the front door, wielding a doll by its torso so its bare rubber feet stuck out in a point like a dagger.

"Mom tells me not to give Susie ideas. Or like, it'll scare her," he said, lowering his voice. We had to change the subject for now.

"Ok, ready to go?" In response to my question, Susie repeated after me, in the affirmative.

The road to the cow field wound away from the far end of the development, and as we walked along it the houses got smaller, some of them older, with rusted pickup trucks sitting in gravel drives, wire fences holding back goats, the bulk of the farmland implied to extend back and far away from the road. The kids seemed happy enough, and the roads weren't too busy, but I wasn't sure this was a good idea. It was innocent enough, I was curious, and even if Cecil ended up saying something strange in front of his sister, Jessica had seemed to expect this would be an issue. At worst, I'd have a story to tell her, finally.

We reached the broadest field, a classic red barn with peeling paint on its far end, self-evidently the spot. I nervously monitored the drivenness Cecil took on, simply ducking through the wire fence ahead of us to enter the field, but there were no animals nearby and the farmhouse down the drive looked dark and empty. There was a line of tall trees bordering the property, so I could prepare a basic lie about a missing ball or remote controlled aeroplane if anyone confronted us.

As Cecil and his sister romped down the bank into the field, I leaned back on the metal guard rail at the edge of the road, which someone had zip tied a corrugated plastic sign to. I glanced down my shoulder to read the sign in reverse, and when I made sense of it, it slapped me with a pang of anxiety and renewed resentment of my stupid hometown. It was the kind of thing that, even though it was probably not explicitly condoned and only required a box cutter to detach, would be more trouble, in terms of local sentiment, to remove than to just tolerate. The faded print on the brittle plastic surface conveyed an ominous order: Fly The Flag While We Still Have Freedom. Of course, the image of the so-referenced flag had long turned pale pink, the blue corner speckled and greenish. I looked out over the field, remembering my own childhood fixations; the possibilities of black holes, sure, but also the encroaching end-of-days, be it from God or the Mayans or Weapons of Mass Destruction. Concern over any flag had always felt like pointless window dressing. I'd hated the flag, before I even had a sense of politics, like when we made little paper window decorations to hearken the election, just after the Millennium had come and gone without incident. It was flagrantly ugly and mediocre, like everything else around here. A year later, I would be looking up at my father, pumping gas into the family car and frowning at the gas station sign. A huge flag at the top of a new, white pole unfurled itself off to the side of him. More and more flags. What, in particular, did whoever had printed and affixed such a sign worry about? Every car dealership had a flag the size of an airport tarmac, so did the Longhorn Steakhouse. I thought, fuck you. I thought about the little pair of scissors I had bought at the Target, wishing they were in my fist.

Cecil calling my name snapped me out of my apocalyptic rumination. I looked over and waved at him. He was standing next to an oval patch of yellowed grass.

"This is where the dead cow was!" He said it with a sort of triumph at finally being taken seriously. I did a light jog to reach him, gravity pulling my boots forward to clomp down the steepish drop, then stood, like Susie, with my hands on my hips, staring down at the dead, squashed grass. It was too perfectly rounded, and probably a place where a large bucket or trough had sat for a long period, some kind of felicitous sign that confirmed his memories rather than where the cow had actually laid. Cecil was deep in his own recall of the sight, though. Thoughtfully, he crouched down next to it and touched the grass where yellow met green.

"What do you think?" I asked.

"What?" he said.

"Just in general. Why do you think it happened?"

He hugged his arms around his knees, looking at me dubiously, then glanced at his sister. Susie wasn't paying attention, wandering back towards the fence near the road to make her poor doll play tightrope between the posts.

"I don't know. It was the day after I saw the lights. And the cow was mutilated, you know? Like its side was all scraped up and open. There's not, like, normal animals around here who would do that, mom says so." He shifted uncomfortably on his feet, screwing up his mouth. "Don't talk to my mom about it, okay? She doesn't like it."

Even with a child, it was easier for me to roll through the question than to lie. He seemed to say it more for my benefit than his, anyways. If I wanted to get along well with his mother and make a good impression, I wouldn't bring up topics she had a concerned, disappointed reaction to.

"What about the lights?" I asked.

"It's like I told you earlier," he said, impatiently, maybe a bit suspiciously. "The day before I saw this, I got up in the middle of the night and I wanted to get a glass of water from downstairs because I was thirsty. I felt kind of hot, maybe. And while I was downstairs, the light changed, you know? So I looked out the window, and there was this big red ball. It was glowing, like, a ton." He spread out his hands in front of him for emphasis. "It wasn't a car for sure."

"Yeah?" I said. "What do other people think?"

"I don't bring it up at school unless people ask, obviously," he said. "And when they do ask they end up saying 'are you some kind of moron' or things like that. So why ask me stuff like, do you believe in aliens or what happened to your dad in the first place, right?"

"That sucks. Kids can be assholes," I said.

"Mom says she doesn't want to discourage me," he went on, relating the word 'discourage' with theatrical sarcasm, a direct quote. "But also that I should keep it to myself." He shrugged, pushing himself back up to his feet. "But if it's real, and it ends up being something I can prove, the first time someone really proves it, I'm being really calm about it, you know?"

"Yeah," I scanned the edge of the field to make sure Susie was still preoccupied. She was trying to loop the slack of a stretch of wire around her doll's neck.

"What do you think?" He asked, his voice surprisingly direct. I looked down at him, feeling put on the spot.

"What do you mean?"

"I mean, my theory is, if aliens are why my dad's plane disappeared, of course they'd show up here. Maybe to take me too, or at least let him see us." He looked back at the patch of grass. "Or apologise, anyways. But then, when people try to explain away alien stuff they say it's because something bad happened to you in the first place, that you think it happens, you know? That you're crazy."

"Yeah," I said. He waited, like he was expecting me to go on.

"But if it was caused by the aliens in the first place, I can't just be imagining it, right?"

Susie called me from the fence, trying to weave her way through the gaps between the wire, and I could sense eyes from the house watching us, though it may have just been the pressure I felt from Cecil's question. Did he want to be reassured, or did he expect a genuine theory from me? Or, maybe, he wanted to know if there was an actual theory that would reassure him.

"Let's go," Susie yelled. "I'm getting sunburn!"

Cecil frowned and rolled his eyes.

"It's a possibility," I said, giving a limp non-answer. "I don't know. Weirder things have happened."

♦♦♦

The invitation Martin texted me on Thursday evening was so casually dashed-off, like he was half-expecting me not to respond, so I assumed the cookout by the river would involve a whole uncomfortable crowd of people, but it was just Martin, Mollie and me. Maybe without me he had, rather than valiantly achieving the hometown belongingness that I had abandoned any hope for, instead opted for continued isolation closer to home.

He had strapped a portable grill into the front seat, setting it atop some beach towels so it wouldn't scuff the leather. He could have put the grill in the front seat for an egalitarian, fair-minded reason, or so he could anxiously stick out his arm to steady the top of it every time we went over a pothole. Either way it meant that Mollie and I bounced around in the back seat of his car as we went, not bothering with seat belts.

The gravel dispersed where the path ended into a patch with soft, uneven edges by the riverbank, and spread out all the way up to where the stones started to be swallowed up by the mud. You could walk right down to where the water, slightly amber brownish, would pool around the front of your shoes. I tested the waterproofing of my banged up boots as Martin set up the charcoal grill and Mollie unfolded some crumply nylon camping chairs. When I turned around, Mollie was standing off to the side with her arms folded, while Martin alternated between patting the front and back pockets of his windbreaker several times, the back-and-forth motion traced by orange day-glo accents that ran across the muddy camo print on the back and sleeves. I thought, with private amusement, that he never would have been caught dead wearing something like that in high school. It was corny, an article of clothing that immediately marked you as a committed townie, but ultimately slightly more attractive on him than his endless track jackets.

Martin finally said, "Shit," under his breath, and went back to the car. Mollie flopped into one of the chairs and gestured at the other, inviting me to sit. She looked on edge.

"You don't smoke, do you?" she asked.

"Nah." I said.

"He forgot a lighter."

"Oh," I laughed. She sighed and rolled her eyes. Behind us, the car started up and pulled down the road.

"Guess he has to go all the way back and get it…" Mollie said, watching the back of the car pull back down the gravel road. It was so like the Martin I knew to charge off without a word, though now it left me alone with Mollie again. The afternoon we had spent watching films until Martin's shift ended was uneventful. Watching something on the couch allowed us to remain apart from each other in a way that the intimacy of having to squeeze together to look at a laptop screen wouldn't have. Mollie's selections were *Mama Mia!*, agreeable enough, and *Moonstruck*, prefaced with, "This one is my favourite." She watched both silently, almost as serious as the bakery girl sniffling when Nic Cage screamed about slitting his throat with a bread knife, then visibly relieved when things worked out. When the film ended, Mollie said, "Wasn't that fun?" and I'd agreed, even though what was most fun was finding out that Martin was dating someone with taste in movies so opposite his own.

Now, sitting across from me with the inert grill between us, her attitude was completely different. She winced with that sort of embarrassed frustration straight girls always put on at their boyfriends being childish or inconsiderate, when it's more about the scuffed illusion of the relationship than a specific thing they can expect an apology for. Unhappy, she looked so much like me. I must have been smiling, thinking about this, because she fixed her own face into a smirk when she glanced up.

"Oh well," she said, sing-song. "It'll only be a few minutes."

"Yeah, no problem."

I began to think that maybe our visible similarity didn't matter so much, or that cultivating my attitude towards it as not having any particular meaning, of being a kind of redundant, banal observation, was best. There was always an element of accident in resemblance, after all, but believing that on its own ignored the significance of the context that allowed the comparison to be made. Maybe how I ended up reassuring myself that our similarity didn't matter every time I thought about it was the more significant thing; but what, then, was the subconscious meaning it pointed to? I couldn't come up with anything to ask her directly. My thoughts scuttled in my head like a hamster in a wheel, and I knew they wouldn't go anywhere near my mouth. I assumed Mollie didn't think she looked anything like me, because she was younger and she hadn't known the me she resembled. I didn't have a sense of myself changing over time until later, either. She stared back at me, into my scrutiny.

"You can come over any time, you know. If it's hard to be at home."

"Why would it be hard to be in my own house?" I asked.

She frowned. "I was just saying, if you need the space on the weekends… If I'm off I'm never up to much, especially if Martin's at work."

"Oh," I said. "He told you I don't get along with my mom or something."

She didn't say anything, only returned to her half-hearted smirk, then adjusted it to look more placating.

"What a little shithead." I added, after a while. This made her laugh. "It's complicated. He's one to talk…"

"Mmhm," Mollie said and kicked a piece of gravel so it clanged against the side of the grill. "He practically needs a restraining order to deal with his dad. I have no clue how he got through high school living in the same house as him. Cats and dogs, right?"

"Yeah, it was crazy," I said.

I racked my brain for a small talk hand-hold that would help me understand her. I was at an extreme disadvantage. What else had Martin said to her? How much did she already think she knew about me? I fidgeted in the chair, awkwardly adjusting the angles of my elbows and knees. Every position I took seemed to throw it slightly off balance, heightening the nervous disorientation of being in a situation I had never planned to return to. City girl! I was supposed to make my real friends in college, become cultured and have the uniqueness that marked me as too weird here confirmed as what made me interesting out there. Instead, I had been just as at a loss, and now I was back, living with my mom, hanging out with my ex — a situation of such obvious failure Mollie felt compelled to charity towards her boyfriend's high school sweetheart.

Mollie hadn't gone to high school with us, she wasn't even from around here, so it wasn't just her perception of *me* that was inaccessible. Her affection for Martin must be something totally different than what mine had been. He was physically attractive in a different way. I supposed I was too, if I was feeling generous. He was an older boy, with a house and a car, and she was the type of girl who confidently and securely desired that.

We had both been quiet for a while. Mollie peeled a softened sneaker off one of her heels with the other foot. "I'm going to go in the river for a bit," she said. "It's finally getting warmer." When she pulled off both of her shoes, I noticed she wasn't wearing socks underneath and cringed. She walked delicately over the muddy gravel and bent down to roll the cuffs of her pants up once her toes were in the water. "Come on, you might as well," she called after me. "If we have nothing else to talk about."

We were far from the main road, it was quiet, and the

shadows were beginning to get longer. I hesitated, then bent down to undo my bootlaces. I had to shift my weight back suddenly as the chair tilted off two of its legs, and Mollie looked back at me and laughed, fluid and charming, that laugh that had been jarringly familiar to me and yet also so much better, so much freer than my own. She was already up to the middle of her calves in the water.

Even if there was no point to it, I seized any small window of opportunity to make a girl like me with a competitive edge. So her taste in comedy was pratfalls? I'd give her plenty of material. I pulled off my socks and balled them up, tucking them into the boots. The gravel poked painfully into the soles of my feet, and I remembered how I marvelled at how thick and tough that same skin used to get during the summer, cultivating it. It would always go soft again. I dipped my toes, bare toes this time, where the water lapped at the soft mud. It was cool, not quite cold.

"You know, I saw a UFO while I was swimming in this river once," I said. "About two hours away, where I went to college."

"No way. You seriously believe aliens would just drive by? Here?"

"It's not so weird. 'UFO' technically means anything in the sky that you don't know what it is, right? And the nuclear reactor at Three Mile Island is just up the river, too."

"They'd scope that out?"

"Yeah, to warn their kids about the consequences of half-assed work."

She laughed again. "Okay, what did it look like?"

"It was like a flash, and then a yellow and white ball with a long tail. I saw it going up, just as it was getting dark."

She shifted back and forth on her legs, coyly indulging me by thinking of a sensible explanation.

"Ball lightning. Or the International Space Station. Whatever. What were you doing in the river at night?"

"Skinny dipping with some other girls," I replied. This really amused her. "People are really sociable their first week away from home."

"Come in then, if it's nothing new for you," she said, kicking an arc of water at me. I pulled my own pants up to the knee and sloshed ahead. I made a show of running after her, lurching between river stones on momentum and intuition, trying to bank waves in her direction. As I got further out I could feel the cuffs of my pants getting heavier, filling with water, clinging to my legs. I lifted my foot and kicked, getting her with a decent blast, and she screeched. I reached down to dip my fingertips into the stream, flicking light droplets at her.

We were toeing the realm of horseplay. It would have been natural for me to reach over and graze my hand on her arm, grab it even, but I didn't cross that line. Pressing too far, even with innocent intent, could provoke girls to pull back and go quiet, screw up their face in confusion, the inscrutable point where they'd scoff and go 'ew'. It was something they seemed to understand about me before I understood it about myself. So I shrunk back from accidental touch, from getting too close, making me come across even more unnaturally than if I had thrown myself at her.

There was the sound of a car trundling over gravel again, we turned around to see Martin parking and getting out. I slogged over the river stones on the way back, scraping the arches of my feet and twinging my ankles, as Mollie returned to the shore as casually as she bounced down the steps, or padded across the linoleum floor in her socks at home. She wasn't giggling, but had an air of laughter still hanging around her. Martin was already crouched at the grill, poking a long barbecue lighter into it until some of the coals started to glow. He stood up, closer than me to Mollie, and caught wind of the mood. Looking between us he said, "Should I be concerned?"

"Fuck off," I said, automatically. He took it playfully enough. He may have only heard in scandalous second-hand about the cumulative circumstances that led to me coming home. I didn't have a sense of how he would respond to it; it wasn't even an idea either of us could have articulated while we were dating. Together, Mollie and I teased Martin about forgetting the lighter, how mad he'd looked, as he laid out turkey burgers on the grill and they began to give off steam, then smoke. I hoped the material could prove infinite, preventing the topic from turning to me, but it didn't. The patties were scraped off the grill; Mollie insisted on handing me one of the least-mutilated looking ones, and we ate off flimsy paper plates that started to blow around as the sun set. I had a face full of food when she asked me, "So, how is it, being home?"

My hand lifted to my mouth as I chewed, giving myself a few seconds to think. I tried to be funny about it, rather than express my primary feelings: grim, anxious.

"It's alright. I needed a break from being broke and unemployed in the city, at least."

"I can put in a word for you at the store. It's probably too far from your house to be worth part-timing at, though." She frowned. "Martin, can you think of anything?"

"I have a job," I said. "Not really a super formal one, just babysitting for this woman in my neighbourhood who's had to go back to work recently."

"How's that?"

I was truthful. "It's basically fine. They don't get up to much."

"Are you good with kids?"

"Absolutely not," I said. "They kind of stress me out, they can be very intense."

"But they don't get up to much?"

I shrugged, looking at the glowing coals going grey at the bottom of the grill.

"Martin said you got some art supplies when he took you to Target."

"Yeah," I said. "Maybe I haven't totally given up the dream."

"Oh, you're an artist?" Mollie leaned forward with interest. To hear someone in my hometown say it, after I had gone so long describing myself in more and more roundabout ways in the city, felt strange. Still, to most people here, I looked the part, or the part of an eccentric at least.

"No, uh," I laughed, acting as if the burger on my plate was really visually interesting. "I studied art. Like in college."

"So what do you do?" she asked.

"Nothing much, yet."

The sun had gone behind the trees now and the dark was setting in. I was thankful the particular details of her face were softened.

"Your ex is very mysterious, Martin," she commented, leaning back in her chair.

"That's new," he said.

"Ha, ha. Very romantic." I dug into the burger with more

focus now, since it had started to cool down, but also so that I could glance up between bites to peek at Martin and Mollie, to get an idea of what sort of affection passed between them in quiet, casual moments.

"What's up?" Mollie asked, catching me looking. I turned towards Martin, who was more used to my middle-distance staring. It was like he could sense the provocative retort I was coming up with, something like: "You know me, I like looking at interesting couples."

It would fly right over her head, I predicted, but Martin still frowned at me, heading any implications off at the pass.

"Sorry. Just zoning out."

Martin packed up the grill and Mollie folded up the chairs and gathered the garbage into a bag. There was an unlabeled bin screwed to a post nearby that we shoved everything into. I stood at the edge of the river, looking upstream, in the direction of the towers, though their pillars of steam weren't visible anymore. Behind me, Mollie and Martin's voices gradually took on the cadence of an argument as they packed everything into the trunk, but I couldn't make out the exact topic. I didn't turn around and kept still, feeling queasy while thinking of all the ways it could be about me. A car door opened and slammed a bit more abruptly than necessary.

"Ready to go?" Martin called. He didn't wait for me to say anything before getting in the driver's seat and closing the door. I scanned the far bank of the river. At first it felt like a strange floater was jagging my eye, but then I knew there was some kind of red light on the opposite shore, by itself and bigger, brighter than headlights. I squinted at it, and caught a whiff of air that felt unnaturally dry, pulling in my nostrils with a smell like burnt hair. A headache began to throb in one of my temples, and my vision seemed to narrow around the light.

Then Martin honked the car horn and rolled the window down. I glanced over my shoulder, took a deep breath, and the strange feeling dissipated.

"Come on, I've got work tomorrow."

"Alright." I turned, not looking back over the river, though I was able to take another peek when I opened the door. The light had dimmed, or disappeared behind a tree from this angle, or it really had been just some stupidly modded up car light that had pulled away. Either way, my eyes couldn't pick it out anymore. I climbed in the back of the car, next to Mollie, who seemed tired and bored. I watched her rest her head on the window, nuzzling with her dark reflection as the car began to pull away down the path. Martin didn't say anything.

"Sorry," I said, after a while, feeling compelled by the tense mood to apologise. "I just thought I saw something."

Physically, I could tell I was changed: singed nose hairs and the strange, happy adrenaline of the fated encounter, ways that were private and undetectable by others. Martin and Mollie were closed off around me in their tiff, but as I sat straight up in my seat, me, the one that was always slouching, I understood that I was now familiar with a tiny portion of the feeling that had convinced my father to leave.

Chapter Five

Deep summer arrived, stretched out, became unwelcome. Inside, I would get goosebumps and dry skin from an arid, over air-conditioned tundra; while outside, the roads baked in the sunlight, the wavy haze rising off of them a stern warning that I'd start going pink then red as a lobster if I lingered too long without meticulously covering myself in sunscreen.

I hated how much I sweat and how direct sun made me squint, how everything began to smell vaguely of softening plastic or tar. There was always a smell, the chemical tang of wood pulp, the great cloud of manure passing over on certain days, calamine cream and greasy tubes of Banana Boat SPF 50, but under it all was the whiff of hot, dry asphalt. With the kids, I perched on a hill of long-neglected, displaced soil on the very edge of the development. We had found the new frontier of half-aborted construction projects and prospective family lots that had been my childhood domain. We just had to walk fifteen minutes in the opposite direction from the road that led to the farms and, eventually, the combined elementary / middle school.

It was nostalgic to supervise the kids climbing the piles of loose dirt in various states of being grown back over by grass, to help them down into the half dug out basements and foundation pits to explore. I thought to myself, feeling clever, that the building / bildung had been put indefinitely on hold, so long as we could play here. Part of me was amazed I'd gotten away with so much, crawling around in abandoned construction-in-progress sites right in my own backyard as a kid, without even considering it particularly rough and tumble. The appeal, of the mounds of dirt especially, was undeniable. Up here there was maybe a little breeze, the air could be a little fresh.

Susie slammed a poor naked Barbie doll into the dirt like it was a hand trowel. The smooth rubber legs splayed and bounced her arm back up, but she didn't seem to get bored of it, her fingers gripped around the knobby breasts until her efforts gradually formed a little pit in the ground. I had asked her earlier if she ever felt like anything else, you know, playing with her animals or Cecil's old cars that he didn't use anymore — but now I saw why she turned me down. The mystery and gravitas wouldn't be the same. She left one doll lodged in a pit of sufficient size. "Omigod, she died!" she nudged the other into saying, tilting her back and forth in her fingers. "I gotta go get some grass to cover it up." Susie switched to concentrating on pulling up handfuls of grass.

I checked my phone, frowning at a picture message Mollie had sent. She was resting her elbow on the clear plastic divider that went over the front of the long counter where they kept all the toppings that could be added to the frozen yoghurt, and made an exasperated-yet-composed face underneath the green visor of her uniform as she angled the phone to show that the store was completely empty. *soo fckin bored* read the message that came immediately afterwards. She had sent it to both me and Martin, so the sentiment was clearly sincere, but I hesitated to respond with any more substance than *lol same.* Would it be taken as too eager? I clicked the phone lock, leaving the message typed but unsent, and looked back up at Susie, who had harvested a respectable mound of shredded grass already.

Her little dramas required the dolls, even if it seemed like a morbid fixation, because they were about the limitations and transformation of the body, so far as a five-year-old could understand. On cue, she unearthed the dead doll from the hole under the pile of grass. "I have to go… she can't see me," Susie made the doll whisper, as she stole away on curved toes.

As I was watching Susie play, Cecil flopped down next to me. He had been dragging his razor scooter up the hill and riding it down again, seeing how far he could make it slide sideways before it either ground to a stop or pitched over. His face was flushed and he was covered in dust and grass stains. He seemed to go about every activity with focus and roiling frustration, as if playing outdoors in the summertime was most like repairing a malfunctioning appliance or watching a losing sports team.

"You alright?" I asked. "It doesn't seem like you're having fun."

"It's not fun," he said. "Can we go inside."

"In a bit," I said, not looking forward to enforcing the tick inspection then coming up with some novel and satisfactory response to their almost immediate need for snacks. If I diligently managed it, though, I could cherish the reward that would come. Jessica never seemed to mind if the kids' play clothes were deposited in the hamper in rough shape, she'd say something like, "I'm glad they're getting outside so much," and smile, with that glow that made me stupid.

I thought of the light I briefly saw over the river, as Cecil and I sat on the thin layer of grass that had grown over the unsettled dirt. Down the slope, Susie had both of her mutilated dolls laying side by side and was sprinkling shredded grass over them.

"I just wanted to talk to you for a second," I said to Cecil.

"About what? Did my mom tell you to say it?"

"No, but you don't even know what I'm asking yet."

"Ok, fine." He seemed to be in a worse mood than I had even been able to observe.

"Have you seen anything weird again lately, you know, like the stuff you told me?"

"Shut up! Mom did ask you," he said, moving to haul himself up and take the scooter with him. This made me feel like, instead of dealing with the unpredictable moods of a child, I had blundered a delicate and consequential matter, high-level existential negotiations.

"No way!" I said, making a show of bluffing even though Jessica's curiosity about his UFO talk had been pretty restrained since the first time she had asked me at the convenience store. It was, at most, a mouthed implication snuck into the typical, day-to-day chat about how the kids were doing, if anything interesting had happened while she was at work. "I wanted to ask because I saw something too."

He looked at me, rightly suspicious. The whole conversation felt vaguely like manipulating a child even though I wasn't lying. Validating his perception, or presenting something as a factual event from your adult vantage point, which, most sensible people would agree is some kind of alternatively explicable delusion, was, excluding the easter bunny and a few of his comrades, probably considered harmful and vaguely immoral as well.

"What did you see?" He asked after long consideration, during which he glanced at Susie over my shoulder.

"Well, I was down by the river on a Sunday night, like a week ago."

"What were you doing there?" He asked. Okay officer.

"I'm an adult," I said. "When you're grown up you can go places at night for no real reason." I paused for him to raise a further line of questioning, but he didn't, so I went on. "I was looking over the river and I saw a red light too. A really big, bright one, obviously not a car. Just like the ones you saw. So I was just wondering."

Cecil thought about how to respond to this, caught between the easy conclusion, calling 'bullshit' or whatever age-appropriate term, and the more difficult aspect, to consider that his private metaphysics for understanding, not just where his dad went but the alienating, incomprehensible nature of the universe in general, had a corroborating witness. I sympathised. My own thoroughly rehearsed personal fantasies formed a long list: that I could, through acting the part privately, groom myself into being a genuine prophet of God (5-7 years old, fully sublimated into atheism combined with a general obsessive tendency to narrativize); later, that thinking of the outcome of an event would bring about its opposite, or at least eliminate what I had envisioned as a possibility (high school age to ongoing, though partly diffused through a Mephistophelian embrace, or at least expectation, of the negative); finally, that a mysteriously defined and antagonistic cohort of 'good people' in particular could sense dirty or cynical thoughts coming off me like an odour (took hold sometime in my early 20s, becoming instantly intractable). Within my perceptive apparatus, the daily nuts and bolts of making sense of the world, these things were absolutely feasible and usually true, or worth acting as if they were. If someone outside of my head referenced them, much less acted like they were an actual, existing phenomenon, I would be terrified and also think they were insane.

"You're just trying to be nice." He said it sadly, a strange synthesis of dismissal and wanting to believe.

"No, I really saw it," I said. "But I understand if you don't believe me."

To see something unbelievable could only be isolating, now I knew this in a minuscule way. Cecil was already aware of the way alien experiences were normally dismissed, a traumatic substitution for a banal, awful thing that the individual's mind couldn't accept; a displacement of rape, kidnapping, domestic violence, prejudice, abjection, being shoved out of their world. To be supposedly 'understood' in that way would hurt him horribly. He must have felt really marked with it, like he wore it everywhere, the weirdest and most upsetting thing that had happened to him. But the opposite was impossible, to instead be understood through something so strange that known, collective reality couldn't contain it, only your own. Even if one other person acknowledged it, the ominous enormity of the implications became so startling, the instinct had to be to shrink away. There was no resolution. Half-hearted incorporation as some sort of trauma or misunderstanding was probably, ultimately, easier.

"I haven't seen anything lately," Cecil admitted eventually, ripping up a handful of grass. "It's like they're really gone, or weren't even there in the first place."

"Maybe they're just somewhere else," I said.

"So? Then it had nothing to do with me anyways."

"Sorry," I said. "I just thought you'd want to know." It felt like a forgoing of my implied authority, pathetic even though I knew, objectively, it wasn't, to justify myself to a child I was babysitting.

"I'm not stupid, you know?" He said. "Even Susie knows he's basically almost certainly dead. Though she doesn't really get it, you know? She hardly remembers him because he wasn't home much, so 'being dead' is just like, oh, he's in 'Texas', or whatever." He threw in one of his mother's affectations, an eye-roll and air quotes around phrases that were set off from the rest of the sentence, but didn't quite make sense to treat in that way. "Like her understanding of dead doesn't include that it's this whole permanent thing."

I wondered, did mine? Could anyone's, without being paralyzed by a purely instrumental relationship to time, planning for optimization that could never be realised? To run up and down this pile of dirt, to sit at the top of it, to put on an operatic cycle of deaths and rebirths, unity and deception, simply for your own enjoyment — all of these things were to act as if you weren't going to die. To look back at my childhood was to be aware of so much empty time, stuff I didn't particularly remember or which didn't add up to anything about my current self in any discernible way, a stretch that only tended to come back to me in momentary snatches and/or regrets.

"But," Cecil went on, "If there's one really slim possibility that things are actually ok, I have to follow it, right? If the other thing is, like, 100% definitely permanent." I had to admit, it was the logic of taking death absolutely seriously. It was also an enormous, incomprehensible weight, an unattainable standard. Still, I remembered thinking that way, as a child, when everyday things felt impossible and painful.

I went too long without saying anything. Cecil got up impatiently.

"Can we go inside already?" he asked.

I called Susie and we walked back through the empty lots and along the road back to the house. When we got back, I checked her hairline and socks for ticks while Cecil silently picked up his tablet and climbed the stairs to his room. After furnishing Susie with her ham roll-ups and string cheese, I opened my phone again, looking at the message Mollie sent with what I'd typed still sitting in the text box. Martin hadn't responded with anything. I deleted what I had written and tried something else.

at least you look cute

I picked out the emoji, beaming with the little hands by its face, to accompany it.

Her response was instant, worse than nothing.

Lol

♦♦♦

Jessica returned at only a quarter past five that day, and could sense the sullen mood. I opened the door to the kitchen from the garage so that I could corner her in the mudroom. Cecil was still upstairs and Susie had gotten absorbed into an animal show on the TV. Concern shadowed her face but she did her best to look happy to see me. I frowned, what I had planned to say scattering in my mind like a handful of marbles dropped on a table.

"Amy, what's up?"

"Uh, Cecil's not in a great mood," I warned at last.

"What happened?" She lowered her voice and tilted her head.

"He seemed really down about stuff with his dad today," I said. "I just let him go up to his room and have some time to himself." She turned to the side, frowning, thinking. Even a little upset, or maybe especially a little upset, it made my heart thud to look at her.

"Okay, that's good," she said, even though she was

hardly happy with it. She glanced over my shoulder, wondering why I was still blocking the way.

"I'm sorry. I might have brought it on, a little."

"Don't blame yourself," she said. "I'm glad you told me. I'm sure it wasn't anything you did." As she said this, Jessica did the little shuffle people do when they're in front of each other on a narrow sidewalk. She moved her hand down, sliding close to my hip, to try and nudge past me. "Amy, could you?" I flushed, moving out of the way. I retreated backwards into the kitchen and went to the fridge to pull out the casserole she'd prepared in advance for tonight.

The casserole dish was heavy, a bright yellowish-orange enamel Le Creuset, and I stared at it for a moment when I set it on the counter, producing a surprisingly loud and sharp thump. No lid, foil crimped over the rim instead, but I still recognised the tiny handles that curved out so perkily, sending a wave of anxiety through me. In the presence of luxury lifestyle investments, my brain tended towards calculating whether I had been paid the equivalent of their price tag for my own artistic work or not (I had still not been paid one Creuset's worth); I also hated these things because Josie had owned an identical, powder blue one, that would come out of the cabinets once every three months or so when she decided to give caring for someone's extra sourdough culture a go. It was sooo cute, it was an investment for homemaking. The teasing disbelief she'd reacted with the first time she'd asked me to get it out, and I had no idea what it was, had been destined to spark an unhappy association in my brain. The highly pressurised and somewhat underwhelming reality of my long-awaited First Relationship With A Woman came from moments like these that exposed the ways that

I was an inadequate, awkward, undesirable, ill-fitting, shoddy woman myself.

"I can put this in for you, actually," I said, fumbling to start the oven timer. "I mean, I can start it while you're at work, so it's ready as soon as you're home, you know."

"It doesn't make a huge difference," she said. "You should let it preheat, by the way." She leaned onto her arm, perching herself next to me and tilting her chin up a bit cockily, like she was amused. Her gaze seemed to come down from even higher than the normal advantage in height she had over me. "Like I said, I'm sure it's fine. Everyone has off days. You've been great so far."

"That's really nice of you to say," I watched as my hands slowly peeled the sheet of tin foil off the top of the casserole dish. "I guess I felt like I should try doing more. Be a little more helpful, you know, so you don't have to keep working when you get home, too."

"You don't have to do that," she said. "No, I mean it. Leave the foil on." She gently pressed my wrist down and I bore it until it was possible to calmly move my own hand away, and laughed.

"Sure," I said, "Sorry. But really, let me know if there's anything else I can help with, during the day or whatever."

"I feel bad asking for any of that," she said. Her tone was going short, even as she tried to keep things pleasant. She had gotten more comfortable letting me see how tired or frustrated work made her, and, right now, negotiating my randy over-enthusiasm and insecurity was even more work. "I can't pay you like it's a real job."

"What are you talking about." Cecil had come down from his bedroom in the meantime. The sense of how close Jessica and I were standing felt even more immediate, and odd. Even she sensed it, moving back a step.

"I was seeing if Amy wanted to stay for dinner. Well?"

"I think my mom had something planned."

"Too bad," she said. "You should sometime."

"Yeah," I said. "I will, definitely, I've just gotta go." I went to go out through the front door as usual. As I stepped outside I looked back — Jess was smoothing down a cow-lick of Cecil's hair, his face still twisted in a curious, irritated pout.

♦♦♦

Martin was working on Saturday again, but I nagged him to drive me out to a convenience store on his lunch break. This time, I didn't bother coming up with an excuse, opening with *lunch break soon?* and offering only *idk i need chewing gum lol* as justification. When his car pulled up, he didn't step out, and I could feel the oppressive cloud of his bad mood as soon as I opened the passenger side door.

"I was just fucking around," I said, still standing outside of the car. "If it's really a pain in the ass you can go."

"No," he said firmly. "It's not you."

I got in. The problem was Mollie, actually. It was funny that I had texted him, he started, because up until a few minutes ago he *was* going to be busy during lunch. His tone, while he described the subsequent events, was sharp and annoyed, like when he related the unreasonableness of teachers, the track coach, his dad, everyone but me, while driving me home from school. He prattled on, each thing opening like a thin-walled nesting box carrying more digressions and parentheticals. She was being so weird lately. Like, always complaining about being bored or alone at home because they're cutting her hours at the frozen yoghurt place (though they won't tell her why, just deny it, actually, whenever she points it out), or, also, that he works too much and doesn't hang out with her enough (but then when they do hang out she never comes up with anything to do), so of course, being the one who has to come up with things, I (Martin) thought, why not take her out to lunch then, on a day she's off. So I called her, but she seemed off and was like, this is kind of sudden, I don't really want to, so I asked were you still asleep and she said well they don't want me at work so it's not a fucking crime, or whatever, to sleep in, like I was the one giving her a hard time and not going out of my way to do what she asked me to, anyways.

He pulled up to a Sheetz on the highway and I got out, purchased a pack of gum and returned to the car. Something about, if not analysing, simply stating the constitutive elements of the situation calmed him down, like he could get a better grasp on it now.

"By the way, do you mind stopping at the bank," he continued, when I got back in. "I have to do some paperwork for my job."

"Sure, why not."

The bank Martin stopped at was perched on a little commercial island that had been installed on a corner of an intersection. It was surrounded by a small parking lot broken up with oblong green spaces that drivers exasperated each other over as they moved around them in a halting spectacle. One of the curbs was torn up badly, and a pane of plate glass in front of the building had been reinforced with some plywood and tyvek. The situation that presented itself to me, taking in the details as I waited in the car, was that someone had rolled straight through the intersection, over the curb, into the bank's lobby. It was reported regularly on the news around here, old people driving, drunks, and it often happened at night, so probably no one had been hurt. The duct tape holding the plastic sheets in place looked brittle and ready to peel away, but business went on as usual inside. I leaned back in the car seat. It must not have been a priority to fix. After a few minutes, Martin came out, trotting over to the car like he had done to humour my non-enthusiasm in high school gym, and rapped on the window, my side. The switch to lower it clicked hard, which made me think that, despite driving Mollie around, he must not have a shotgun seat passenger all that often.

"Yeah?" I said.

"Do you have a pen? All the ones in there are dead."

"Don't they have any behind the counter?" I asked.

"There's a line."

"Sure, fine." I unzipped my bag and grabbed one that was hooked into a wire-bound notepad. "That might be the only one I have on me. So make sure you give it back."

"What, you think I wouldn't?"

Of course, by the time he filled the deposit slip and returned to the car with several signed and stamped documents, he had a new passenger bobbing in the front pocket of his polo shirt, which he'd forgotten.

Martin had developed an almost freakish vivacity now, going around, depositing his bonus or whatever. He looked healthy but in a heightened way that felt closer to death, the way a truly peak-performing athlete's heart could burst or tendons give out at any second. It was the type of energy he had when I attended school track and field events to provide moral support, a slightly manic 'runner's high' enhanced by the pain of pushing your own body and will to meet the rewards of small-scale, conditional social inclusion. Now it was exactly the same; he could work himself so hard at such a stupid job because of the tiny patch of normalcy it enabled him to pull together, something to lord over his father, Mollie, me. It made him happy, all the more when it was a response to an immediate problem, some sort of fight, an annoyance or an embarrassment.

I also knew from experience that this was an emotional state where he never wanted to have sex, and seemed to actively dislike it as a distraction that emerged from baser desires. He'd get annoyed at me and drive me straight home no matter how much seeing and fantasising about his compulsive exertion turned me on. It entertained me a little to imagine Mollie getting pushed off of him later.

"Martin," I said, trying to keep my tone flat. "You're acting kind of intense right now."

"Sorry," he said. "I'm in a weird mood, with all this shit going on today. But I'm glad you texted me, really."

"Oh, so it's not a total drag to drive me around?" I asked.

"Of course not. You're joking, right? Want me to swing you by the house?" I hesitated. He meant his house, again.

"Sounds like you want me to patch things up with your girlfriend for you."

His laugh sounded harsh and overly loud inside the car. "You were just saying I drive you around so much… I don't know. Just take her mind off things a bit."

I winced at this. This sort of bitter, condescending misogyny was one of his worst features and strategy of last resort in moments of frustration. It was specifically infuriating because I knew that he was smarter than actually believing in it, making it a shallow exercise of whatever shoddy power he could cling to for its own sake. But I also felt anxious about the position I was being drawn into, even though I was curious about Mollie and Martin, and found them more tolerable than I imagined reconnecting with anyone else from my high school class would be. They had both started leaning on me as a buffer between them, sopping up the overflow of what they couldn't say or couldn't give to the other.

"Where did you even meet her, anyways?" I ended up asking, when Martin didn't add anything else.

He sighed, feeling ambivalent and sore about the memory now. "I don't know. I went to the frozen yoghurt place one day and she was there."

"Come on. It doesn't just happen like that," I said. He rolled his shoulders and looked impatiently at the other lanes in the four way intersection, as if they would secretly get away with another light cycle without his careful watch.

"Fine, at one point I said something like 'you must think it's pathetic that I only ever come here alone'."

I scoffed. "You're kidding."

"She said it meant I was honest with myself, or something like that."

"To get frozen yoghurt all alone?"

"Yeah. So I asked her out to a movie."

"That's nice," I said. I meant it, but worried Martin would think I was winding him up, because it was the type of story most people would make fun of. He didn't say anything, but had stopped fidgeting so much.

With Martin alone, emotionally cracked-open by the

tiff with Mollie and the topic of how they met, I wondered if it was a rare window to broach the topic of her looking so similar to me, not now, but how I had looked in high school. It was unpredictable how he'd respond, but probing into it would produce a ton of information regardless. He could deny it vehemently — that meant something was obviously up. He could deny it casually, or respond dubiously, like maybe he just didn't see it. Maybe he would, begrudgingly, acknowledge it, either feeling caught or compelled to admit it was something strange that he had been considering but unable to vocalise. But how to ask it got diverted again and again on the path between my brain and the back of my throat.

Stalled in backed-up traffic, Martin took his eyes off the road to look at me, his face curious and open. I managed to return his look for a second. Thoughtful, calmer, done up in his work shirt, I wanted to know him well again, rather than feeling like it was merely expedient.

"Penny for your thoughts?" he said, turning back to the road as the cars began to move.

"What?"

"You looked like you were thinking really hard about something."

"No, it's nothing. I'm just sitting in the car."

"Sure. You're always thinking about something, the way you hardly ever really look at people. It always made me feel like I was missing something."

I went silent, feeling embarrassed. I knew I couldn't unselfconsciously project effortless listening, effortless response. At twenty-four, I already had a crease at the top of my nose, on the left side, from how my eyebrows would scrunch themselves together.

"Do you remember that one time you had to ask me to drive you to school early for the Honors Society induction?" Martin went on.

Folded cream programs, a black and white dress code I struggled to find an acceptable outfit for, it must have happened at one point.

"Yeah," I said. "Vaguely."

"You didn't want to ask your mom because the stuff with your dad was pretty fresh, I guess. But when we got there, they made me stand outside the auditorium the whole time."

"That's so stupid," I said. "I'm sorry, I didn't remember that. I mean, it was so pointless. I wish I hadn't gone."

"I'm not jealous," he said. "It just made me realise everything about high school was arranged to make sure you felt humiliated about one thing or another. I felt dumb. The cross-country team was barely a sport compared to football and shit, right? So as soon as that was over I'd just have my boring-ass life. And you did well at that stuff but felt like a weirdo."

That made it sound kind of internal, which is how ill-fit was always conceptualised — a problem with the piece that didn't fit. Martin wasn't dumb; it wasn't like his mediocre GPA was an inevitable, biological process that exuded from his body. When I thought of him I remembered never getting tired of pinging back and forth on AIM, to the point where we'd both be practically comatose in person the next day. Or watching him watch some weird movie and knowing that he was fascinated, taking pleasure in the thoughts it seemed to pull out of him. I only felt weird because everything that seemed significant to me tended to go down with snorts of laughter or silence when I told anyone else. I felt isolated because everyone seemed to already be so closely knit to each other, there was no gap for me to slide into. Hanging out unsupervised in his dad's refurbished basement, watching him fiddle with a burned CD-R or trying to get the entertainment system to recognise files he'd torrented from the internet, knowing we'd be lounging against each other, watching a movie it felt like no one for miles around would ever give a shit about, was almost as good as feeling sexually desired for the first time; maybe it was more important.

When he closed his hand, took that away from me, there was nothing left, no reason to stay. I felt my point slipping out of reach, scattering into some ugly feelings and impulses I couldn't organise into words, or ones I couldn't open my mouth and say. Even just something like: "Aren't you kind of weird too?" Maybe I could blurt that out, but I held my tongue because I knew he wouldn't say so, not now, anyways.

"What's your point?" I asked.

"No point. I was just thinking about it. Or, I guess, feeling glad it's over."

"Me too," I said. Then, "Okay, I'll stop by the house."

♦♦♦

Mollie had just woken up again. She was stretching and yawning on the couch when we arrived, treating the whole thing as a really indulgent occasion, but stopped, acting more attentive and serious at the possibility that Martin was still annoyed. After he left, I sat with her in front of the flat screen TV teetering on a cheap particle board electronics cabinet. The TV and couch were centrepieces in an otherwise under-furnished living room, a statement of personal taste, a symbol of the nature and compensation of Martin's gainful employment — the familiar portal to something, anything else.

Martin had always scrounged for whatever films he could get at the bottom of used DVD bins, and then the massive frontier of internet piracy opened up. The cabinet under the TV still held a few of the brittle, scuffed DVD cases, especially cherished, but it also contained a huge external hard drive with hundreds of nesting, overflowing folders hooked up to the flat screen.

While we waited for Martin to finish the second half of his shift, Mollie and I plumbed the folders on the hard drive, looking for something to watch to suit the strange mood. Everything I scrolled past was a hard sell; even the few chick flicks I had a feeling had been downloaded specifically to cater to her tastes didn't seem to make her happy.

"I'm not in the mood for anything," she said after a while. "Sorry, you can just pick whatever. The work stuff is still pissing me off, even though it's my day off, I know."

"What's up?" I offered, skimming through what seemed to be 30 to 40 Takashi Miike films. "If you wanna just vent about it."

"It's not even worth being mad over, like, I get it, it's a budget thing. Even if it feels like they're giving me less hours it's not personal, if that's all the time they have to schedule. And it's not even a money thing, like, Martin can basically cover everything, he doesn't need me to work. But I dunno, it seems like, even though they know I'm looking to pick up more hours, no one ever talks to me if they need someone to cover. Or even stupid stuff like offering to carpool, or hang out, even when I try to be friendly. I know, I'm being paranoid. Everyone's great otherwise, and we get along..."

Was it really as easy as just being friendly? Mollie acted like she believed this. The girls at work were 'great', approached with the right attitude of openness and trust. I started to have the feeling that she was getting treated the same way I had been, as a conditional. Lovable when you were passive and a means to shore up someone's sense of being 'a nice person', but always, inevitably, guilty of pushing that generosity too far. When it came time to cut hours, or, more trivially maybe, decide who to hang out with outside of work, invite along to something, to swap phone numbers with, she was the first and easiest to shut out.

What did she do that was worth bullying her over? (I recognised myself, a few years younger, in her, so perhaps it was narcissism or maybe a kindness to her and myself to call it 'bullying'.) She dressed kind of like a 'hot girl' bit character from a mid-aughts teen comedy, all the gaudiness of a Disney channel kid but with tits. She became seriously involved with an average-looking guy who showed up at her workplace alone and deployed a really pathetic pick-up line. Worst of all, she hadn't been around forever, her mom didn't know their moms, all that shit. So basically nothing. It was enough to throw her overboard at the sight of a cloud on the horizon. This was how I expected people who felt a part of something to behave, though sometimes I still felt it was a rank I could aspire to join, or at least berate myself for failing to.

"I only really have one strategy for those situations," I said after she trailed off.

"What's that?"

"Fuck 'em." I tabbed into another subfolder, 'Industry – Franchise Horror', and a long list of files dropped out of it like a drawer. I glanced to the side and noticed that she took it well, smiling now. "Do you mind blood and guts?"

After a series of negotiations on how gross was acceptable, then in what way was best, we went with a spontaneous decision: *Hellraiser II*. As we got comfortable on the couch, I realised hanging out in private, with neither of us having anything to do or anywhere in particular that wanted us, was re-familiarizing me with what it was like being around straight girls, how to enjoy it but also bear the weird gap — like images de-synced from an audio track — that would always exist between me and her.

"Mm, that's what institutions will do to you, Kirsty," I joked as the actress on-screen frantically tried to reason with cops, then mental ward orderlies.

Mollie didn't laugh, absorbed in the problems of the film, but she started to look bored when Kirsty started to explore the psychiatrist's weird, puzzle box mansion, revealing a cache of plot-significant photos and artefacts. I watched her when I felt like I could get away with it. After all, I agreed, the way they'd wedged in screen time for props from the first movie was kind of bullshit. Mollie sighed and shifted around a bit, and without even looking at me suddenly moved her shaved legs over my lap to lie across the couch. I envied how it was something she could pull off so casually; meanwhile, I was left having to be hyper-aware of where I'd put my arms. The old sensation of inflamed female friendships was coming back, blood running down the wall, the sinking uncanniness of a flayed subjectivity in your own mind you didn't fully know yet, always stinging, always giving yourself away: I Am In Straight Girl Hell Help Me.

When Julia came back from hell, a damp, red exclamation point of taut muscle, she went on to seduce the poor mental institution orderly who helped Kirsty escape.

"Come here, come to mother," she said, in a dark, audacious voice. I thought of Jessica and felt a pleasant shiver over the top of my stomach. Mollie gave a fluttering laugh at the line, and then Julia sunk her fingers into the guy's skull. He made a horrible sound like the very bottom of a milkshake. The feeling in my guts turned to queasiness.

Martin announced his arrival home with the familiar sound of car up the driveway, garage door, door inside, splash of keys on the counter, while the film was working down to its obscure, incoherent conclusion, and he observed as much.

"Who picked this?" He asked. "It doesn't make any sense." Mollie was ignoring his question, so after a few seconds I tried to come up with a response.

"I like Tiffany," I offered. On the screen the mute girl's actress was done up in braids and screaming 'mommy' to unconvincingly convey that the scene was depicting her childhood trauma.

"She hardly even says anything."

"I like Jessica!" Mollie interjected, glancing over her slack body directly at me for a moment. Then, cowed but not blushing, she quickly corrected herself. "Julia, I mean."

She looked back at the TV where the now monstrous psychiatrist was getting torn into chunks at last, and I stewed, knowing *my* cheeks were going red. The whole scene, happening outside of the TV, I mean, was domestic and convivial — Mollie's legs laid casually across my lap and Martin coming home from his shift in fucking khakis, lightly grilling our taste in films. Mollie's weird slip (seconds later, it already felt like an unreliable apprehension, had I imagined it?) had me contemplating the worst turns I could imagine this warm, friendly situation taking, like being engineered into some relationship-enlivening threesome.

"I have to take a piss," I said, sliding out from under Mollie's legs. I closed the bathroom door behind me, which was bright white and flimsy enough that I could kick through it. Alone, in what felt like a thin-walled cupboard with plumbing, I tried to clear my mind, make myself relaxed and sociable again. A fluffy cluster of tissues was tucked back into the top of the tissue box, like it was in a hotel. This is what people did, pair off, buy a house, watch old movies on an enormous TV. Muted yellow lights in the lamp over the sink made my reflection look softened, almost pretty. I pulled at a lock of my hair to see how long it was getting, started to feel claustrophobic, then sat on the toilet and made myself pee a bit, flushed the toilet and ran the sink for a while before going back to the living room.

"Besides, sentimental stuff about children is always so jejune anyways," Martin was saying. I winced at his stilted pronunciation, throwing hard emphasis on the shortened 'e' of the first syllable. Martin had the same problem I used to have, which still slipped through inevitable cracks in my desperate edifice of sophistication. It was the impoverished pronunciation of the self-taught, isolated book-learner or obscure forum-fed loner; knowledge being spoken aloud, nervously, for the first time. It was the same sort of thing he would have said when we were both sixteen and waiting in the Borders' parking lot for one parent or the other to come collect us, and I would have agreed. I frowned, thinking of Cecil's stoic evaluation of the difference between his own knowledge that his father was dead and his sister's, then looked back at Martin; he was addressing the statement to me, expecting me to respond.

"Right, but," I thought for a second before going on. "It's kind of funny, in the context of something so morbid going on, and that makes it kind of more real? To me."

Mollie looked over the back of the couch at Martin and I standing in the kitchen and squinted like she was thinking. My cloud passing over their moon.

"What?" I said. Her face relaxed and she turned back to the TV.

"I'm glad we're all getting along."

Chapter Six

Outside, there was an orgy of cars lining both sides of the street. Walking slightly ahead of my mom, I could already hear the sound of far off conversation, a radio playing. It was the 4th of July and we had been invited to Jessica's house, for what I assumed would be a low-key, intimate event. As I began to grasp the scale of it, its presence stretching way down the road, it felt less and less appealing. Obviously Jessica, the angelic image of a perfect PTA mother, would have a life bigger than I had imagined, and I was just a minor part in hers, even though she seemed to take up so much of my own. Each car represented an imagined relative, work friend or social contact — it made me turn in on myself, the times when I felt Jessica's proximity floating closer to me falling away.

"What do you look so miserable for?" my mother said. And then, "You really need to do something with your hair."

People arriving from their cars padded through the lawn, past the curvy, shaped flower beds that bordered the house, straight to the backyard, where someone was tending a charcoal grill and a plastic awning had been set up over a long table. I put my mental effort into becoming invisible, splitting off from my mom as if I had somewhere to go. Business-like, head down, I consulted the buffet table, putting some cubed watermelon, Bar-B-Q chips and a scoop of potato salad onto a paper plate that buckled under the stress. I scraped at the largest chunk of potato salad with a clear plastic fork, trying to cajole it into smaller pieces without sending everything on the plate tumbling onto the lawn. Feeling the prey animal response of eyes on me, standing alone, I tried to ignore it through devotion to this task.

A stifling feeling of what-the-hell-am-I-doing-here took over. From fourteen or so, every time that I had been around a large group of adults, at church, around the neighbourhood, during school functions, I was keenly aware of my status as the insufficiently lovable child of a man who, the up-to-date muttered third-hand accounts speculated, had gone fantastically nuts when the lightning rod of home internet touched to his brain, jolting it with raw SETI data, green alien gifs and the entire history of rumoured parapsychological studies, compiled and annotated by amateur web design kooks. This infrastructure had provided the connection that enabled him to fuck off to who-knows-where his talents were apparently needed by these shadowy, semi-scientific circles. But why have this abnormal response in the first place? A light on the horizon? One of those moments of inexplicable mutual intuition, which I had to admit, regularly passed between the twins? My overbearing mother, tamping down on his fantasies until he absolutely had to blow a gasket? Or could it have somehow been me? Disappointingly sullen, an eternally, intractably sad and difficult eldest daughter — at the time I couldn't be loved enough for him to stay. Objectively an insane theory, but one that haunted the halls of my low self-esteem, a shadowy hand still reaching out of the dark at my worst moments.

Standing at the corner of the awning, while families with young kids or middle aged men in shorts milled by, I caught someone looking directly at me. It was Mollie. She perked up, or at least altered the face she was making into something friendly rather than openly gawking. Martin was next to her, seeming possibly as out of place as me, an effort I appreciated. He was shifting his weight to the side, slightly away from her, holding a case of beer cans.

"Amy! This is so crazy." She walked over, taking Martin's other hand to pull him along. He'd picked up the tic of leaning back a bit and looking disoriented when a girlfriend led him by the hand, as if he'd never walked through a crowd before, which made me glad I had been too timid about grabbing his hand in public to ever do that to him.

"It's not that crazy," I said. I looked around for a trash can or a tucked away ledge to dispose of my picked-over plate. "I babysit for Jessica and I live down the street, so."

"Oh, that's cool," Mollie said. Next to her, Martin dropped her hand and nodded to indicate that he was going to drop off the cans wherever the cooler was, which she hardly acknowledged as he drifted away. She was studying me, incorporating this new detail into whatever mental picture of my life she had.

"How do you know Jessica?" I asked.

"She knows my parents," Mollie said, blowing through my question as if the explanation came to mind automatically. "She's so nice, isn't she?"

It was such an obvious lie (where, remotely, were her parents?) that I wanted to tease her about it, though how quickly, dauntingly almost, she produced it, like she wanted me to challenge her on it, made me uneasy.

"Yeah, she's great," I agreed. Martin returned, having upgraded the cans of beer he arrived with to a bottle, still damp from the mysterious cooler tucked away somewhere.

"Where'd you get that?" I asked. Martin looked down at the bottle in his hand, tilting it to read the label like he had never seen it before.

"It's inside." I rolled my eyes, but, since I knew the interior of Jessica's house so well, I could narrow it down to two or three places.

"Hey, it's a little crowded here," Mollie said, pitching forward a bit as a guy in a yellowing dress shirt with a bolo tie pushed by her to get to the food. "Let's spread out a bit, huh?" I got out my phone and checked the time. It was a quarter past 1 PM.

Standing out in direct sunlight we had to deal with the aggressive press of midsummer heat and the glare reverberating off of the white awning of the tent. Rather than being nudged constantly by the steadfast crowd around the food table, we now scanned the sky and side-stepped to avoid two kids who were tormenting a badminton set that had been left in the grass. I cupped my hand over my eyes to examine the crowd more closely. Jessica the hostess hadn't made an appearance yet, which meant that she was probably in the house, preparing something or other that would need to be run outside. Cecil would appear briefly, sometimes with his tablet still in hand, to bring out a fistful of plastic forks or another bag of chips. How habituated I was to keeping an eye on him kicked in, and I followed him, picking up a large, empty platter and taking it back inside.

"I wish there were more chairs," Mollie said next to me. Conversation wasn't coming easily, so we settled on observations about logistics.

"Yeah," I said. I looked around like I was treating this as a problem to solve. The few chairs that matched the house and patio furniture were held down by older family friends and people who were just dropping by didn't bring their own. We'd be standing until the party started to clear out significantly, probably early evening. Despite their image as leisure at its finest, holidays were a test of endurance for me — the home and backyard re-engineered so peace and quiet became as scarce as possible. I hung on with white knuckles as everyone else, allegedly, enjoyed themselves.

There was a murmur and some light applause among the crowd on the patio. Jessica was coming out of the back door with Susie holding it open, practically dangling herself from the doorknob. Jessica's hands were occupied, carrying a platter newly piled with burger condiments. Seeing her smiling and rushing towards the appreciation of the cluster of people under the awning I felt a rush of my own energy, like a car had backfired next to my ear. I was newly aware of my pit sweat. This sort of existential, life-or-death wrangling type of crush hadn't struck me for ages, maybe since middle school. I wanted to go to her, but watched my mother walk over as soon as the platter was out of her hands. She approached like she was opening with an apology: How's it going? Sorry if my daughter is *so* difficult. Jessica fanned a hand in front of her face and laughed. Not at all! I could practically hear her say it.

In my peripheral vision I saw Martin slug back the rest of his beer, watching me staring intently at what was happening near the house.

"Want anything?" He asked, looking between me and Mollie.

"I'm fine," I said.

"The fruit salad looked good," Mollie added.

Martin returned with another bottle of beer and a styrofoam bowl of bruised and paltry fruit salad pieces sitting in pinkish juice that already seemed to be fermenting. In the bowl, a plastic spoon ill-suited to the task ahead of it was held down by a cubed piece of cantaloupe. While gathering this stuff, he had also managed to loop himself into a conversation with my mother and Jessica, who, of course, had both been so happy to see him and followed him over. He exerted an effortless ease with them, talking about moving into his own house and his really sweet, really lovely girlfriend, sliding an arm around Mollie's hips as she dug into the fruit salad.

I watched Mollie eat, tuning out the conversation. Even though the fruit was slimy, she ate it with enthusiasm, awkwardly hacking pieces in half and scooping up chunks with the plastic spoon, then savouring them like a swanky gourmet dessert. The spoon squeaked slightly on her lips as she pulled it between them, almost like they were made of clinging latex rubber. Noticing that I was looking at her, she stared back, a bit confrontationally. It made me feel like I was the one being staked out. What was she curious about, my own purely businesslike and only aspirationally close relationship to Jessica? She finished eating the fruit salad and turned away to find a place to toss the empty bowl, leaving me the lone silent member of the group. I tried to pick up whatever the conversation topic had become.

Martin was bullshitting expediently, bordering on optimally, probably on his third or fourth beer. He discovered a hack that worked for him, probably the same his father had at one point. During high school, neither of us had snuck much booze at all, and I remembered the stiff way he interacted with my mother, hoping to impress her, trying to convey a self completely incompatible with any sensual desire. How far he'd come by going nowhere. I managed to latch on to some key terms. The topic was his recent promotion and the additional responsibilities it demanded, but also that it let him buy a new car.

"Hopefully Amy gets a break soon too," my mother was saying, a 'break' not being a scenario where I could take a breather from fussing over job applications, seeing the amount in my bank account dwindle, or being stuck in conversations that demanded precision micromanagement of my interpersonal relationships. She meant an instance when I could exploit one of these structures to hoist myself up into a successful life trajectory.

"Well, Amy is a genius, so if she can get out of her head for five minutes, she will." I looked at Martin as he said this, wanting to tell him not to talk about me like that. It felt cruel.

"That's really kind of you to say, Martin," Jessica said. "I'll miss having her around when she moves on to something bigger and better." I blushed at Jessica expressing even mild sentiment about me, and thought — *now*! Say something about anything, like what you're hypothetically saving money for, make up some job you'd like to do, but my mother hopped on to the conversational beat before I could.

"Martin would know as well as anyone what she's like. They were high school sweethearts, after all." I closed my eyes. What a nightmare. The way our relationship had flamed out bubbled under the surface of appearances — distance and nostalgia smoothed over everything. And now Jessica was going to be pulled in to the charade. I felt pinned down and wrong under a raking light.

"Oh!" Jessica laughed. "I didn't know that."

"Amy, are you alright?" Mollie asked. She had returned after getting rid of the bowl and was throwing my helpless silence a lifeline.

"Sorry, sun's just in my eyes," I said. Martin was finishing another beer. "Could you get me one too?" I asked.

He looked surprised at the request. Across from me, my mother frowned, like she had been expecting me to do it. I had to ruin the mood somehow.

"Well, I should go say hi to everyone else," she said, excusing herself. Martin returned and had swapped to drinking something out of an opaque plastic cup. He handed me the beer bottle he had in the other hand, oblivious to how the conversation had stagnated.

"So," he said to Jessica. "Be honest. Should any sensible parent trust this woman to watch their precious, irreplaceable offspring?" It made her laugh, but Mollie's mouth didn't even twitch.

With my mom on the other side of the lawn, Jessica stood closer, mothering me. She would put a hand on my shoulder when she brought up something funny that happened while I was at her house, or something I'd done well, touch my wrist when I said something that made her laugh. My cheeks felt hot and slightly puffy, like I was having an allergic reaction, and Martin took this in attentively. I drank the beer he'd handed me, probably a bit faster than I should have, and started peeling the label around the neck just as Jessica was gushing about how well I got along with Cecil.

"That's not really something I'd expect from her," Martin cut in bluntly.

"Really?" Jessica asked. "He's hiding inside now because it's a boring, mostly grownups thing, but the kids really seem to love having her around."

"Amy never seemed interested in kids at all."

"Martin," I rolled my eyes at him, compulsively picking at the corner of the label with my thumbnail, making a light, repetitive plonking noise. "I was like, seventeen. Of course I didn't."

Jessica rested her hand on my shoulder again, and then let it trail downwards. I was only wearing my bra under a thin t-shirt, so it felt like her hand could phase through to the naked centre of my back. Her fingertips touched me through the fabric in an arc that seemed to leave a trace, the singed circumference of a laser aimed straight through my heart. Like the pierced hull of a starship, too much of this and I'd depressurize and burst. She pressed in lightly, levering herself against me to turn and look back at the patio.

"I should go and check on the food again," she said, pulling her hand away. "I'll be back in a bit, though."

"I'll help clear the empty dishes," Mollie offered, following her. "I need to talk to you about something anyways. Is that okay?" She looked back at Martin, who made a sort of resigned face and shrugged.

"No problem."

I dawdled along with Martin as he sought out more groups of distant acquaintances to catch up with, so I would still seem engaged with the party. He forced himself on, obviously drinking too fast now, and the desperate maintenance of the far edges of his normal life began to feel pathetic.

I excused myself to go to the bathroom, and on my way back I saw Mollie and Jessica talking, standing close together in the living room. It wasn't a surprise to see them there, but the opacity of what it meant, their shoulders nudging together at an angle pointed away from me, felt worse — more of an urgent, disorienting shock, than if Mollie had walked across the room and slapped me in the face. I was already not taking the party, which seemed like a spontaneous mass demonstration against the specialness of my connection to Jessica, well. I was convinced by this point that what I had wasn't even a connection to her, really. It was just a dusty window ledge I could go up on my toes to catch a glimpse of her through. I had no idea what Mollie, the ostensible orphan, the bedraggled, sad frozen yoghurt shop girl, had to say to Jessica, but it was demonstrated in front of me there, between the familiar couch and entertainment centre, that it was more than I had.

Jessica glanced over her shoulder to smile at me.

"Need anything?" she asked.

I pressed my lips together and shook my head.

"I'll be back out in a sec," Mollie said.

The cooler was in the second place I had considered, tucked under a slight ledge at the end of the kitchen island. When I came back outside, toting a beer for myself and another I anticipated Martin would need by now, I felt utterly depleted. I moved alongside him again, but went inside myself. Martin's attention prickled at that; by his old measure, I began 'acting stupid'. But if I came across as acting, or in a meta sense, consciously wielding my shyness to be 'condescending' or 'insincere' or 'frigid', it was only because I sincerely felt stupid. I couldn't keep up with all the talk, I had no idea what was going on. The sun tired me out, the same as the endless parade of introductions and don't you know, don't you remembers.

Mollie came back, too late for me to feel like it relieved any of the mire collecting like silt deposits in my brain. I never knew how much to lie in these circumstances, or how to lie, while I assumed other people did it instinctively and with minimal mental and physical effort, not even thinking of it as lying, but as the formal requirements of conversation. I began to swelter as the calculus of what to say got knotted up in my head, deciding what was feasible but not true, because the 100% honest answer would end the conversation and make me seem like a bad sport.

I was horrible at lying, not in the typical sense, because even as hyper-aware of myself and my panic as I was every time I made something up, most of these lies seemed to pass without comment. But they grew; they got bigger and more elaborate to maintain in my mind, completely out of proportion to what I'd begun lying about in the first place (maybe: feigning an interest in sports, claiming to have seen a recent film, saying I had done a standard pro-social recreational activity over the weekend). Even though they had only fallen over on rare occasions, each time I racked my nerves with the assumption that it would tumble over, inevitable as in a game of Jenga.

Martin bore this pressure and even invited it, a sick demonstration of vigour I couldn't bring myself to share. Past a certain point I realised, feeling uneasy, that he was definitely drunk at the neighbourhood cookout.

Mollie even said, after a while, "I could use a break, huh? From talking to so many people." Martin looked at me when she said this, and I stared back at him, which clued her in to the fact that something was happening here, unrelated to her. "Martin, I thought you didn't drink," she said. It wasn't a question. He looked at no one in particular and swigged the back third of a bottle of beer.

"Special occasion."

Next to me, Mollie's skin was as pale and even as ever. Mine, I was sure, had started going pink and blotchy.

"I'll just dip back inside," she said, after a tense silence. "I think I'm getting too much sun."

We both waited an expectant, weary interval for Mollie to come back, or for one of us to pick up the conversation again, but I didn't want to talk to Martin. I was feeling sweaty, insecure and desperate to go home, even though wanting to be around Jessica — on the assumption that I might miss out on some chance (at what?) — wouldn't let me leave.

Mollie's absence stretched longer than a bathroom break or even a chat with Jessica, leaving me to babysit Martin when he started to look a bit absent and peeled off from the party. I followed a few yards behind as he wandered around the corner of the house, past an overfull bag-a-bug trap on the edge of the property swaying on a bowed wire stand. It seemed to squirm in the corner of my eye when I found Martin spewing into a cheery rhododendron plant in full pink bloom. The flower bed had just been mulched, so the bitter smell of digestive enzymes at work already hung around the side of the house.

The sound of him retching, of the vomit hitting the leaves and landing on the soft ground, was muted by the noise behind me, but everything else felt so far away I may as well have been witnessing it in a private room. Martin threw up like he was embarrassed, sort of delicate and restrained despite how gagging tensed him forward, distorted his usual features, with the huge pink flowers reflecting a flush back up onto his peaky skin. My hand rested on the corner of the house as I watched, feeling a queasy pulse throughout my body, which had gone taut and attentive, responding to the excitement and comfort in returning to being a sort of spotter for Martin, having loyal access to his grossest and most shameful moments.

When he finished, he braced an arm against the plastic siding, still hunched over, and looked up at me miserably when I walked towards him and placed a flat hand in the centre of his back. His shirt was damp most of the way through.

"Shit, sorry," he managed at last, too shy to say what he thought he was apologising for, which probably wasn't what I wanted him to feel bad about anyways. I watched his face, staring down at some of the spattered leaves, and let my eyes crawl along his profile, towards a chunk clinging to the side of his mouth.

Being trapped in a classroom or bus while someone else spewed used to drive me into a tearful panic attack as a kid. Just as mysteriously, I realised that childhood part of me that felt so wrenching and raw had, at some point, turned off. I wanted to pull closer to him. I was remembering how when we kissed years ago I'd think about how the corners of his mouth sometimes smelled like faintly sour milk.

"Are you feeling better?" I asked. "Usually you feel a little better afterwards."

"I feel stupid." For a moment Martin was still attentive to any sign that he wasn't done. I was only slightly buzzed, but spilling his guts seemed to have snapped him sober.

"You drank too much," I said. "It's fine. You were being kind of a shithead and then you threw up. You didn't like, die. Or become your dad." He glared at this barb.

"So it's not a big deal to you."

I just hummed softly, rubbing his back in small circles. I wouldn't give him the pleasure of getting mad at such a half-assed counter-retort; I wanted to come across as the responsible one in this situation, to keep things together while we were in my workplace, around Jessica and the kids. Sensing eyes on us, I looked up and saw Mollie and Jessica tentatively observing from where I had been standing at the corner of the house.

"He's fine." I said. "Just making sure he's alright." I gave Martin's back a final pat and he straightened himself up, moving back towards Mollie. I scanned Jessica's face for approval. Look at me being the good one, the mature one, the kind one. But she was unreadable. Instead, I saw Mollie wince.

"You have something on your mouth still," she said softly, and Martin turned to look at me with pissed-off disbelief.

♦♦♦

By dusk, most of the people at the cookout had dispersed, tired out from the heat, put off by the insects, retreating to their own homes for dinner or seeking their own separate vantage points for the fireworks display. I hung in like a champ, tolerating dry burgers for dinner and occupied myself with peoples' comings and goings, how they acted around Jessica and how they moved around and through the house, even though it didn't add up to any confident conclusion.

Martin and I sat on the front porch, waiting for the fireworks to begin as Jessica saw off my mom and most of the other remaining guests down by the road. Mollie had gone back inside the house not too long after Martin had been sick in the flower bed. She had come out again in the first place to say that she was tired from work but didn't want to make anyone drive her home, and Jessica said she could rest in her room like it was the easiest, most instinctive thing to offer, which made me burn with miserable, confused jealousy again. Martin was happy to wait, making a big show of fully sobering up and redeeming himself as a patient, soft-touch boyfriend before driving them back home. Next to me, he looked like he was relying on the tradition of watching fireworks to carry himself, otherwise he wouldn't have known what to do, queasy and distracted despite only toting around a plastic cup regularly refilled with tap water. In front of us, Cecil ripped through his own pack of fireworks, reading the gory names aloud, most alluding to typical implements of American self-aggrandisement: Multi-Shot, Gulf War, Cylinder Shell, Sky Patriot Missiles.

"Snakes," he said, with equal enthusiasm, pulling out a small packet that only had a few black pellets inside. He stared at it, then grinned and started poking his finger through the plastic film to get them out. I could tell his imagination produced some sort of colourful, writhing spectacle that would burst forth from the weird compacted lumps.

"Don't get too excited," I warned. He placed the pellets in a tight triangle on the bit of sidewalk in front of us that led up to the porch. Martin said nothing, just clicked the barbecue lighter, touching it to each point of the triangle in turn until they started to smoke. There was a moment of anticipation, on Cecil's part, at least. Martin shifted closer to me as he sat back down on the step. Probably unintentional, I thought, as I stiffened and leaned away, because he was so tired by this point, and his knee wasn't touching mine, just hovering at the exact point where I had to worry about accidentally leaning into it. The snakes unceremoniously elongated into slight black curls in the dark. Then nothing happened.

"What the fuck," I heard Cecil say under his breath.

♦♦♦

I used to cry at everything. Before any other names, my primary designation among my peers was being a cry-baby. I cried if a kid threw up at recess. I cried if I lost one of my nice pink erasers when one end was only barely scuffed. I cried if I got more than two questions wrong on a test, or if I was scolded for leaving too many loose papers in my locker. It always became a public curiosity, when I was mortified, desperate to be left alone. People never got tired of asking what was wrong, and I couldn't answer. My voice, which could so reliably chant along during read-aloud, felt like it was stuck under my throat, and pulling it up only dragged out tears, mucus and whimpering. I was turned against myself, there was something I was holding on to tight inside my body. I couldn't go easy about anything. Even when I first kissed Martin, my first kiss at all, adventuresomely stolen, I had expected — credits to some movie rolling, dull brown corduroy couch beneath us — to have a sense of completion, of actually feeling secure, figured out, that I desperately desired but by now had given up on. A similar farce replayed on my third date with Josie (though, expecting the ambiguity, I had prepared myself to conceal it). There had been no divine light of epiphany, and after a disappointed few seconds I sat back on the couch and quietly cried. Martin had been very understanding and didn't ask me what was wrong.

After the firework display faded to a dim remnant of smoke over the trees and the soft smell of gunpowder, I walked home and lay in my bed, trying to sleep. I was excruciatingly aware of the hotness and dustiness of the room and sleeplessness obliterated my ability to think clearly, not even offering the mercy of unconsciousness to make me unaware of my brain's capacity to follow its own contours disintegrating. I only felt the itch and discomfort of every inch of skin. Years ago, in a bustling city art gallery, I'd stood in front of a Louise Bourgeois drawing, done in the midst of her own deep insomnia, felt cracked open and wept. I could always finally sleep after a good cry.

Why wasn't it so easy anymore? I thought I had earned the respectful neglect of the few people in my life who would see me begin to tear up and smile about it, my funny quirk. But since coming home I hadn't cried, hadn't even had to swallow the urge, even when I felt suffused with anxiety and despair while I sat with Martin watching the fireworks. It was like a biological process had been activated when I resigned myself to coming home, with the solemnity that a caterpillar decides it's time to turn itself into a chrysalis. I was stuck in the stage where the interior of the chrysalis turns fully to liquid, unsure how to respond to anything or what my eventual capabilities for response would be.

Next to my face, my phone glowed and I checked it, some garbage email notification. I also observed with some dread that the clock read 2 AM. An entire hemisphere of my head was a throbbing ache. Time would march on without the will of my mind, or the relief of a span of empty sleep.

My mom must be out cold by now, I thought. One of my large suitcases still sat in the middle of my bedroom floor, the bottom unpacked. It was the one that I had tucked my wand vibrator into, wrapped in a pile of clothes I rarely wore and even more rarely expected to need when I got home: the few blouses I still hung on to that were my absolute most desperate play at 'making a good impression', usually for job interviews. I'd have loved to throw them out — if I thought I would never need them again I would. It was tempting to push the last layer of blouses aside, take out the vibrator and expediently obliterate myself until I was too tired to move or think, but my mother was a light sleeper, standing awake in the dark probably as many nights as I did. Even now I could sense that we were probably more like two ships on a stretch of contested waters, a subconscious part alert and listening for each other. It was the only trait I had inherited from her.

I wanted something that felt as uncontrollable as crying. I was jealous of Martin for getting so drunk, even though it was a really pathetic thing to let yourself do at a neighbourhood cookout. For a moment, he could detach from grinding consciousness, go around the party saying things about me (his little genius!) so effortlessly, and attend only to a single physical urgency.

Did he like me? Would he still fuck me, I meant. I didn't expect Martin fully liked or trusted me, the way we still seemed to be in an extended stand-off, the back and forth of comments that made sure the other knew we could still reach for the worst weapons we had. Why would he talk to me and let me hang around him so much though, if he wasn't at least a little curious? Even if the curiosity was tinged with distaste at how much I'd changed, I would take it. I had stuck to his side the entire cookout because otherwise I was too vulnerable, my presence too unjustified.

And then. My brain caught, like a deep record groove repeating over and over again: the image of him throwing up over an expanse of vivid pink flowers, light casting up magenta onto his face, his mouth, eyebrows screwing up, arm braced against the side of the house. Why hadn't I freaked out? It was like I'd been piloting myself not just from miles away but from a disjoint in time. For once I acted like I knew what to do.

He threw up. In my desire to dominate him I attentively rubbed his back, observed the film of sweat on his forehead, because it was the best thing to do. I remembered him catching his breath, looking miserable, tensing to determine if he was going to hurl again or not. He had a chunk stuck to the corner of his mouth. I observed it in my mind over and over. Inappropriate, regrettable vitality made me feel hot under the covers, like I was a swooning, agitated Sieglinde and he was the Wehwalt who crossed the threshold of my home, spewing on my rug — though he'd hate the comparison — like a dog, here to entrance me and derail my life.

Wagner, really? It was funny to me that this was the scene that came to mind. The disgust of sibling incest, especially twin-incest, maybe was not entirely located in the way it destroys the wholesome family unit, or even in the possibility of inbred children, but the factor that was relevant here: the current of intense narcissism underneath it, of only being able to desire what was already practically you. A shallowness, a type of stupidity, at only being able to recognise as your equal elements that reinforced your sense of self — this was what fascinated me about him. Usually I'd channel these feelings into some sort of art, which I currently saw no capability to realise. So what was the point? Where could I put these lurid associations that kept coming forth even on the edge of exhaustion, that I seemed to cook in, up to the back of my throat, no, now up to my eyes?

Martin was really like my twin in certain ways, in that

a twin enables you to witness the practical outcomes of your own thought experiments in self-narrativization. I was always jealous of my twin sisters, a closed set, more like my mother, and they appealed to my father's scientific sensibilities. As individuals, though, they seemed uninterested in this phenomenon, only entertaining it as one of their dad's quirks. Why didn't he notice (he didn't stick around long enough to) that Martin and I were the real two of a kind who had found each other, all sullenness, teenage cynicism and rage, boredom and unapplied intelligence. What if I had stayed? What if I had settled down with a nice girl and committed myself to an eroding but stable, practical job? The predicted hypothesis wouldn't hold, that was the result today, wasn't it? I would be even angrier, even more self-destructive, equally aimless, equally pathetic.

But maybe together it wouldn't be so bad. Fucking Martin would be so easy. I already knew how to do it. It would give coming back home, this sort of miserable temporal cul-de-sac that made me feel like a child again, some sort of narrative arc. It would please my mother, so long as the infidelity of peeling him off Mollie didn't cause much of a scene.

My thoughts had gone ugly, not just because I had seen him weak and sweaty, but because I saw the relief of my proud retentiveness through him. I wanted the abandon of spewing, the calm emptiness afterward, without the obligation of sickness. I started to feel sick, like I couldn't slow my heart down, though I knew I wouldn't vomit myself unless I had eaten something seriously dubious. Too bad. My hand slid below the fatigued elastic of my underwear. I took a breath and ran a testing finger down the middle. It came back wet, and I held it in front of my face, thinking, watching it catch light even in the dark of the room.

If nothing else, it couldn't make the situation worse. I tried to imagine my heart cushioned on the radiating pink light of the rhododendron flowers. The side of my other hand bumped against and then rested on my half-open mouth. In my mind Martin could be peaky and pale or wearing a flushed glow, both at once, ideal. It could be like he was wearing that blush palette Josie had been so protective of, what was it called, *Orgasm*? Nausea, pounding headache, my overcrowded imagination elongated the process I typically could speed through with relaxed focus. Something was holding me off, blocking me. My mind wandered to how Jessica had looked at me, the same as always today, but cast in a new light by the extended relationships all around her. Jessica turning to look at me from her conversation with Mollie, and now her smile read as pity. I disgusted her. It was hopeless now, because it always had been. I refocused on Martin, winded, bracing himself on the wall, replaying the tape until I could regard it with perfect calm. The fantasy started to get imprecise, abstract feelings, wrapping my arms around him from behind, pulling him up off his knees (but, he'd been standing) then, back around in front, sliding my fingers into the foetid, wet warmth along lips, past teeth, under tongue, hooking fingers, pulling out and open, almost tearing—

After a point I got off as quickly as the thought had occurred to me, rolled on to my side and wiped my fingers off on the ass of my underwear. Uncomfortable, I rolled over again. I felt like an oven left running with the door open at mid-afternoon. I was sweating from my cunt out. Kicking my legs out from under the sheets, I moved on to my back again.

Sprawled on the bed, my mind didn't empty out but raced down more frantically spiralling paths. *Things were getting very strange,* I managed to dictate to myself above the noise. And also, I had to get laid.

Chapter Seven

Of course, I was a husk the next morning. When I arrived at Jessica's house, she already had a mug of coffee waiting for me, there on the counter in the cow mug, which seemed really sensitive of her. She wasn't bustling around either, sitting across from me at the table as we both quietly emptied our own cups. After a few minutes, she asked, "Did everyone get home safe last night?"

It was a gentle way of acknowledging that things were rough and awkward from the afternoon before. I sipped the coffee, thinking. I hadn't heard from Martin or Mollie after they left.

"I guess so," I ended up saying. "I didn't hear anything bad, anyways."

"That's good, at least." She put the mug down and leaned back in the chair, looking off towards where the kitchen opened into the foyer to listen for sounds of the kids getting up. "I'm glad you knew a few other people. Sorry we hardly got to talk, since I was so swamped."

I kept the mug close to my face and pressed my fingers around it, like I needed to absorb its warmth. I was trying to hide how happy this made me. The cynical edge — that she was this way with everyone, just the type of person for whom being kind was easy and who could make everyone feel loved — still jagged at me. It wasn't a bad thing if she was like that, it was only a matter of my pride — of having overestimated the station I held in her life. But now I couldn't help my ego inflating again. She had to dash around for so many other people, but no one else got to sit opposite her at the kitchen table.

This gave me an opening to ask about Mollie, but I didn't. I wanted to hold off learning the exact nature of her closeness to Jessica. Of course it wasn't sexual. I put the mug down on the table and stared into the low pool of coffee that was left as I thought this, its surface as black and blank as what came up in my mind when I tried to entertain that idea. It was still enough to make my stomach sink. A clearer picture of the emotional intimacy, of what had come before, would smart even more.

"It's fine. I mean, it was good to see you, when I got to see you."

After Jessica left, I slumped on the couch, the world filtered through the low-level grimy feeling, the heaviness of head and limbs that came from poor sleep, but at least the children were sympathetic, in their own ways. Susie was still depleted from the all-day whorl of activity. "My headache hurts," she reported at one point, lying on her back across the carpet.

Cecil was residually pleased about how he'd managed to hide out in his room most of the previous day, only coming out for the cookout food and fireworks show, but sometimes I caught him looking at me with surprisingly direct curiosity. Maybe he was wondering the same thing I was, who were those people I glimpsed you with? I sank into the cushions and watched TV, flipping my phone right-side up every fifteen minutes or so to see if Mollie or Martin had messaged me.

I didn't expect it then, but that line would go dead for a week or two. Even though I was turning it over in my mind, troubled by it constantly, neither one of them followed up on the events of the cookout. I spent my weekdays caring for the kids and coming home to dinner, and my weekends steadfastly tolerating sharing the house with my mother, going out on her whims. I thought less and less of the tension between them, the unexplained fight at the river and the time Mollie spent hiding out in the house at the party. Probably, they had more important things to be doing, and I receded into the background of their dynamic.

It was easy to convince myself I wouldn't have wanted to intrude anyways, and the small ways I could extend my role in Jessica's life made acting on this principle easier. Starting with preheating the oven and putting in whatever she had prepped for dinner, a list of tasks I could do and imagine her feeling thankful for later spread out before me like spider web craquelure. I'd let myself collect on one or two before leaving, a pleased gasp that I'd loaded and emptied the dishwasher, or rinsed off and lined up the kids' stack of dirty shoes in a neat little row, but I'd never stay too long, not enough to join them for dinner or exhaust what I'd done. Jess began to attune to the way I passively expressed my pleasure at other people being around. Usually I was too embarrassed to say so aloud, blanking on the pleasant small talk that implied it, but whenever she got home, her relief and my happiness at seeing it started passing back and forth between us, like a tight circuit.

I got bold and started taking her bag off her, tucking it away in the coat closet when she got home. I was sped up by my inability to come to rest anywhere, like a gust of wind trapped in a blind alley. Touching her would be terrifying, panic-inducing, I had worked myself up into believing, but I could swirl around her. I could touch things in her house, tent my fingers on the smooth countertop and slide them a few inches side to side from hers. Watching her eyes drop briefly to follow them, to see what I was doing, pleased me. I was acting like a pet, testing how much it could be loved. Jessica would look at my hands, then back up at me, seeming amused. Unlike with Martin, it didn't really bug me if her interest was only humouring me; I was happy to have it.

"I feel so bad I can't pay you more," she said, from the opposite side of the kitchen island, the one closer to the front door. Another Friday evening, we had come to a standard move in our game. Jessica smiled comically and apologetically, handing me the bills pinched up in her long fingers while she leaned over the counter, propping herself up on an elbow. This let me look at her from a rare high angle. Even from below, the way her eyes tracked me didn't let me feel superior. I felt like I was being put on the spot to improvise more than ever.

Somewhere between chess and a ballet lift in terms of competitiveness versus cohesion, the intended next move on my part was to take the money, careful not to graze her hand, too much, and casually begin, "No, it's fine—", then insert something about the job I found pleasant or worthwhile, like, the kids are so fun! Your house is great. I totally raided the refrigerator. In a slightly non-standard move, I said, "It makes me happy to see how much easier it is for you, when you get home."

She wrinkled her nose, her eyebrows knit together, but she was still smiling, a sort of delight that I had moved in an unexpected but not unpleasant way.

"I really mean it when I say I wish I could pay you more, Amy." She slowly raised herself from leaning on the counter. "And I did pay you a bit more this week, since you've been doing so much. But just this once, okay?"

I fanned the 20s out, there really were thirteen, no, just twelve, rather than ten. Had she outplayed me?

"That's really kind of you, thanks." I tried to say as evenly as possible.

"I don't want you to feel obligated to do all the extra stuff." She said this a bit hesitantly, not like she wanted to explicitly discourage me, but more like she was worried I'd take it hard, pull away in response. "But we'll miss you once you move on to greener pastures."

I thought of responding with, "I wouldn't have to if you made me your stay-at-home husband," but I knew that was too aggressive, even if I said it in the most self-effacing, screechingly jokey way possible. Against someone who had just preemptively turned the tables on me, without even needing to think about it — I made a shy, tactical retreat.

"See you next week," I said, then slipped around the counter, letting myself out the front door. When I heard the latch close behind me I let the curve of my back nudge back against it and slowly blew out a sigh as massive as Riff Randell improbably swooning over The Ramones.

That was acting, a moment when I could play at the goofiness and futility of my aspiration. I knew! It was a purely emotional affair, entirely from my side. Jessica was as incidental to me as a beam of light, the sun passing through a window the perfect way for an afternoon hour, that I could warm myself with. How could she be anything but indifferent to me? I rubbed the bills between my fingers, shoved them deep into my pocket. She only wanted to do right by someone she recognised her standing over, without placing any of the awkwardness of our mismatched expectations on me. And because she was kind, and because she was the kind of person who had her life together, she was able to.

♦♦♦

On Sunday, I woke up at 8:30 AM, without an alarm, instead of stumbling downstairs around noon. I was feeling remarkably healthy, once I'd clawed back a few nights of deep sleep after the cookout, energised by a predictable routine and how the zip pouch where I tucked at least five of the bills Jessica handed me every week was starting to have some heft to it. Moved by genuine internal momentum I showered and dressed, and arrived downstairs just as my mother was leaving for church. She seemed not just confused but almost distressed to see me.

"Did you want to come along?" she asked, as if I was demanding something both unexpected and unreasonable by appearing.

"Oh, no, of course not!" I laughed, and she pulled a worse face, turning towards the door.

Once I was sure her car was out of the garage and pulling down the driveway, I made a guesstimated three cups of coffee in the coffee machine and took a few pieces of fruit out of the fridge. When the coffee was ready, I scrolled through images of dogs and engagement rings for a reasonable amount of time and drank from the mug when it was the right temperature. I said, "Ahh," like I was ready to face a busy day of mowing the lawn and putting a new shrub in down by the mailbox. I assumed I was experiencing a snagged portion of the degree of confidence usually alien to me, that separated me from people whose actions implied a totally unfamiliar relationship to their own concept of the self.

I typed a text to Martin: *want to get lunch?* I reconsidered, took another sip of coffee, and changed it to *Let's get lunch,* capitals and all. It felt assertive, bordering on aggressive, but he had been quiet and aloof for so long, I had to provoke him. I hit send and waited, putting my phone face down and only looking again when I had finished the coffee and fruit I'd pulled together. When I checked, the grey bubble showing that somewhere in the world Martin was typing flitted in and out of view. Then a message appeared.

Sure. Why not

I remember studying the message, though I didn't interpret any particular subtext. If I think of him now I can see exactly what this message conveyed — bristling, entertained, curious, all-over misery. Another message appeared under it.

Mollie and I broke up btw

Or are like taking a break

Tho probably you texted her before me

I was surprised, but didn't feel like having an extended exegesis about the context of his responses via clipped, asynchronous little text bubbles. I scrunched my face up thinking of how to respond, the shine of the morning already wearing off. I had the sense of getting myself into some absolute dog shit.

no, you first

what time?

♦♦♦

By 12:30 PM, I was perched on an uncomfortable metal chair at one of the high, narrow tables that seated two or four in a pinch, near the bar at a Longhorn Steakhouse. My feet dangled, the chair's 'back' hardly reached over my ass, and I constantly had to rearrange my weight in some way to reach for something, to relieve the way I was clenching a certain muscle to keep my balance, or to scoot out of the way of someone sidling past. The lunch menus were paper place mats that clung to the table's surface. Even though it had been sprayed and wiped down in front of us, it still felt sticky. The menu insisted that I would have some kind of bacon cheeseburger, and I didn't feel like further scrutinising the images for an alternative. When the waitress came by, Martin ordered a strawberry lemonade, such a contrast to my most recent memory of him, getting himself wasted, that it caught me off guard.

"Just a glass of water," I said, when the waitress turned to me, forgetting what I had wanted. "That sucks about you and Mollie," I added, once she was out of earshot. "She's a nice person. And it seemed like she really liked you."

"Yeah, for once, right?" I rolled my eyes and laughed, determined to take it as a joke. "It was a while ago. Like right after the cookout, she brought it up. So she's got a room with a friend of a friend through her job now, or really, like, just some girl she knows. I don't know. It's not one of the girls she works with, but her little sister, or cousin or something."

"Oh, wow," I said. I didn't say that this seemed like a really bad situation for Mollie, though it worried me, and the conversation stalled. The decor surrounding us was newly immiserating after a few years away. Wooden barrels as side tables and cartoonish murals of 'country living' grated on me more; before leaving home I had a sense of more being 'out there', but I didn't anticipate being received as fundamentally provincial once I arrived. This was what I had been marinating in for almost two decades of my life, so who could blame them? I winced at an image of a tarted up blonde woman in pigtails and a dress that seemed in colour and design more like a child's onesie, leered at by a cowboy type for baring plenty of cleavage and a missing tooth with her grin as she set beer mugs onto the top of a barrel. Equally bad, I considered, if this nightmare decor order had come from above, a pastiche exported to locations across the US determined by committee, or if it was a special directive by some fuckwit manager of the joint, proud owner of this particular, uniquely miserable iteration of franchised establishment — both sets of middlebrow sadists united under the banner of acting dumb for their imaginary public. Some local colour, meeting some corny, received idea of 'the people' where they are with what they want; supposed 'observational humour' uniting across demographic lines, grotesque women, pervy men, stupid poor people. Whoever made the call on decor here loved middle-of-nowhere life and was also precisely what made it so miserable. When I began to understand, as a trapped teenager, that there were people who determined how space was divvyed up, how to manage it, who it was for — they all started to seem the same, my enemies: the fucking owners, small business tyrants with nice shoes, bosses who want to be your friend and your mom's friend while still reserving the right to ice you out if you get a stomach flu when you're supposed to come in, milk monopolists who buy the high school a football field, megachurches and their zipcode-size parking lots, Martin's dad and his stupid dog. But hey, lighten up, why don't you ever smile?

Around Martin I became newly aware of how my negativity had marked me as a loser in the city. When he was angry the way I got angry, or did other things I had learned to be embarrassed by, it pulled an almost painful cringe out of me to look at him. But it was a tender, addictive feeling, like twisting a hangnail. While I was in the city I sometimes missed recognizing this in others, and desired it, rather than continuing the doomed project of remaking myself to fit in with people who were in a world that was always already their own, and the centre of everyone else's. They didn't seem to know why I sneered or sighed at things, of course, but equally what to make of the things that excited me, that I felt so strongly about. It was gauche to move your response to anything outside the modulated, reasonable environment of the friendly studio crit. Everything was worthy at its core, even if the outside gave, at most, slight pause. I figured this was because they had always been seamlessly integrated into an order that allowed them to relate to everything in a benign, upbeat way as 'interesting'. But a lot of things weren't interesting; this was the most intimate insight of my life so far, or that more things were only compelling in how repulsive they were.

I glared down the list of combinations of cheese and extra meats you could put on the hamburgers. Mollie's resemblance to me now seemed especially irrelevant, or maybe a trick my own anxiety and wounded pride had played on me in the first place. If they had really parted ways, she couldn't be some kind of impostor who had stolen my life, or representing the life I should have chosen. She was just a person who had incidentally entered and exited Martin's life, just as I incidentally re-entered it.

"You did go a little wild at the cookout, but moving out, I dunno. I thought you two were pretty serious."

He sulked, not giving up any reference point for how serious he considered the relationship to have been.

"Party boy," I joked. "I don't think I ever saw you drink in high school."

"I was 18."

"It's not like it wasn't around," I said. "I'm sure some people thought you were like, straight edge or whatever." I referred to the omnipresent sense that other kids, the ones cooler than us, were partying and getting drunk constantly, but it meant something different for Martin, who didn't share my practically dry household where booze was a prized component of adventures away from home. Wanting to bite my own tongue, I preoccupied myself with peeling the paper wrapper off a straw, looking around like I was on the edge of my seat anticipating a cup of water.

"I was in a weird mood," he said. "Okay? It's not like I drink often."

"Yeah, alright," I said. "No wonder you spewed then."

The waitress returned, the huge, overfilled drinks almost spilling over their edge as she placed them on the table. She tucked the tray under her arm and asked if we were ready to order. Waiting a second for Martin, who seemed to be not so much staring at the menu but at the table underneath it, I selected the most standard bacon cheeseburger with fries, and, when the waitress turned to him, Martin ordered the same. As the waitress left, not even making a note of the orders on the pad tucked into her belt, since the place was really dead, I poked my straw through the layer of ice cubes that had gathered at the top of the water and noticed that Martin was watching me do it.

"Trying to flatter my great taste?"

"What?"

"Getting the same thing as me."

Was I getting somewhere? I smiled at him and he

huffed a bit, turning away as much as he could on his own uncomfortable chair. He was the most uptight person I had ever fallen for, maybe even the most uptight person I had ever known well, but I could find his emotional constipation somehow noble, it was endearing how easy he was to embarrass. If he had ever been capable of relaxing even a fraction more, the type of guy who would have let me stick a few fingers in his ass while we were hooking up in his junker car, maybe I could have fixed him, but would I still like him? I looked across the table and thought: I understand you like scrabble tiles. Not only the letters but their distinct point values, the numerical proportions of each aspect of you were printed on your surface in flat black ink. Still.

He turned back to me, starting with a deep breath, like he was remembering something that he'd planned and had to work himself up to say. "Thanks for sticking around, though. It made things slightly less depressing."

"It was nice," I said. I sipped my drink, acting nonchalant, because it had taken me so off-guard to hear him say something so sincere. "Did we ever watch fireworks like that, back in high school?"

"Are you kidding? Of course we did. What else is there to do on half the holidays around here?"

"Nostalgic, then."

"Not if you don't remember."

I let him have that. He seemed to take it as amusing cloud headedness on my part, but the gap between our memories stood out; watching fireworks with me still counted as an interesting episode in his life, while it had totally dissolved into the white noise of time passed for me. I watched his expression shift, becoming friendlier and a bit unsure for once, like he wanted to please me somehow but didn't know if he could. He was playing up being miserable about the breakup, about being reminded of what happened at the cookout, but underneath it all he still must have thought having lunch with me was kind of a nice thing to happen.

"Are you still happy to see me again?" I asked, into his attentive silence. A smirk.

"What, to be having lunch?"

"I mean, when we first saw each other, we weren't expecting to ever speak again, right?"

"We already had this talk," he said, straightening himself in the chair and rapping his own straw on the table a few times to break it out of the wrapper.

"That was, like, the no hard feelings talk. But I dunno. We've been hanging out now, things are fine. So it makes me wonder, you know? What you think of me now. And vice-versa too, of course." I leaned back in the chair, at least the thin angle that it allowed me to, unrolled the napkin with a fork inside it that was resting in front of me, checked the packets of sweeteners lined up in a dish next to a tented specials menu, itched at the inside of my elbow — all as I said this, to come across very busy, business-like almost, and not have to look directly at Martin. And then, stopping up the water in my straw with the tip of my finger and pulling it out to drop back into the glass, prepared myself to evaluate his response.

"What? I mean, you're different, but I feel like it isn't really my business." He fidgeted, resting his head on his hand and turning to the side evasively. He was smiling now, maybe pinpointing exactly what I was getting at. I had always been pretty easy to read, so, I thought, let him read me.

"I wouldn't ask if I didn't want your stupid opinion," I

went on. "I mean come on! We took each other's virginity at one point."

He frowned and looked into his drink. Little chunks of red strawberry pulp clung near the surface of it. He seemed to resent being reminded of this, or maybe felt embarrassed that it was said by a girl like me, even in a near-empty restaurant. I caught the heels of my boots on the rung of the metal chair and adjusted myself forward so that I could rest my elbows on the table, even though it felt like a thin gross film reached up from the surface to grab my skin.

"Yeah, it's nice to have you around," he admitted. "I was surprised how we get along the same. It seems really stupid now, to have just totally left each other's lives like that."

"Ah-ha," I said, proudly.

"I mean, I understand why. We were fighting all the time, and we had totally different plans, but it's like we're on the same footing again, now." For him, the same footing meant a slim leg up on me, but we could painstakingly relitigate that later. Letting him feel slightly superior was, now as always, the most straightforward method to feel out how far he was willing to go with me. "You're still the same in a lot of ways too."

To hear that made me feel like my guts were glowing dimly, almost like a hot stove. I had wrenched confirmation out of him, word of god, that the strange closeness, how he would treat me in offhanded moments, wasn't all in my head. What could be more beautiful, I thought, sitting in a truly awful chain restaurant strategically placed in the prime retail zoning of the endless parking lot of my hometown, than to feel my mouth on his, to press and measure our bodies against each other again, years apart.

I started wanting it like a magnet pulls.

"Oh, well. You don't clean up so bad yourself," I said, and swallowed, feeling myself take on the camp line delivery of the bad boy from the first five minutes of any romcom, the one who is so blatantly a bad fit for the protagonist. Martin lifted his head and put the hand he had been propping himself up with against the table in a loose fist. He looked at me with a happy but troubled knowingness. I was being ironic, glancing between the corners of the room, presenting my face in a narrow selection of preening angles to keep myself talking. "What were you thinking," I went on, "Chauffeuring me around and watching fireworks with me and shit when you had such a nice girl at home?"

He laughed. "I don't think she was worried about you. You seemed to get along so well I thought she'd be the one you'd go hang out with."

"I know, I was just joking." He let my comment hang for a few seconds, looking at me seriously.

"Joking how?" he asked, his voice dropping a bit into a low, blunt register.

"It's like, we're so different, when you're dating a girl like her, she wouldn't even consider…"

"I don't think you're that different," he said, going on with the same serious tone. "You're staring at me a lot, when you talk," he added, after a few seconds.

"Is that unusual?" I asked.

"For you." He looked to the side, like he was curious about what was taking the food so long. We had only been sitting there a few minutes. As he scanned for the waitress, my eyes lingered on his cheek, his temple, his forearm, measuring out how much softer he'd grown, with the pleasure of encountering a favourite paperback, years later, read and reread and thumbed through.

"I was a little worried, not hearing from you for a while."

"Yeah, sorry. It was nothing you did. At first I didn't know what to say about the breakup. I guess I got worried that whatever I did say, it would come across, you know, an imposition or whatever."

"No way! It'd just be knowing what's going on with you." Calling up the willpower it'd take to shove my fist into a threateningly bristled shrub to grab something I'd dropped, I reached across and deliberately placed my hand so the side of it was lined up against his. "It's fine. It's not weird."

Martin was exerting an enormous effort to not respond in any particular way. When I leaned closer, tipping my hand against and then into his, he squeezed it for a second, then shifted away, pulling his arm back and resting the other on the table instead. I knew some compelling bit of regret or shame had jolted him away, but it still thrilled me for a second, to be touched.

I leaned back too, almost losing my balance on the cheap, teetering metal stools all these shitty places seemed to have. Neither of us said anything. My hand was in a fist, held in place on the sticky tabletop. The back of my mouth felt slimy and bitter with indignity as I realised Kid Rock was playing over the restaurant's speakers.

"What!" I said.

"Amy, come on."

"I know you and Mollie just broke up," I tried to outmanoeuvre his hesitation, but it was already pretty clear: while it was totally agreeable to me, if a little predictable, obviously temporary and doomed, the threshold was one, for some reason, he thought he couldn't cross again. "It doesn't have to be, like, serious." I rolled my eyes and grinned, trying to be disarming. "I'm just curious."

"No, I mean, I don't know. I don't feel like it would work out, you know, in *that* way."

He tried to place a friendly, now completely de-sexualized hand on my wrist as he said this. I pulled my arm back off the table like a snail's eye that had been prodded, the surface pulling at my skin.

"What's that supposed to mean?" I said. This frustrated him; he wanted that vague statement to be enough to close the issue, which meant that he let himself be careless.

"I don't know, just look at yourself."

After a second I laughed, because it was the only utterance that could process amusement, disappointment, anxiety, anger, sometimes all at once. I had given his small life the benefit of the doubt, but his second- or third-hand reports of what I had been up to, combined with his gut evaluation of my appearance, had him thinking he understood me. Hoisting myself off of the stupid stool to walk away made me, humiliatingly, much shorter than him. Martin looked across and down at me at a slight angle, and I looked back up at him, framed by the bare cement floor.

"Sorry. Hey, I just meant, I felt like it would be awkward, for both of us, how different things are now. And it's too soon, anyways."

In my head, deciding what I wanted to say was as simple as reaching out to pick up the salt shaker would've been. He was being ridiculous, cowardly, prudish, uptight as ever, and at my expense. It always had been! But to say any of that? My gut flipped over on a gruelling wave of anger and I flushed, embarrassed at how stupid feeling this way was; of course it was his right to turn me down, being so forward right off a breakup, even if the reason wasn't a lack of interest but anxiety over being caught desiring it, even privately or casually.

I turned away and weaved around the chairs and tables and booths and prop barrels and waiters standing in the winding path out of the restaurant. Pushing open the glass front doors blasted me with light and heat again, and, with nowhere in particular in mind, I paced out onto the mostly empty extent of asphalt. Soon I stood in the shadow of a great wreckage of my high school years: the half-empty shopping centre that had once been a conjoined Borders and Circuit City. It was a regular haunt for Martin and I, where the possibilities of some elsewhere were occasionally, preciously material. Gutted now. What had I expected? I sat in the shade that fell on the curb and pulled my knees up to rest my forehead on, feeling small, how I must have felt constantly when I was a child, but also horrendously ugly.

My gamble had not just ended in sexual humiliation, but what felt like a failure of understanding. Now I knew I would never win that prize, especially not here, even though it was a hard expectation to finally extinguish. Surprised disorientation, like missing a stair in the dark, still accompanied the capacity for being hurt in this way that I somehow still had.

I thought of Jessica. The complexity of mutual understanding didn't need to enter the picture with her, since I had such an easy role to satisfy. That satisfaction was why I felt so healthy, so astonishingly confident lately, right? I lifted my head and scrolled through the contacts on my phone to select her name. In the beating, direct sunlight, so bright I squinted at the screen to make sure I was prodding the right name with my thumb, my hands were cold. I looked back at the restaurant, far enough away that I could imagine it was a flat cardboard model. Martin wasn't coming after me. The phone was against my ear, and right away I heard Jessica's voice.

"Hello, Amy?"

"Hey, um, could you come pick me up? If you're free." I said. My voice seemed to come out too loud and I looked around, like the few people going by in their cars, circling for a parking spot, were eavesdropping on me. "I'm at one of the old shopping centres, outside the Borders Circuit City one," I said, and then craned my neck around to correct myself because she hadn't been there, she wouldn't know. "Or, it's the one that's half empty and half a 'Bed Bath and Beyond' now."

"Sure, I just dropped the kids off, so I'm nearby. Are you alright?"

"Yeah," my voice pitched up in the affirmative, unconvincingly. "I just had a really, really shitty lunch date. So I'm too embarrassed to call my mom."

"I'll be right there."

♦♦♦

In the seat of Jessica's minivan I felt like a specimen cradled in a cushioned display case. She had pulled up to me in the parking lot about 20 minutes later, rolled down her window and given me a tentative grin.

"Hey," she said, a bit sing-song, a bit conciliatory.

"Oh my god, thank you," I groaned, pushing myself up from the curb. "I'm so sorry about this."

"The guy didn't do anything to you, did he?" She

asked, when I came around to the passenger side.

"No, it was one hundred percent stupidity on my part." I felt around for the latch of the seatbelt. She was watching me, just to ensure I had fastened it before she started driving, but it still made me feel flustered, and I fumbled getting the tab into the slot at least twice. When it finally snapped together, I braced my arms, resting my hands on my knees, and pushed myself straight back into the chair as she pulled out of the parking lot.

"I'm sure you're being hard on yourself. And if he got that upset you probably wouldn't have gotten along anyways."

"Yeah, it's nothing." I was a bit red, holding in the information that the guy in question was someone she knew, had even cooed over as kind and sensible in front of me. "So you were just dropping Susie and Cecil off somewhere?" I asked.

"There's a youth group thing this afternoon," she said. "So I'm basically free. Did you get to eat? We could go somewhere."

"I didn't make it to the food arriving," I said and smiled self-derisively. She returned it, stopping at a traffic light.

"Let's grab something then."

"Oh, no, I think I just want to go back home." I winced at how I turned her down, a reflex action running deeper than any thought or desire.

"Makes sense," she said. "Don't worry about it."

Familiar intersections and side roads passed as we neared our neighbourhood. Jessica and I sat mostly in silence, a financial advice program mumbling on the car radio. Even though I had said so (in momentary terror of, what, having lunch with Jess?), I didn't want to go home. My mother would be back soon, but I didn't have a strong preference for being alone, either. What was the most comfortable position to be miserable in, did it really matter? I had an urge to remove the burden of choice, even if it meant glomming all rejection together into one really shitty day. Thinking that would be easier, or even just out of desperation to rebound or wreck something out of impotence, I spoke up as we neared the final turn onto our street.

"Wait, Jess—" I folded forward in the seat, one of my knees anxiously bobbing. Past embarrassment, I felt slight terror when, car still moving, I couldn't call up what to say next.

"Did you want to stop somewhere?" she asked.

"No, I mean, it wouldn't have worked out."

"Getting lunch?"

"No, with the guy."

She hummed at this, giving me a warm silence to elaborate into while she stared out over the steering wheel.

"I don't think it would have worked out," I repeated. "Because I have the most obvious, stupid crush on you anyways."

That got her to pull the minivan over to the side of the road. We were parked in front of someone else's house. She was looking at me, not unhappy, and I looked across at her as well, wearing a lilac blouse of light but stiff fabric that stood up in peaked ruffles at the neckline and a greyish pencil skirt that went down to her knees. I watched her calf muscles flex slightly as she lifted her legs away from the pedals and turned her knees towards me. With her eyes on me, I knew, but couldn't meet them, I rushed to explain myself.

"I'm always thinking about doing things for you. Like I like it too much, you know?" I realised I had set my eyes at the arm rest at her side as I was speaking, which probably made it look like I was staring at her breasts, and turned my face away.

"You're serious?" She said.

While I had been trying to make myself act strategically, forcing myself forward from a distance, like a remote controlled toy, I suddenly felt viscerally embarrassed that I had led her to ask this question. I looked back at Jessica, all of her, framed by the curved window, the lumpy seat, centre console and dashboard.

"Of course I'm serious!" My own voice sounded wretched. She seemed to go inside herself with thought after that, her lightness and sensitivity briefly vanishing. I thought the worst, she's annoyed, she has to find another babysitter now, even though her face didn't seem irritated or even disgusted. It was the look of someone compelled, by an equation or crossword or a piece of art — to make sense of it.

She leaned across the centre console and reached a hand onto my shoulder, as much to lever herself forward in the cramped, awkward space as to caress me. With my eyes shut, I felt her kiss me, so deliberately, as if she was testing out how far she could believe me. I went hot from the back of my neck forward, imagining someone peering out from the front of their house into the car window behind me. The kiss was reserved, not wet, no tongue, but it stretched out in time, and demanded a huge amount of concentration. She held it until we crossed the line into breathing each others' breath.

When she pulled away, I looked down at my own chest, rising and falling, like a creature out in the sea, something that could go deep underwater for hours at a time. Whatever she was testing, the kiss had satisfied her too, and she pulled the van into her own driveway, leading me into the house and upstairs by the hand. I followed without saying anything, easy as I had fantasised it would be. In the bedroom, I stood at the corner of her dresser as she started to remove her clothes.

"You still want this, right?" She asked, looking at me with the complicity of a question that suggested its own solution, before undoing the second button of her blouse.

"Yes." I couldn't have said anything else, which I knew was a bit shameful. In every context where I felt needed, up to the task, a lolling puppy eroticism took hold. My most rote and predictable frisson, what could be said except that it always worked, and now Jess would know the full extent of it.

"Okay," she said, stepping out of her narrow skirt and curling her legs under her on the bed. "Come here."

The backs of my thighs strained as I bent straight down to fumble with my laces. Righting myself to kick off my boots made me dizzy, not just from nerves, and I grabbed the corner of her dresser to steady myself, watching her hands mesh together in front of her breasts, undoing the rest of the tiny, polished buttons on her Sears Catalog blouse. The soles of my feet in thin socks sank into the bedroom carpet, and I let my jeans pool at my ankles, tugging my feet out of them as I walked towards the bed. My hand rested flat on top of the duvet cover, shiny and embroidered with flowers, that she had left undisturbed.

Jessica was sliding the blouse off her shoulders slowly, watching me with a calm smile. She was still wearing her stockings, which only dug in to her compact torso very slightly. She slid her arms out of her bra and squared her shoulders to me, looking completely relaxed. And then she extended her hand out, drawing me in. I practically stumbled on to the bed; my legs couldn't take me forward so I crawled. The mattress was firm, memory foam too, the same texture that repeated across the surfaces of my dreams, forgiving and nonspecific.

Kneeling upright on the bed, Jess pulled me up and turned me by the shoulders, almost impatiently, so her stomach and breasts pressed close against my back. One thigh nudged between my legs to coax them apart, then I felt an arm snaking around my hips, beginning to feel around. When I curled over myself, caught off-guard by how fast things were moving, she hoisted me back up, setting a splayed hand across my neck, thumb and forefinger hooked under my chin, to hold me flush against her body. It was like she wanted all of me exposed, reflected in the large mirror above her dresser with my skin puckering in the chill of her central air conditioning. She seemed to touch me with an absolute clarity about my desires, the intensity, the friction, the level of pain that turned me on without pushing through into distress. It was like she could read my flesh with her fingertips, or like she could dip into me, mind and body, for the purpose of fully wringing me out. It was almost too much like I was touching myself, which intermittently scared me, the thought breaking through in moments when I was uncomfortably aware of my heart pounding. I felt my thighs straining, crude internal valves opening and contracting, vivid mortification, a hot and wet feeling running down my thighs. I groaned and turned my face away, and she pressed her mouth into my neck until she'd made me come.

Jess let her arm go slack and I slid down onto the bed cover, though it felt more like she had tossed me. She nudged my shoulder with a damp hand to roll me flat onto my back and laid her body alongside mine, running the same hand up under my shirt. As if I was a waiter attuned to the tiniest implicit demands of a wealthy diner, I jumped up onto an elbow and reached around my back to undo my bra. When I'd unlatched it, she slid her hand beneath the underwire and was able to buck it out of the way with the back of her hand. We kissed for a long time, and I began to feel self-conscious about the ungainly excess of my own breasts, soft stomach and hips, next to her body that was more like an aeroplane fuselage. It abated, the sensation of the excessive, watery saliva that ran from her mouth into my own, like rain water down a slate cliff, warmed in my mouth and became indistinguishable from the drool pumping out of my own glands. I became placidly aware of this permeable, receptive feeling as a sort of natural state of my body.

She pulled away for a second and I sighed hot breath directly into her face, which made her laugh at my complete pliability, how I had abandoned my stiff aloofness about closeness or touch so quickly. With the same modulated roughness she climbed on top of me and held down one of my wrists next to my face. She stretched herself over my body like it was a narrow ledge she had to lie compacted and low to fit on to, pressing up and off of me like a cicada exiting its moult. Along with the skirt and the blouse, she had discarded the remaining parts of her that the obligations of her position in daily life required. Now there was something new and direct about how she looked at me. I couldn't decipher it and gave up trying, turning my face away, feeling my breath collect in the increasingly disturbed sheets. Evaluating how I was squirming against her thigh, she reached between my legs again. Bare curiosity — *like a child who had never been hurt picking up a cat,* I thought, letting my face roll to the other side, burying it into a throw pillow with a beaded appliqué that left a print in the shape of a dragonfly wing on my cheek.

♦♦♦

Afterwards, we lay together in bed, grinning conspiratorially as she stroked my shoulders or combed bits of my shaggy, grown out haircut with the tips of her fingers. She still had on the slim watch with the face that sat on the inside of her wrist like a teardrop. As the light changed outside, it caught the corner of her eye and she got up, putting herself back together out of the scattered clothes on the floor.

"I have to go get the kids soon," she said.

"Oh, yeah." I tried to sound airy and casual but must have looked agitated. Snapped out of being able to just soak in her affection like a sponge, I thought — was this it, did I now have a new familiarity with how adults conducted their affairs? It was the first time I had slept with someone in a way that wasn't the tortured outcome of an explicit process that could only lead to either ghosting each other and / or fucking. She had guided me through a portal where sudden, and what I was used to considering inadvisable, urges could be met. When she was fully dressed she stood next to the bed and rested a hand on my head.

"Take your time, but be dressed when we get back, alright?" I made a funny, disembodied-feeling noise of assent and listened to her walk away, lying still until I heard the sound of her grabbing the car keys off the hook by the door, then opening and closing it on her way out.

I didn't make it anywhere. Once I was alone in the empty house, I closed my eyes to better take in the sheets I was cocooned in, with the aim of sorting out my own thoughts. Of course, nothing much came before I fell dead asleep. It had only felt like seconds passing when the sound of a door latching shut jolted me awake. Jessica was standing there with her hand over her mouth, though slowly I could see a grin spreading on her face, wider than her fingers could cover.

"Amy, are you OK?"

"Shit, I fell asleep, I'm so sorry," I said, trying to keep my voice as low as possible. I pulled the sheets close around my face.

"It's fine, but the kids are back. Do you want to just go back to sleep and I'll get you up early?" she asked.

"You mean spend the night?"

"Yeah, if you're quiet."

Immediately, I began to think through how I could explain this scenario if my mother noticed or confronted me about it the next day. The kids had been at a Sunday evening youth group, which she would probably know about, so I couldn't say that Jessica had needed me for some late night thing and I had just fallen asleep in front of the TV. Dreading the conversation didn't move me from the bed, though. An explanation was less urgent and less interesting than pricking my ears to listen to Jessica getting the kids ready for bed, following her footsteps until the door opened again and she was back inside. I was speechless with that absurd, infatuation-level sort of tenderness as I watched her slip out of her clothes again, pull her hair up in a bun and put on a loose t-shirt and sweatpants. She got into the bed next to me and pulled me close to kiss me at my temple, a brief touch, before rolling over.

When I woke up, I could tell it was early from the quality of the light, a gentle glowing stillness I usually only faced when hungover or fighting to meet a deadline. Jess had left a pile of rumpled sheets next to me that made the king size bed seem obscenely wide. I got up, found my underwear on the floor and pulled on the t-shirt and jeans I had been wearing the day before.

Once I was dressed, I stood in front of the sink in the small bathroom that was attached to Jessica's bedroom. The muscles in my neck and jaw were clenched up, and I had a headache that made the inside of my skull feel like it was pressing out, like my thoughts were bumping up to the edges, as floaty as they felt. Under a line of round, white lights, I looked at myself, frowned, then stuck my tongue out to peer at the back of my throat. Something back there felt warm and slightly swollen, like my tonsillar crypts were irritated, or the glands around my neck and chin were fighting off a low-grade infection. I pressed around where I thought the glands were, up from the bottom of my chin, and tried to gauge if they felt 'large' or 'hard', even though I rarely examined them any other time. Then, I prodded a finger as close as I could get to my tonsils without gagging, watching with fascination at how I could provoke my own salivary glands into weeping.

Maybe pressing at the edges of the dominion I had over my own body was one of the most interesting things I could do in the small radius accessible to me, now certainly bumped ahead of experimentally rekindling things with Martin. The other most interesting thing had felt definitively out of reach until a few hours ago and now felt like something I could ruin at any time, like picking a winning lottery ticket off the floor; I wasn't sure why it had happened to me, or whether it was, within my recent understanding of how life tended to go, something that was even allowed to occur. I couldn't even predict how Jessica would receive me downstairs, though I could faintly smell coffee. Letting these things happen for as long as I could, seeing my own involvement as a liability, had always been my strategy; maybe that was why I had passed out in her bed. Whatever happened, it would be surprising. I couldn't bring forth a single convincing prediction about it as I stared the inside of my own mouth down.

My hand squeaked on the hardwood bannister as I padded down the steps, the tile floor of the kitchen was cold on my feet. Jessica was staring out the window over the sink, a big pyrex bowl of pancake batter and a whisk leaning against its rim on the counter next to her.

"Hey," I said, too shy to just watch her.

"You're up." She turned and smiled at me, then tilted her head towards the bowl. "Want to be the test subject for my distraction strategy? If I surprise the kids with something nice, maybe they're less likely to notice anything suspicious."

So she was still happy about it, at least, but wasn't sure whether she should let the kids catch on. A kind but responsible position, which I found both relieving and a little intimidating in its maturity and practicality.

"Sure." I hoisted myself up on one of the wooden stools around the kitchen island, my feet dangling. Jess sparked the stove top to life and let a pan start heating up on it, then pulled the glass cylinder coffee press from the drying rack, upended one of the mugs next to it, and started scooping coffee grounds into it from a jar. Next to the stove, there was also her own mug of coffee and a halved grapefruit. She fussed over the breakfast preparations while the coffee brewed, and then poured me a cup when it was ready.

"Why did you let me sleep over?" I asked.

"I figured a tactical retreat was easier with the kids back in the house," she replied. "And you looked so calm, for once."

I squeezed the mug, and then pulled my hands away. It was still so hot it stung my fingertips. Meanwhile, Jessica slid a sizzling knot of butter around inside the pan and started pouring and flipping dollops of batter. I stared out the back window, built identically to the back window of our own kitchen. The familiarity that spanned all these lined-up boxes was maybe the only argument you could make that they facilitated social cohesion. For the first time in a while I thought about the red lights I'd seen at the river, how they'd made my head ache. This was the same window that had framed them for Cecil. Now, all that seemed like something that could never happen, a momentary error of my own memory and his that had been evaluated and expelled from the realm of the sensible. Getting fucked and doted on by a Hitchcock heroine mommy was ironically clarifying; I was equipped to push down the fear and pain of uncertainty like swallowing a belch.

Jessica slid a plate across the table towards me, looking down with amused embarrassment. Like that, she seemed like any person a little older than me, a person I could be in a few years. I wouldn't have a nine-year-old child, but still, people would see me on the street and think I looked about her age.

"Sorry, I was on autopilot and just did the first one that way..."

The pancake on the bottom of the stack, under two

other normal ones, was three lumps fused together like a Mickey Mouse head. I squeezed some syrup over all of them and then stuck my fork and butter knife straight through the others, into the rat's forehead.

"It's good," I said, after chewing and swallowing the first bite. I ate the entire plate before the coffee cooled enough for me to sip. Jessica stood across from me, watching me eat while she pulled wedges from the grapefruit halves with a spiky grapefruit spoon, sometimes getting them out whole with a weird wet sucking sound. She put them into her mouth and smiled like she was suppressing laughter over a shared joke between us. When she placed the spoon between the carefully eviscerated halves on her plate, the light clink seemed to reverberate back as a faraway wail that grew into a long, dissonant note. It curved down, then another followed. She frowned.

"That's the test alarm for Three Mile Island," I said. I checked my phone for the time, then laughed to myself when I read the date, putting it back in my pocket and staring into the heavy, earth tone mug of coffee Jess made for me. "They're playing the nuclear sirens for my birthday."

She took the news that it was my birthday without comment at first, but then walked to the refrigerator and brought out a bowl of strawberries, deep red all the way through, taut, wet flesh wobbling on the edge of bursting into mould, a late local crop.

"Happy birthday then. A neighbour brought these around. Take some, I can't eat them all." I looked down into the bowl and started pinching up the green tops, leaving a pale crescent of flesh when I bit off the rest of each fruit. I glanced up from the growing stack of tops; her direct, affectionate gaze reminded me of how looking directly into the sun could make you sneeze. The sirens waned and she checked the silver watch on the inside of her wrist, curling her whole arm into her body. A graceful gesture she knew would both get me to stare and to understand that I should hurry along.

"The kids will be up soon, if not already," she said. "At least change your clothes."

"Alright." I dropped the last strawberry top onto the small pile that had formed in the bowl. I paused for a moment, levering a hand on the counter but not pushing myself away, before asking, "Why do you take them to church stuff, anyways?"

"It's good structure, isn't it? Stuff to do with other kids, outside of the house. Why? Didn't your family—" She trailed off. "It's just what people seem to do, around here."

"Yeah, it felt normal at the time."

"Do you still go?"

"I stopped as soon as I went to college. I guess I didn't feel like I even had a degree of belief that I became alienated from or anything."

Jessica shrugged. "It's fine if it pans out that way for them. I don't need them to believe or anything, I guess."

"You don't?" I asked.

"I don't have any strong feelings about it." Jessica looked like she wasn't expecting the question.

"Really?"

"Is that weird?"

"I mean, the expectation kind of fucked me up in some ways. Even if you don't explicitly tell a kid they'll go to hell… Like, I'd think about the girl in my 2nd grade class who said that her family did Hanukkah instead of Christmas at show and tell, and I'll never forget how, when I asked if it really meant everyone who didn't believe all this stuff wouldn't go to heaven, because it seemed like an obvious mistake, the woman in charge of the Sunday school class just gave this awful, wincing smile like 'yeah'."

Jess was silent, seeming unsure how or why we'd landed on this topic over breakfast. As soon as I'd recalled it, I began to doubt. Had I actually asked that question, or was it just the logical extrapolation of what adults were telling me, the obverse implications of the glories and rewards of believing? But the functional outcome for me had been the same, and a bright kid like Cecil would think it through that way too. Talking up salvation always implied hell, and an acceptance of hell eroded you, whether you felt like you were going or not. I tried to clarify my point.

"I mean, if you don't care whether they believe or not, it's kind of morbid to put a kid in a position where there's this abstract idea of 'sin' they have to measure everything against, you know? Or where they might think that anyone would go to hell, or that it could exist in the first place. Cecil is a lot like me, I think, in terms of personality. His obsession with the UFO stuff is like how I felt about getting raptured my entire childhood."

"What?"

"You know, Christ returns at any possible moment and you're just sucked away from life up to heaven. Sometimes I would just get hit with this dread that I'd be yanked away from books I hadn't read yet or getting my favourite flavour potato chips from the Rutters... Normal kid stuff. It didn't make sense to me that everyone else acted like it was nothing."

Jess laughed. I had let the smooth intimacy of eating

breakfast together in the kitchen make me forget that she hadn't grown up here, and even here I was an outlier, to feel these things so literally, so seriously. I pointed my face down at the empty bowl of strawberries as she replied, "I guess I follow the philosophical angle, but you're being awfully hard on an arrangement that just let you get laid." When I looked up, she did the coy gesture and glanced at her watch again. "Alright. You really have to go now." I slid off the stool and she dipped an arm around the small of my back to kiss me before I went. The kiss was fast, but she paused to look at me after pulling away, like a present she was thrilled to receive but didn't fully know the use for.

Outside, I grabbed Cecil's razor scooter from where it rested on the lawn to expedite my trip back and forth between the houses. It was small for me but still usable. Before stopping at my house, I rode over a long, downhill stretch at the end of the development, where they had cordoned off lots of land to build houses, but no houses had sprung up, no foundations had even been dug. They were undisturbed, square plots of only high grass and ticks. I was 25 years old now.

Chapter Eight

I discovered something foreboding about myself — I now understood an ugly shard of the stepfather impulse. It became very hard, when Cecil was being difficult, to not pull up the 'look, little man, I'm fucking your mom, I'm going to be your new dad' routine. I felt frustrated with him, how could I justify feeling threatened, though? His dad was dead.

Susie was oblivious to time passing but Cecil ticked over into worse and worse moods as it became clear that there was less summer ahead of him than summer already used up. Any reminder of this was an implicit reminder of school, which Cecil regarded with undisguised repulsion. I didn't blame him. What was a quaint brick building with recess yards and colourful play equipment from the outside, all very parent satisfying, on the inside had an eternal stale and sour smell, the combination of overcooked cafeteria food and industrial cleaning products locked in an endless, futile battle against the kids spewing and coughing and sneezing all over each other. Now, as it had been for me, kids were hotboxed in managed surveillance with only themselves and their germs, which led to the formation of brutal or merely confusing unofficial hierarchy among the inmates. Even in grade school I lacked the will to be competitive or manoeuvring. I was a presence off to the side that things occasionally happened to, that would cement an element of my status: sad, weird, and/or (eventually) dadless.

Like me, Cecil was good at the clear, directed aspects of

school but everything else about it was miserable: lunch lines, where to sit, how to talk to people, how sitting around reading a book would arbitrarily be admirable one minute, or in one teacher's eyes, and then inadequate and anti-social to another. Day in, day out, you were just getting pushed around over those sorts of things. Was it like that for you too?

I said, "Don't remind me," and he kicked a soccer ball hard against the garage door.

Maybe he felt like I was cool before, but now I had subtly moved to ally with the adults, observing my increased attention to extra household tasks for Jessica and the way I hung around her, the way we joked and smiled at each other like good friends now. In a few weeks I had gone from a new curiosity in his life to a boring old institution, even if he didn't know exactly why things had changed. I didn't try to dig up anything further about his father, or an update on the presence or absence of his UFOs; these were private beliefs now, for him and me.

It was painful to watch him contemplate this on his own, because it reminded me of how consistently agitated, trapped and anxious I felt as a child. I wanted to tell him, you can't be this pissed off all the time, but for me, the only way out had been through. Somehow, eventually, the wild energy and confusion changed into something else, and the way my brain worked now was the product and precipitate of this process, existing together in comparable stasis.

Another ominous indication of how I had become a paragon of social integration was how quietly pleased my mother seemed with me. It practically gave me a glow, she said at one point, to get out of the house and be around children all day. I guess a halo could be applied to anything in hindsight, though my memory of her face when dealing with one of the twins leaving a round, pink bite mark on the other's arm, or sticking her head into my room, where I was trying to privately cry, was a grim grey frown. I bore her compliment, it was better than her figuring out what had happened between me and Jess.

I always thought I was more like my dad, anyways, the slumping shoulders, the round face. It comforted me that I could keep my father around, be an embodiment of his remote presence haunting our household, plus I enjoyed the annoyance I could tell it caused my mother. The twins were always lean and taller than me now, their dark hair the only trait they shared with my father, so mom delighted in compliments about their looks. Mine were awkward and unmentioned. But increasingly I could see my mother in myself, in my thin arms that remained bony and angular no matter how my weight fluctuated, or worse, in my neurotic demands or defensiveness in my least flattering moments. Maybe this was more normal, but I didn't like it.

I frowned at my wrists and experimentally turned my head to the side a bit, trying a few different facial expressions in the mirror in Jessica's bathroom. It was a few minutes before she usually got home. The minutes worked their way down, slower than seemed possible, like Jessica's arrival was a gravitational distortion I was edging up against. It had only been a few days since we had first, I guess, hooked up. We hadn't really talked about it; our schedules, her work and my own, intervened, and so I was constantly waiting for and thinking of more. Every night since, I had pushed my door shut as far as it would go and gotten myself off until I had ridges on my fingers. It was so easy to imagine she was touching me, to see everything about her vividly, as if my body had gained a strange generative power that could only be put on hold by muscular exhaustion. My wrists did feel worn out. Were they getting old faster?

The garage door rattled open and I stepped out of the bathroom to meet Jess at the door. She smiled at me, kicking off her shoes, and dropped her bag on top of the dryer, which was running. She slid an arm down by my side to edge by me, and I let my hand run up her bare forearm for a moment. She paused, looking surprised, but not upset.

"Everything alright?" She asked. I pulled my fingers back.

"Yeah, the kids are fine. Meatloaf's on," I said. "Work went fine?"

"Pretty much as usual," she walked past me into the kitchen. For the first time I felt defeated by this exchange. It had gone on too long to be even a sadistic flirtation. Since it was Friday, she paid me without much flourish — it had become so routine. The bills slipped out of her wallet and into my back pocket without comment this time.

"That meatloaf recipe always makes so much, do you want to stay for dinner?" she offered.

"No, I should go." I tried not to sound too morose. At the family dinner table, I would just feel like a kid again. Jess paused, sensing some sort of gap in understanding, but not having the time or privacy to resolve it with the oven timer about to ping.

"See you next week, then," she said.

I didn't go directly home, instead tracing the old route to the convenience store. The dull stretch of nothing felt longer than I remembered. Usually I liked being alone on this route, aside from a few passing cars, but now it made me feel trapped in my own head, a terrain I usually enjoyed retreating to. I saw the canopy of the gas station, the lights over the pumps just beginning to glow, and regarded with relief what had been an omen of encroaching despair, humiliation and boredom for most of my teen years. Inside, I purchased a bag of neon sour gummy worms and slid into the booth where at the start of all this I had sat across from Jess. With my phone flat on the table in front of me, I opened the bag of candy, ripping the first worm I pulled out in half with my teeth out of frustration. I inspected my message history with Jess, all generic back and forth about what times to show up or if she needed me briefly on the weekends. Slowly, with one finger, I typed something out.

I really wanted to talk to you actually

Would 'We need to talk.' be more commanding? 'We should talk' a bit more casual and chill? I considered it, but didn't feel like revising my first instinct. After sending the message I watched the phone screen until it turned itself off. No music played. Whoever was on shift had turned off the radio, which you weren't supposed to do. I ate a few more of the gummy worms and began to feel oversugared on an empty stomach. My phone screen lit up and I jumped to see what it was, but it was a message from Martin.

Sorry things were weird the other day

As I unlocked the phone, the message bumped up under the incriminating exchange that had led to us having lunch in the first place. He was still typing.

Mollie wants to try to make it work eventually but like living apart for now

Taking a break or whatever

So forget it

And

A longer pause.

I didn't mean you looked bad or anything just that we're both so different now lol

I rolled my eyes, feeling even queasier. Impulsively, I picked up the phone to type a response.

yeah dude that always works

what did you end up doing... eat both the burgers

The bubble showing that he was typing started and stopped for a long time, then vanished.

Maybe

I paid for both after all

I refused to dignify this with more than a *lol,* which he'd take as evidence I was in good humour for now. I tried willing time to pass as I ate through the rest of the bag of gummy worms, still with no word from Jessica. I frowned, let myself wonder why Martin had waited until Friday evening, almost a week later, to send these messages in what I could interpret as a weird attempt to reconcile, but it seemed like the kind of thing that was pointless to expend much mental effort on; he probably hadn't thought much about it either. I got up from the booth and pushed the empty bag through the heavy flap of the garbage can on my way out.

The evening sun stretched out my shadow on the ground and I tried to take on a wide, rapid stride to suit it. In front of a long stretch of empty lots I took out my phone and checked it again. Feeling spurned and miserable, family dinner surely couldn't last this long, I called Jessica's cell phone number, even though it seemed like crossing a boundary. Her phone rang several times and I began mentally reciting what I would leave as a message as I walked, until I heard her voice, and stopped dead in the middle of an empty road.

"Amy?" She said.

"Jess… I really wanted to talk," I replied, cringing as I only repeated my unread message.

"Yeah, sorry, I saw. I was filling the dishwasher."

"Right. Listen, I know it's hard because the kids are always around but," I kept walking, trying to get my head straight. "I just need to know, maybe I'm just stupid and can't tell or whatever, but things between us, was that, you can just say yes or no I guess, a one time thing, or something more like—"

I shut up, losing my train of thought to the sound of a door opening and closing on the line, a ghost of the sound that had punctuated so many agonising conversations with whatever crush I had at the time over AIM.

"Amy, still there?" I heard her voice. "I stepped outside."

I could imagine how she looked, standing in her backyard, casting a shadow across the centre of the patio, holding the phone to her ear with the other arm hugged across her waist, turning her shoulders, lightly twisting on her feet as she waited for me to go on.

"Yeah," I said.

"So," her voice went low and quiet. I could imagine her talking into my ear. "You wanted some privacy?"

"Yeah," I said again.

"What did you want to tell me, then?"

I started jogging, pressing the phone to my ear. She wasn't scolding me, or even annoyed that I had called. She was egging me on, pulling me towards her, answering my question without needing to put it in such crude terms, I could be sure now. It blotted out my mind, like a drop of dye falling into and dispersing through a whole cup of water. I wanted to say something insane; to convey the scale of my feelings, it had to be.

"If I was there," I began. "I would get on my knees in front of you. I would put my head in your lap," I wondered if she could hear my breath going heavy, how it made her feel, to hear me panting again with exertion and desire. "I would want," I hesitated, thinking, feeling the jolts that bounced my body forward as my feet struck the road, "to press my mouth to the inside of your thigh." She laughed and I thought I could also hear it just in front of me, just beyond my line of sight.

I ran across the lots leading to her house and cut through backyards to see her standing there, framed in the centre of the clean new wall of the house behind her. She had hung up on her own phone, but still hugged an arm to her side. She seemed so small, something in a sealed container, with a lock I could solve by crawling towards her on my knees. She looked at me, standing at the edge of the longish grass, and smiled with resignation overtaking it as inevitably as the setting sun started to go orange.

"I'm dead serious," I said.

"Do you have anything going on tonight?" she asked. I wanted to keep looking at her from far away, where I could take her in shamelessly and objectively, but I moved in closer so that we could keep our voices low. When I tried to grin at her, she closed her eyes and sighed, then glanced off to the side, taking on the anxious evasiveness that was usually my forte.

"No one's expecting me." I could tell now that she wasn't drawing me in for an evening of picking up where we left off, but gauging my seriousness. Even then, I felt absolutely at her disposal.

"Then I need to know if you'd do something for me," she said. "Something else."

♦♦♦

We got in the van. There was no suspense building up to where Jessica was driving me. Past a point on the familiar roads I knew there was only one outcome, but what it meant remained, for me, a conceptual black hole. She stopped in front of Martin's house, of course. This connection, which I had vaguely dreaded, was now inevitable, like my paranoid imagination had made it real.

So I said, "What's going on?" Outside it had changed to twilight, darkness coming in almost quick enough to see.

"Go ahead," was all Jessica offered by way of a response. I made no move to open the passenger side door, even as the locks clicked open. "Amy," she started, more firmly. She reached down to the centre console, picking up and glancing at the screen of her phone.

"Are you fucking with me?" I asked, a bit of a laugh prepared at the back of my throat, begging for this to be an extended round of teasing, because I'd been so sensitive and suspicious.

"Just go," Jessica repeated. "They're expecting you." She waited until I got out of the car, I stood still, facing her and standing in the way of the door closing. She fiddled with switches on the dashboard half-heartedly, refusing to look at me. "And it'd be nice of you to let me know if I need to arrange a different babysitter, as soon as possible. I'm sorry this is the best way I could come up with. With some things it's easier to just show you than to say, you know?"

I didn't know, I had no fucking clue.

"Sure, yeah," I said. After I closed the door I still expected Jess to come out of the car when I'd made it half way up to ringing Martin's doorbell and tell me that she was putting me up to some kind of weird joke. But behind me I heard her car pull away, and felt intensely alone facing the front of the house. A few lights were on inside, but there wasn't any sound or movement. I rang the doorbell and Martin answered it, looking nervous. The cold white light from inside the house hit clinging droplets of sweat on his forehead and emphasised the light, round scars across the middle of his cheeks where he used to get horrible acne.

"Jessica dropped me off," I said, trying not to seem panicked or miserable, even though that would be something we had in common. "She should have called or something... I don't know what's going on."

"Oh, shit," he said. He frowned at me, his arms spanning the doorway. He glanced behind him, checked one pocket, then another, for his phone, and scanned the screen.

"Don't worry about it. Can I come in?" I asked.

He stepped aside and I followed him through the empty kitchen and the sliding glass door that opened out to the backyard. The outdoors had that strange early summer night warmth, a brief window when the temperature felt the same as indoors, but the air was damp and heavy outside. The white plastic fence cut through the low light, creating an insulating wall around us. Sometimes a car would glide by on the street, a dog a few houses down would bark, but otherwise the backyard felt like a squared-off island. Next to the door, a shovel was propped against the house, and Martin picked it up.

I trailed behind him to the far corner of the yard, the part with the patch of disturbed earth near the high fence.

As I approached the small mound of dirt that had been moved from the ditch, a sliver of pale flesh caught the moonlight like the plastic fence, forming a smooth line up a forearm, then angling into a limp, delicate hand. When I made sense of it, as an object among the turned chunks of clay, a gasp caught in my throat, and Martin must have noticed my shuddering, sharp inhale. Next to me, he looked unimpressed.

"Shh, fuck, didn't Jessica tell you, like, anything?" He walked to the edge of the ditch in the ground and hesitated before going back to refilling it from the adjacent pile, looking at me, expecting an answer. I shrugged, I didn't know what there was to be told, and he rooted the shovel into the lawn in frustration. "Is there something going on with you two?"

Was there? In any other scenario I'd blush, squirm, laugh in an especially incriminating way, and not even have to say anything. Compared to what was going on in front of me, embodying the trope of the perky, dependable babysitter getting the life fucked out of her seemed like an uncharacteristic achievement in normality, even if it was a version that was gutted and turned slightly askew.

"I don't fucking know, I babysit for her," I said. Martin raised his eyebrows and lifted the shovel again, and I stepped forward to see what part of me already knew was half-submerged in the ground. This was what I was meant to know, after all. Martin had thrown some of the soil back onto her torso, so she was luckily modest, but Mollie's limbs and head were still exposed. She stared up at the moon, dazed like she had been put under laughing gas at the dentist, and squinted when she sensed me leaning over her, next to Martin.

"Amy?" She asked.

"Yeah," I said softly. She ignored it, speaking to Martin. "What's she doing here?"

"Jessica dropped her off."

"Ah, things are getting serious," Mollie said, and rested her head back, like someone slipping back into unconsciousness after briefly sleep talking.

"Who knows," Martin said. He stuck the shovel into the loosened clumps of dirt and threw it over what was still visible of her arms. When most of her body was covered, he packed it firmly around her with the back of the shovel, then knelt down next to her face. Mollie was aware of this, not like she could see him, but like she could sense his proximity, and spoke, her voice very small, but still cut with the detached seriousness she phased into when something made her unhappy.

"Please, you don't have to be so sappy about it." She turned her face to the side as much as she could, from her position. "It should be a routine now."

"Sure," Martin said. "Let me throw it on your face with the shovel."

"Yeah, who cares," she said. Martin reached out a cupped hand to smooth the dirt over her face. I looked away as he did it, with the same uneasy sensation that made it feel wrong to look at a couple while they were fighting, or making up. Out of the corner of my eye, I saw Martin stand up again, taking the shovel to carefully pile the last of the dirt over where Mollie was now fully buried, then pat it into a shape like a raised flowerbed. We stood in front of the mound, then Martin chucked the shovel into a bit of lawn a few feet away and it held itself up out of the ground like a prong. Above the fence, light pollution from downtown glowed orange in the distance, red lights pulled down a far road. The strange glow heightened everything about the scene, as if there was a dim blanket of artificial light flattening everything out, draining away colour. The buzz of nocturnal insects had imperceptibly started over the course of the strange burial. Now that we were silent, it overpowered any other noise. Turning away from the mound, which was perfectly still, we went inside. Martin got a can of Pepsi from the fridge and sat across from me at the kitchen table, without offering me one.

"It takes about three hours, for her," Martin began. So we had plenty of time.

It, referring to the scene I had walked in on out back, was a necessary bodily function, like how bugs grew by moulting their outer layer of skin. There were inexact parallels in *our* nature — you know, here on Earth — no complete match known to science, but enough for certain analogies. The skin left behind was like those dense layers of leaves that collected over gutters and in corners in late November, but greyish, translucent, like the skin that peels off a blister. Thankfully, it didn't retain much detail. When Martin and Mollie first started seeing each other, it was every few weeks she had to do it to maintain her appearance, but it comes around less and less often; with Mollie it was now every three months or so. Maturing into a life that could pass as real was a matter of quietly refining their external appearance, then carefully and subtly ageing. That's why a lot of them got close to members of the species they were mimicking. A companion was not only protection and assistance, but a sort of active camouflage that let them fit in with normal life, alongside the capabilities they had on their own.

"Wait, 'them'?"

"Mollie and Jessica, obviously." My first instinct was to

object, though *obviously* I was being pretty stupid if I was only now catching on. Martin leaned back in the kitchen chair. "And I guess, like, others, in general."

"So wait, then, the kids—"

"What, Susie and Cecil? They're just normal kids," Martin said. I bristled at his immediate, confident dismissal, but I had to defer to his experience. I sat there, staring at the centre of the table, white paint over shallow ridges of cheap wood grain, knowing that he was studying me. He could tell I was taking in his words as if they came down a long telegraph wire, having to slowly tap out each subsequent question.

It took a few minutes of silence, Martin taking a sip of his soda then turning the can with the tips of his fingers, to work myself up to a direct question: how long has this been going on? Not like you and Mollie but this whole phenomenon? How widespread is it? How many of them are there? But he discouraged me with a look like 'what are you, a cop?' before I could even finish. It was unexpected, coming from Martin, who usually found my own manner too spontaneous and furtive. Couldn't he just give me his best guess then? Who knows. It was like I asked him to go to the park and count the starlings. The conversation churned and groaned, like a machine that didn't want to move. Martin resented me for needing it explained, for asking, which almost seemed like an extension of his unremarkable aspirations; he saw the most merit in his ability to accept immediately and bear without complaint even something completely alien. He was pretty satisfied, I'd bet, imagining that I felt a hole in the earth opening underneath me. Did he expect me to be put off, to get angry or run away? I could feel my pulse throughout my body, going fast, but it wasn't the feeling of a cornered animal. I leaned back in the chair, considering.

So Mollie and Jessica were not human, but they were capable of living a mostly very human-like life. Maybe Martin had correctly judged my own aversion to unusual circumstances, but he had overestimated my loyalty to the so-called 'authentically human' holding any sort of special place in my heart or mind.

But the last thing I wanted to ask was if he had any sense of why they were here, and, additionally, why bother with us? He shrugged, shook around the last bit of soda at the bottom of the can. Bugs were one of the oldest things on earth; they probably were in space too. Put that way, I understood how he'd reached a conclusion that didn't bother him. Living long enough on earth would make any sort of alien just another type of animal, like we were, even if it conducted its affairs secretly, in the guise of some other creature. Our perspective was skewed with terrestrial biases, but if something came to us, speaking to us, looking human in a sort of be-not-afraid guise, it would make sense to bet that it wouldn't be like us on the inside, hardly even a mammal. I could accept some type of beetle as a matter of course. In hindsight, more bugs would easily slip in among the others, the entire subtle and omnipresent kingdom of insects, genius architects of mimicry crawling, with no small portion still unseen and unnamed, all across the earth.

"Ok, but why, though? Why go along with any of this?" I asked. "For you, personally."

"I don't know why you're asking all of these questions," Martin said sourly, meaning he was happy trying to shock me but didn't want his own feelings to be on the table. "Does it matter? She's here and it's better if there's someone to help her."

Even though it was evasive, I admired an aspect of his response. It came to him so naturally; he loved her like he had never unhesitatingly loved me. I was challenging, Mollie was simple, her entire nature revolved around this single bizarre obligation; therefore, she was adorable and adored. It felt like something was pulled out past taut to straining inside my head.

"Right," I said. "Of course."

Martin looked out over the backyard and flicked on an outdoor light. A crack of disturbed soil ran down the middle of the mound now, like it was a loaf of bread overflowing the pan. He unhooked a pink bathrobe that was concealed under several layers of jackets on the coat rack by the door and went back outside. I followed, several paces behind.

He had mounded the soil around Mollie with such care, that when she was done, he could crumble it away by hand. I kept my distance, plastered against the rigid surface of the fence, feeling pale and cold despite the humid air, waiting to see how she'd emerge. His hands felt for the surface of a strange withered skin among the soil, stretched and wrinkled but correlating to the dimensions and vague shape of a human body. There was a seam up the middle that had split open in a vertical slit near the waist, and Martin, in a gesture that read as unexpectedly suggestive, hooked two of his fingers into it to tear through the whole length, the edges clumping and disintegrating like soaked newspaper.

When the soil and roughage were pushed aside, I couldn't look directly at her new body, still wet like a worm pulled out of the dirt. Martin helped her to her feet, lifting her straight out of her own pulpy remains, wrapped the robe around her shoulders, and Mollie quickly walked barefoot across the grass, back inside, turning her face away from me. I stared at the lawn, slightly overgrown, looking lush and black in the dark, and heard Martin next to me stabbing the shovel into the ground a few times to turn the soil and break up the greyish strips of dead flesh that were left over. Then he scraped the remaining, displaced dirt that sat over the lawn back into place. Once it looked like an abandoned DIY gardening project again, he walked back towards the door and put the shovel back in its place, leaning on the back wall of the house.

"You know now, right? And you're still standing there, so you're still in love with her."

"What?" I looked at Martin, startled.

"Jessica," he said. "The way you look at her is so obvious. So of course she'd send you over."

"I mean, I like her," I said, swallowing. "Regardless. She's nice, she treats me well." He wasn't convinced by my deflection.

"It isn't so bad, right? The problem isn't 'how can you love me when you've seen me like this?' is it?" I turned to stare at the disturbed ground, the familiar, clumpy texture of damp clay, foundation pits, ephemeral hills. "It's more like how can we have seen each other like this, but you can still be such a dick to me? Or each other." I felt Martin looking over at me, following my eye line. I didn't look back. I could imagine his face, cracked with unhappiness, handsome from being mostly in shadow, angled away from the lights at the back of the house. "I was talking about Mollie, I didn't mean like, *you* — you," he added, trying to get me to face him.

"Yeah, not now, anyways," I said. Next to me, the back door to the house latched open and closed, and all that was left to hear was a low whirr of insect life.

♦♦♦

Inside, Mollie had turned on the TV and sat on the couch with her legs tucked under her, still wrapped in the robe. There were only a few scuffs of dirt on her feet where she had stepped out of the ditch; otherwise Martin's chivalry combined with how apparently routine this process was had kept her beautifully clean. Martin went upstairs, probably to take a shower and, clammy and grimy with sweat, I wanted one too. The water was running, the sound of the heater and pipes dragging themselves to life rumbled through the thin walls of the almost-empty house.

Martin had turned me down as indifferently as a wet cliff face a few days ago, and now his devotion to Mollie had a much larger, more serious context. Still, he had been observing me closely, waiting for me to squirm or flinch, but also searching for something else. Now we both knew we were the only two warm bodies in on this arrangement, so there was a new impulse to carefully follow the other's moods and movements in space.

What would happen if I went upstairs, walked into the bathroom behind him, pressed my face between his shoulder blades or into his hands while they still smelled like sweat and dirt? Doing something so brazen would be cruel to everyone involved, as much as my old urge to provoke Martin specifically craved to. I even felt jealous of the absolute submission Mollie had gotten out of him. Was that what I had wanted from him all along?

Of course I imagined his naked back and did nothing. I sat with Mollie, the movie playing on the TV a strategic distraction from having to look at each other directly. She was annoyed or embarrassed at my presence, even after accepting that it was necessary. While we were becoming friends I had compulsively searched her for marks or tells, this better than life version of myself, whenever she was in my sight line. I knew I was bad at concealing this, it was invasive, and it made my hands go cold with anxiety, so I was happy to have something else to look at.

Mollie had picked, maybe at random, some very European vampire movie that didn't seem to be about vampires at all. Secreting his way into an occult ritual, the protagonist watched as a girl in an airy gown descended a staircase, running her hand, which was awkwardly damp, pudgy and inelegant, down a long, wooden bannister. At the bottom of the stairs she looked towards a woman lying dead, who, in the previous scene, had solemnly pressed a gun to her own temple, and shed a trembling tear. The girl crouched over the body, lowering her mouth to the woman's neck. Mollie was tense next to me. I could guess at how it made her feel, her complex identification with this sorrowful monster. But I was sharply aware that the exact content of her mind was a muted void to me. Then the film dissolved into a chase, a gunfight, the girl was secreted away where the protagonist would never find her… until. With the plot continuing in a predictable fashion again Mollie relaxed, sinking into the couch.

"So, do you know the next time Jessica would need to do that?" I asked after a while. Mollie drew out the hesitation before her response, squinting irritably at the TV. I guess this was gauche to bring up, but she was willing to humour me.

"I dunno, not as often. She's older. And she mostly manages it herself, I think. Though she might ask you to watch the kids overnight. I'm surprised she felt like she had to let you in on it at this point."

"Ah." I said. "How often would the overnight thing be?"

"You sound like a deadbeat dad already."

I willed myself to look at her without glancing away for a half-second. Mollie's skin glistened almost unconvincingly, like a celebrity blown up to billboard scale. She was perfect like a fresh horse chestnut or the inner pink of a seashell, and if I leaned in I imagined there would be that sort of wet, bitter smell of something pried open for its contents. She looked beautiful, how I remembered myself in dreams and old photos, even though I knew that scrutinising myself in mirrors had always made me anxious and sick. She was glowing, but Mollie's temperament was like the exposed skin under a scab picked away too early. Anything I could do would sting.

What I really wanted to ask was: how much older, exactly? Like Mollie, I folded my legs underneath me on the couch, trying to keep myself remote and give her space, but she sensed my curiosity.

"I mostly keep myself looking the same." She went on, flashing an ironic smile. "But at her age you have to be careful, make sure to look a little bit older every time because it's the only chance you get for a while, unless you want to just, you know, give it all up and wake up looking like someone else altogether." The couch cushions lurched a bit as she shifted her weight, turning to look at me straight on. "Well, does it freak you out?"

I didn't answer, at least not directly.

"I dunno. I mean, what's going on here?" I asked.

"Here?"

"Yeah, is it a pilot program for taking over the world? Like, why are both of you here."

Mollie shrugged, looking back to the film. "We didn't plan to end up together or anything, it must just have been what was feasible for both of us."

"So it's more like, figuring out a particular way to live?" I asked.

"Not formally? Like not more or less than anything else decides what to do, I think." Her responses started to get frustratingly conceptual, pulling me into a philosophical back-and-forth rather than giving up any information. What I really wanted to ask was basically her life story, from her first memory of coming to this town, to meeting Jessica, to explaining herself to Martin, all things I hardly had a right to ask for.

"How did you end up here, though?" I tried again.

"Why did the chicken cross the road? Why go anywhere?" She took a sing-songy, sarcastic tone. "How about some practical questions? Don't you want to make sure you dig deep enough for Jess?"

I clammed up, sensing that saying more would open up a genuine rift between us. Martin was coming down the stairs, his hair still damp from the shower. He had changed into jeans and an old band t-shirt, the closest I'd seen him look to how he dressed back in high school. Mollie ignored him and ignored me turning around to look at him.

"Mollie." She waited a few seconds before turning from the TV, as if the movie was at a particularly absorbing moment, and then looked at Martin over the back of the couch. "Do you want to go home now?"

"Sure," she said.

"I'll wait here then," I cut in. It seemed like the right thing, to give them some privacy where I had intruded, but Mollie bristled at this, finally angry with me.

"Why do you need to hang around?" She said it as if I was something to be dealt with, like a dog who would gnaw on hardwood furniture they didn't even have if they left me alone. "Can't you drop her off first?"

"Yeah, sure," Martin said, uncharacteristically timid. "It's just in the opposite direction of your apartment, so I thought…" He considered going on, clearly wanting those moments of privacy with her too, but didn't. We left the house together, Mollie snapping off the light switches behind us. Outside only streetlights and signs for a few 24-hour places glowed on the horizon. I was alone in the back seat as we drove through the empty streets.

When we neared my development, I spoke up just so that the entire ride wouldn't pass in an unpleasant silence.

"Drop me off at the corner."

Martin pulled up and stopped, releasing the child locks and glancing at me through the rear-view mirror in lieu of direct acknowledgment.

"Thanks," I said.

He nodded and I caught him trying to smile at me, which made me almost smile in return, mirror images — each wanting to assure the other that it was fine, that we could tough it out. I waved at the car after closing the door and watched it pull away, hoping, even if Mollie hadn't moved from her spot, leaning in a daze against the window, that she'd have at least glimpsed me and tried to go on with no hard feelings.

I waited until the car's headlights had completely vanished. Jess felt so much closer and more accessible now than she had when, across town, our situation was being so drastically recontextualized it felt like something had opened the top of my head and moved the chairs around. Most of the houses only had a single light on by the door, which lowered a new veil of privacy over what I could do — just go up to her door and knock. When I thought about what I could give her, I felt the gentle buzz of sun on my skin in the middle of the night. I could tell her I didn't care, it was easy, that I could do any of this for her, I could relieve her. Striding across the wet-looking grass and knocking on the door, skipping the doorbell, seemed as natural as anything under the cover of darkness. I went still, tensed for the slightest movement from inside, and waited. Just before I could start to worry, Jess came to the door in a loose t-shirt and pajama pants, her hair down. Instead of the relief I expected, she looked unhappy when she saw me, and the confidence that had carried the spontaneity of my decision evaporated.

"Is that it? Thanks for letting me know, at least," she said, heading off any explanation from me.

"It's not that," I began.

"Then what?"

"I don't care. I really don't care. I'll take care of it. That's what you wanted to know, right?" Jess glanced off to the side as I spoke, only holding the door half open, looking like she wanted to end the conversation and close it all the way at the first opportunity.

"Amy, it's the middle of the night. You haven't had time to think about it." She seemed tired, like she had been sleeping, but restlessly, and not in her bed.

"I don't need to," I said. "Can I just come in and we can talk about it?"

She pulled the door open a bit more to look at me, frowning almost suspiciously. At the top of the stairs, staring down at where the porch lights gently spotlit me, I could sense a child standing in the dark. Cecil, just as sleepless as his mother, watching me.

"I'll try to get the kids out of the house for a bit tomorrow," she whispered. "Goodnight, Amy." I grabbed her wrist as she went to close the door, but couldn't come up with anything to say beyond the plea I had already made. She closed her eyes, the corners of her mouth twitching, then set in a frown again. "You're going to have to learn to be patient, okay? Actually think about it." Her voice was so low, it reached my ears at the same level as the sounds of distant crickets and cars. I let my hand fall to my side and she closed the door.

Patience felt lofty and unattainable, and, unable to give the gift I thought she wanted, it began to go bad and spoil in my stomach. What had I expected? To run into Jess' arms with the correct answer, to be eternally in uninterrupted delight and carnal bliss from that moment on?

Alone, the weight of all the unresolved questions became apparent. There was a list of things I couldn't dismiss, avoid, or dispel by producing the correct response: why was she caring for the kids? How had she so seamlessly taken that place? Did things like that just happen? Again, at what scale? And, most of all, why me? To trust with this duty and the associated information? Saliva filled up a tight, sour feeling at the back of my throat; no longer bathed in the sun of randy, desperate love — I knew what she had meant.

When I entered the house through the front door, trying to shut it silently behind me, my mother was in the kitchen, wide awake, leaning on the counter with a tall glass of ice water sitting near the heel of her palm. Sleepless nights had proliferated all across town. Maybe it was the weather, or something in the air.

"Where were you?" She said, hardly looking at me. When I said nothing she asked, "Are you drunk?" Her voice was tinged with disgust, made me feel all the shame I was capable of all at once, even though I hadn't wanted or touched a drop that evening.

"I'm going to bed," I said. She wanted to object, but didn't know how, and I didn't wait around to give her the opportunity. In bed, old sweat sat on my skin like a film, maybe like the carapace Mollie had shed into the dirt felt to her, just before. I couldn't shake it off. I could only be patient, wait for sleep and then whatever I was supposed to expect to come next.

Chapter Nine

Manic birdsong, the absolute joy of another day of life on this planet, woke me before my alarm, and I couldn't get back to sleep. Hadn't I been patient enough already? Hadn't I been so good, all my life? I soaped my body meticulously in the shower, covering inch on inch of skin. I scrubbed my hair. I wanted to chase the damp of the night before out of me, but like fungus took to dark, wet places — it had taken root. I dressed, I made my coffee. It was too hot for me every time I tested it and I winced back, until it was stone cold. Time was immobile like a heavy stone block, until it vanished. I dumped the coffee in the sink.

Saturday morning was a holding pattern where nothing could happen, nothing would, it seemed like. My mom was out on a jog that seemed to take hours. When she came back, she said, "Aren't you up early." So much was unspoken in her comment, that I usually slept in, that I was usually tired, and, especially, that I had come home so late and looking so ragged last night with no explanation, no acknowledgment of my prior absences. But it also expressed a sort of helplessness, that the window in which it was practical to put the screws to me, to extract and control this information, was closing. I could recede from her and become inscrutable, a boring mystery, different from the little girl, her daughter, who had always been unhappy, panicked, crying, a problem to solve.

When Jess called in the early afternoon, my body leapt at the phone — muscles, glands and organs all. I tried to smother the rest of my response as my mom looked up in basically the same way, trying to puzzle out what missing piece of her cumulative view of my life this could be. I kept my spoken replies flat and businesslike, "Yes, sure, makes sense, I'll be ready in a sec," while beaming, with my mind, a column of light in what I imagined was her direction: "I was waiting. Did you notice? Can you hear how much I want to be alone with you?"

"It's Jessica," I said. "She needs me for something all of a sudden."

"How nice for you," my mother replied.

I waited at the end of our driveway, and Jessica's car came from the far corner of the development, almost as soon as I glanced in that direction. I pulled open the door to see her, only just holding myself off from softening like a flesh-warm pitch drop of sentiment and longing, and folded myself into the passenger side seat. In the back, Susie bopped excitedly in her own seat while Cecil sulked with headphones on, but looked up, unable to suppress his curiosity for a second before going back to his very deliberate scowl.

"Hey," I said to Jess. She looked placid, happy but slightly troubled, and didn't say anything at first, pulling the car away and down the road once I had my seat belt on.

"I'm dropping the kids off first," she said, turning out of the development.

"Yeah, of course," I said.

"Why're you picking up Ms. Amy?" Susie piped up, kicking a leg into the middle of my seat in case it was unclear who she was asking about.

"She wanted to come along to the farmer's market with me," Jess said, then added, "Since she can't drive."

Of course, a five- and nine-year-old wouldn't judge me for that the way anyone in my peer group would. Jess teasing at it still embarrassed me enough that I was quiet until the van stopped in front of another house in a leafier cul-de-sac, one of the more established neighbourhoods adjacent to a country club with a driving range for those who had paid off their mortgage when the going was good and had no other ideas about how to take advantage of the low cost of living and the local abundance of empty space. I sank down in the passenger seat as Jessica apologetically handed off the kids to a warm, effortlessly dressed woman, then returned to the driver's seat looking slightly rattled.

"I managed to get a last-minute play date arranged with one of Susie's school friends," she explained, avoiding looking at me by manoeuvring a complex three point turn to go out the way we came. "Though Cecil was in a hell of a mood about having to go along."

"I'm glad you worked something out," I said. Neither of us added anything for a few minutes, and I tried to seem calm, even though I wanted to launch into reassurances again, like I had last night.

"I have to be careful, you know," she said after a bit of driving, and I knew this was the harshest reprimand she would use on me. "Not even because of what you're thinking, but as a mother."

I wanted to apologise but held back, since she hadn't broached the subject directly. So Jessica felt that this life was shaped by her responsibility to the children, even if they weren't her own. How I should interpret this seemed to depend on the children's real mother, Jessica-in-absentia, whatever her fate was. At best, it was some spontaneous act of charity, intervening where a woman had tragically died to prevent both Cecil and Susie from becoming full-on orphans. It was a fantasy that fit my idealised image of her. At worst: murder, deceit, brainwashing, some exotic cordyceps fungus analog I was yet to find out about — I could take my pick.

"Where are we going?" I asked.

"Well, we have three hours. I was thinking we could stop by the farmer's market first."

"Oh, you were serious."

"Yes, sorry," she smiled. I rested my arm along the car window, where the sun came in, trying to soothe myself into relaxing. Despite how much had happened, my time was still mostly taken up by tangled bundles of errands and logistics, steered by nudges of necessity and desire as they became more and more muddled into routine. I used to have an internal sense of dynamic momentum, travelling towards what I wanted like the arc of something being thrown, just do this, now, this, and then — but I had arrived somewhere very different than I expected; I couldn't trace what exactly my trajectory had been at all. I was almost happy for the distraction, another instance when I could klutz around, carrying groceries and testing for the freshest-sounding cantaloupe, deferring the answer that would finally solidify what was going on.

"I just need a few things," she said. "That's fine, right?"

"Yeah, of course."

The farmer's market was in an old building on the edge of the parking lot for a Wal-Mart Supercenter that spread out so wide on the horizon it could swallow your entire eyeline. The retail chain insisted on itself, inside it could make you think there was no outside. Like the boxy houses, the cordoned off lots, the sterile, institutional walls of my high school, from gymnasium to auditorium

— it seemed massive enough to be the sucking centre of my life. Inside the farmer's market building, narrow like a church chapel or bingo hall, plain dressed people stacked vegetables, conducting their particular business, while a more disparate group, in age, manner and dress, oversaw stalls for tea blends, baked goods, soaps. Either image of entrepreneurship felt like play-acting at this scale, offering a fantasy encounter with the less alienated, the lucky, warm, passionate, or real, as a self-evident component of the transaction.

Nothing felt real. Thinking of where I grew up, I felt there was no 'here', here, and hokey displays like these increased the conviction. Jessica picked up a bruised green paperboard carton of peaches and got a frowning woman in a bonnet to put them into a bag. I made anxious eye contact with the girl working at a pickle stand, behind a counter stacked with white plastic vats. For a moment I had mistaken her for Mollie, who could be adrift in any food service position now, but looking at her straight on, she was just a local. Like the woman fussing over the cartons of fruit, she frowned too, but not in a way that telegraphed stern, proud toil. It was more like the misery of being trapped and shaken around like a bug in a jar by the undignified options you were presented with. In that expression, I felt a shared hometown at last. When Jess stepped in front of the counter to survey the different types of pickles, the girl fixed her face immediately, a vital component of the parcel of skills valued at, I speculated, eight dollars an hour, just above minimum wage and paid under the table, with no guarantees or recourse. The girl ladled chunks of garlic chilli sliced pickles from one plastic vat into a personal sized one.

A young suburban mother, floral prints and over-the-shoulder bag, was waiting with a pleasant smile for the scowling teen girl ladling pickle chips into a plastic quart drum to place it with another filled tub in the plastic bag that stood on the counter and pass it over the clear divider. Experimentally, I tried to superimpose what I now knew about Jessica onto the scene. The depth of her mystery seemed to set the entire farmer's market on rope bridges over a sheer drop; tendrils of her otherworldly intelligence could have filled the room up to the high point of the ceiling, like a tree canopy, for all I knew. I stood still, because I could imagine it truffling all around me, as she waited for the pickles, as she got out a little coin pouch from her bag to pay for them. She pulled out a tight coil of bills and then looked up, directly at me. I smiled, because I thought it was the thing to do, and then genuinely felt it. It was like smiling at a mushroom, a human-comprehensible outcropping of a life that couldn't fit into the standardised container of a boring, singular self. She smiled back. The mystery in front of me was not *what* Jess was, but that despite that, she had taken a personal, affectionate interest in me.

"I love those," I said to her. She handed the girl a ten dollar bill and looked me over as she waited for the change.

"Yeah," she said. "I'd noticed we were running out." I grinned, thinking, you are so lovely and attentive and careful. Get me out of here. We walked across the wide parking lot back to the car and I valiantly carried both shopping bags.

In the car, I balanced a carton of blueberries on my lap, so they wouldn't tip over among the other produce. Jess let out a long sigh, once we had pulled out of the parking lot without a fender-bender.

"So how was it, at Martin's?" she asked after a while.

"It was fine," I said automatically, then corrected myself. "I mean, it was surprising, of course. When I first met you, I was like, okay, she's so normal. She has her life together. But I don't feel betrayed. It's just your circumstances, isn't it?"

"I'm glad you're not upset," she said, sounding unconvinced. "I didn't want to hurt you, but I hadn't planned on..." She shook her head slightly, trailing off as she pulled to a stop at an intersection. "I was a little worried when I found out Martin was your ex, you know? Things felt really tense between you."

"It's all old stuff," I said. "It's not important."

"Well, I'm sorry I kept it from you for so long. I'm sorry I sprung it on you."

The conversation was stiff, out of context it just sounded like an average misunderstanding between lovers. She drew it out almost painfully, encouraging me to really think it over, but I felt like my desires had made my mind up, that I was happy to be entrusted with her secret, subject myself to her needs, at least for the foreseeable. Saying aloud that the reason I accepted her so easily was because I privately sensed that something being good for me, someone being kind to me, would have to come from space anyways, would have been true but too revealing.

"Amy, please be honest with me. Is it hard for you?" she asked then, like she was attuned to my hesitation. Her expression was anxious and open, like it had been troubling her all along, maybe even making her feel inferior that she couldn't offer me some baseline of normalcy that would unite me with fellow humans. Until then I felt transparent to her, and would have responded that of course it was hard, it's always been hard, with anyone, always feeling like the other person held all the cards. It was a shocking question because it implied that I was still opaque to her, and knocked away the notion that she already saw through me, was some kind of omniscient, powerful antagonist; instead, she was just another organism, with a different life cycle, different sense organs, but an equally unknowable interiority. But nothing about Jess made me feel as alienated as things people had done to me, elements of life within and around my home planet's comfy local fixtures that had left me feeling violated, exploited, that communication was impossible.

"In the grand scheme of things it's huge, right?" I started, speaking slowly. "But I'm just thinking on my own level. I'm not scared. Like, the idea that humans were special and alone always bothered me more. So does it really change that much, for me? I don't know." My hands had gone a bit cold and I looked down at the blueberries in my lap, as if I had to closely monitor them.

"It will," she said firmly. "This is a more personal situation than just accepting another form of intelligent life, right? You seem ok with it when I make things hard for you, and I feel awful about it. And when I try to be kind, you act uncomfortable."

"I don't know. Maybe I'm more used to having a hard time. Or maybe it's a clearer role, you know, to be treated like you're obviously below someone. Martin can be sarcastic and rude to me, but who cares, right? It's our dynamic." I waited for an indication of her feelings about this statement. She didn't seem to follow how this was a sensible conclusion. "I feel more anxious when it isn't as clear, you know?"

Still looking over the steering wheel, checking the intersection we were driving through, she asked me, "Why do you think that is?"

Her tone was even and arm's length, like a therapist's. I squirmed in my seat. To convey the sense of personal failure, the feeling that my inability to fit in with ease somehow implicated and marked me because I never could clue into what I was meant to be based on what people seemed to assume, was all very complicated and embarrassing. Pursuing women always ended up having a totally interspecies feeling, for example, maybe just within big city art world circles, where a mysterious discrete quality of women's art and women in general was the object of fascination. At some parties it felt like the most hopeful paragraphs of Nochlin that rang in my head and heart like a bicycle bell long after I'd flushed the rest of HONS 400 Women in the Arts out of my mind existed to be debunked. Dating a woman, socialising with them, eventually figuring out what I was meant to do in bed, even when I learned the basic scripts and effective mechanics — it still felt like the disappointments and missed expectations stacked up out of my own control.

It was second nature to fall back into the weird resentful groove I had going on with Martin, even to briefly think it could lead to something. He had been excessively legible, because I had squirmed my way into relating to him as basically a guy with tits, a guy he could fuck, and if he could swallow any initial distaste about my odd looks or careless appetites, we could get quite comfortable; though this had, in the end, never inspired loyalty. With men or women, when I started hoping I could break through neurotic awareness of romantic and sexual 'rules', something made them put the wall up even more firmly. I always ended up frustrated, longing for the instant flashes of mutual understanding that made me really fall in love with someone — how Jess looked at me with curiosity or satisfaction above anything else. Clear, and when I felt close to her, like she was sunlight shooting through the slit in the curtains and landing in a bright slash on my bed. Why can't it always be like that?

"Can't you just be satisfied with being a little mean to me?" I said at last, once she stopped the car at a light and looked at me. I rested my arm next to the window, turning my face away. "Not even mean mean, you know? Just how you tease me, and drag me around. It's easier. I enjoy it. It's practically ideal for this sort of thing."

She smiled, stepping on the gas again as the light changed. "But I want to be able to make you happy in other ways. When I made you breakfast, and you didn't even tell me until afterwards that it was your birthday—"

"I was thinking of other stuff!" I objected.

"It seemed like you were just bearing it. Like you were waiting for it to be over." She frowned at the traffic. "It felt like I did something wrong. I was worried I seriously misunderstood you."

"It's not you, I always feel like that," I said. It was the fear of the open hand closing, pulling away, the moment that always came. We were going around the long curve that went past the convenience store, the last possible stop before home.

"So you're not unhappy?" She looked at me expectantly, as if I would ask to get out of the car, or be dropped off at my own home, but I stayed, cradling the blueberries on my lap.

"No more than I tend to be, I guess," I said. "Sorry if it's not a very good answer."

We unpacked the groceries together, but stopped halfway. Jess stroked the side of my face, then rocked one of the peaches against a butter knife in her hand and made me eat a wedge from her fingers. I began to feel pliable again, like a cheap plastic picnic table deforming from hours of direct sunlight.

Upstairs, Jess sat me on the edge of the bed, undid my pants, knelt in front of me and pushed me onto my back with her fingertips. I settled into her hands as they cupped around my hips, pulling me to her and not letting me squirm away. When I could curl up my neck to look down at her I saw blond strands of hair darkening and sticking to her skin, her eyebrows knitted together. Things felt backwards, I wanted her to lie on the bed, so I could feel like I was the hero, loving and comforting her properly. I wanted her to touch herself, to show me how and let me watch forever. I wanted to say to her: you don't have to pretend, to have my sort of body for my sake, just tell me instead of letting me feel so disoriented. She stood up and then lowered herself close to me on the bed, with a splayed hand next to my face, her stockinged knee rubbing into my crotch. She tossed her head to the side, grinning and wanting me to beg, or at least ask for what I wanted.

"Jess, would you…" I tried, but rather than the words catching in my throat, I found myself coming up short in the first place. Articulating my desires, which, sex-related, were usually obvious, felt like alchemizing gold from air. Would you, could you, do you want to, is it okay to — which made the most sense to ask? Telling her to keep eating me out was easy, that made sense, but what could she, in theory, be doing it with? Do I call it her real face? No, I didn't think so. That was already in front of me. What was the relationship between the inner body and the outward appearance moulded on top of it? What made me think that what was deepest within, closest to the centre, was more real? Did it make actual, practical sense i.e. my gall bladder more illustrative of myself, or of any sort of truth, than the betraying movements that passed over my face, inevitable as weather, like an internal organ that runs even when I didn't want it to? I tipped my head back into one of the huge pillows on her bed, unsure of my own expression. "Please, I just really want *you*."

She considered the vulnerable length of my body across the bed. I thought I could see a black fissure in her face extending up her chin, a crevice she seemed to sink her finger into and pull aside a triangular portion of her face, like a missing piece of pie. The lower half of her face disappeared past the curve of my stomach. My body was cold, I realised I was shivering. With excitement? Fear? Wondering what it would feel like, bracing for it to feel the same, or even better? I felt something solid and slick on my inner thigh, like a narrow, curved piece of varnished wood. A multitude of gentle pricks, like hair from a beard but lighter and more fine, teased lightly at the base of the object against my skin, raising every hair on my shuddering mammal flesh. Everything felt intense, edged with unreality, like a dream I thrashed around in, trying to wake myself up from. Jessica lifted her head and the fissure in her chin neatly closed itself as though it was never there. I thought: did that actually happen?

She climbed off of me and went to the bathroom to wash her face. Even though we had ended up in bed together again, I felt uneasy, unable to pinpoint her desire for me. If I couldn't fully believe it was sincere, I would start worrying about it being an obligation, or manipulation. I turned my face to the side and my mind drifted, sleepy but vulnerable to that sucking unhappiness. I began to imagine scenarios where we'd fuck and then afterwards Jess would look at me with perplexity and amusement, but also slight shame, like when you wake up to more beer cans than you expected by the side of your bed. In the daydream I wanted to wail, back in reality I just waited in anxious silence as the faucet squeaked off in the bathroom and Jess paused to smile at me before going back downstairs in her slightly rumpled clothes.

I lay there with my jeans still around my ankles, hanging off the edge of the bed. Jess trusted me and seemed more interested in me than I could believe. I wanted to make her happy, even though the element of that process which seemed to involve my own happiness was challenging. Trying to discern the future was ridiculous, though I knew some features of it; like Martin I would have to take up a shovel to become a sort of protector, whether our sexual chemistry lasted or not. I pushed myself halfway up and out of the damp spot under my ass and fumblingly pulled my pants on, then wandered downstairs. Cecil and Susie weren't home from their play date yet. Jessica stood at the island in the middle of the kitchen making fluffernutter sandwiches with her head slightly bowed like a Renaissance Madonna. She assembled three of them, putting them on a large plate. One for Cecil, one for Susie, one for me.

When she heard me walking into the kitchen, Jess looked up. She smiled, like a decision had just occurred to her.

"Amy, come here. Get on your knees," she said, gesturing to the floor directly in front of her with the butter knife. I took a few steps forward before beginning to crouch. My knees crunched slightly and I winced up, a grimace of desire, as I knelt down on to the cute chequered tile floor and tilted my chin towards her hand. She slid the butter knife, with peanut butter and marshmallow fluff still clinging to it, towards my face. I could tell immediately that to see me like this pleased her, even if we had both started playing out this fantasy semi-jokingly, as a way to laugh off my willingness to conform to her whims, or how quickly she could draw this out of me. Her pleasure of indulging me, the material security from having me in her thrall, both rooted themselves deep in my own body, hot enough to radiate on to hers. I bit playfully on the tip of the blunt, flat knife, grinning up at her. Like this, I could touch her and thrill her.

"Clean it off a bit before I stick it in the dishwasher." She knew I'd respond well to a direct order.

I leaned my head forward to take the butter knife in my mouth, salty and sweet with the faint tang of metal underneath. Gradually, I moved my mouth up the sides of the knife until I was deep-throating it, beyond getting every bit off. Cold, prickling patches of sweat surfaced on my body, a nostalgic type of panic I hadn't really had since the all-consuming experiences of teenage crushes, or in childhood, the way splattering sounds made my brain feel like a rat trying to scamper up the sides of a translucent plastic box. It was hardly a blade at all, but if it rubbed against the back of my throat I'd gag, maybe accidentally jam it deeper, and what would happen then? Her magnetism pulled me around the knife, she was rocking me against it like the peach. The flesh at the back of my throat seemed so soft, easy to slice into.

When the kids came in, after the doorbell rang, I was retching over the sink. I managed to catch myself before I threw up, but a thin string of mucus stretched down from the corner of my mouth and fell into the sparkling clean basin.

"Is she ok?" Cecil asked, taking on that particular child's tone of undisguised suspicion and disgust.

"Don't worry!" Jessica said brightly. "She was just having a drink and some of it went down the wrong pipe, right?"

With tears welling in the corners of my eyes, I gave a gamely thumbs up.

♦♦♦

By August, I wanted to retreat into the crisp air and damp ground of fall, like a salamander under a rock, but the summer digressed and looped back around in on itself like the worst attempts to sensibly describe a dream, or what the mind spits out under hypnotic regression.

Jess could abduct me into her own pocket of strange time that stretched out and then went by too quickly, my bus stop metaphorically passing while I was nodding off. I was always feeling her hands on me, wet mouth, damp fingers, damp thigh, but she never sweat, and her skin was matte and firm, it didn't hold heat in the right way. If I looked directly at it, I'd clearly been seduced by something completely alien, but in a way that didn't feel like a horrific folly revealed. I was knocked over by my capacity to feel tender towards her, especially after I knew.

But it had not given me any direction beyond my attachment to Jess. The game we'd played with the butter knife had established the terms that suited me. It had refreshed my focus in a way that uncertainty had prevented; I could go on calmly and proficiently waiting, being patient, moulding our meetings in private around the false front of the babysitting and of being a dutiful daughter, saving up to move out to a responsible job and respectable life. With focus, I could separate these things in my mind and mechanically act them out, even though I couldn't see a future where the two halves would resolve into a life that made sense.

It felt like my mind was elsewhere, making my reactions in real time feel stiff and my stomach go sour. Now I knew, from my own eyes, what was out there. More and more I reminded myself of my father shortly before he had left, agitated and distant, like I felt trying to make myself eat cereal and go to my babysitting job. The possibility, depressing and tantalising all at once, was that my father had found something he believed in more than my mother, my sisters, me. Now that I knew of something just as unbelievable, I also knew I couldn't have stopped him. How could I want him back, both for what it said about what he was on the tail of and what it said about me? A direct transfer to my mother's bank account still showed up every month, signalling he was still alive, working, likely alone. It quietly dissolved into the twins' tuition costs, mom's groceries. No remainder.

I was jealous of the ease everyone else seemed to carry themselves with, all the time but especially now, especially Jessica. When she talked about something annoying that had happened at work that day, she didn't get angry or sullen while recalling it. Whatever happened beaded up and ran off her beatific attitude like gentle rain, and this capacity of hers to gracefully maintain her life felt unfair when she was something completely different under the surface. The same evening she could pull me against her breasts and murmur, adoringly, *oh, my unsmiling girl* into my hair. Did I look that miserable? I was happy when I could touch her, so happy that a part of me didn't even believe it, but it must not have reached my face.

Her loving care was untainted with the tiny resentments born from the social function of a relationship, what we were meant to do for each other. She didn't have an intuitive understanding of the small jealousies and scorekeeping that maintained the idealised romantic drama. She also didn't seem to worry about how I reflected on her as a partner, maybe coming across inadequate, unkempt, improper, weird. It was as conceptually alien as Christ-like love, except it actually touched me, fingers learning how to curl inside me, watching my respiration and taking my bodily fluids into itself with fascination.

And yet, seeing Mollie in the dirt like that was also turning over in my mind. Food would taste dead in my mouth. Feeling nauseous, I'd throw the rest out, as much as an injunction against wasting food had been ingrained into me. Whatever I ate, it didn't go dry and flavourless, like dust. If that was the case I could have kept eating. Food had the pungent, rich tang of decay. My tongue would only sense the flavour lurking at the deepest layer, implicit to all organic material. My mind was turning like tilled soil, and one day it would be.

I couldn't stop thinking about death. Okay, situationally I could. I could eat the most processed, rainbow-coloured candies and not taste that shadow in them, and when Jess would lay me down on the bed, her hands rushing over my thighs, I would say yes, god, please, like a kid funnelling sweets straight into their mouth, working themselves into a sugar high then stupor.

It was harder trying to do the same for Jess. When I tried, my body felt inadequate, like it was a strange vehicle I was piloting, or an unfamiliar tool I had to use. I thought about it like a frustrating math problem and frowned every time. How can I please you with my body?

Each time she leaned into my touch or sighed, was it play-acting at pleasure? I felt sandwiched between chastising myself for not trusting her response and equally scolding myself for only making a confused effort at understanding her.

There is an idea, maybe one I had believed, that only in communion with an alien element, which is presumed to be outside and above our sad gendered and sexual baggage, would liberated sex be possible. Mainly it was confusing in practice. Whenever I tried to touch her I had the sense of her anatomy recalibrating while I was away. Maybe she was figuring herself out through hands-on investigation, but I had the feeling that, as assured as she seemed in our relationship, she was subtly changing things, testing her own understanding of what was attractive or what excited me most.

My existential questions were no longer about the loneliness of humanity in the cosmos or my own banal loneliness but why Jess was doing any of this, pursuing me with such open fascination it could make me feel naked standing in the kitchen across from her, fully clothed. There was the normal self-loathing impulse to, when I was feeling aimless or depressed, seriously wonder why anyone would want to engage in such close quarters, bizarre activity with me, except as some kind of joke. Now there was a whole new layer of speculative possibilities to consider that could make me feel just as bad.

Reproduction was the wrong angle of approach. We both had the appearance of human women, after all. But that only made it more mysterious, going by the assumption that an unknown intelligence would use us as a resource to colonise, inevitably, surrogates or servants or food or funny pets at best. She didn't look at me like that.

I felt shy, and could never bring myself to ask in a way that really conveyed what I meant. It was always incomplete, stammering, like, "Why do you… you know… if I can't tell what you get out of it, I mean sexually, or…"

"Amy! You don't think I couldn't tell that you were interested in me? Or that I didn't want to be close to you?" When she reassured me, it washed over me — a warm sea of relief. She put it so bluntly, what the mysteries and restraint imposed on love left most people to gesture at. Of course she was an alien.

Take my hands away from me, wrestle me onto my back, shove your knee into my crotch. I was too easy, too obvious. Everything human about me followed a pattern, everything I had done before seemed so easy by comparison. On human bodies, I felt up nipples and genitalia like points of perforation that bent one way or the other, easy enough to figure out. My rule of thumb no longer seemed sufficient. What was she made of, to look so human, like the emanation of Kris' wife on Solaris? Could I slide my finger into and under her skin, like she had? If I peeled the form of her face away to see something underneath, would it be something true? Was it necessarily a deception, or just a way of making herself look a particular way? With a little pressure under the line of her jaw, I could do it, I thought. I could sink under her 'surface', but I didn't. To pull away at her form to reach some kind of core truth would be like someone shaving my head and clawing at my scalp in hopes of kissing my skull. When I was closest to her I fantasised about taking that changeability for myself if I could. But I also felt like I had to conceal the idea that Jess changing, too much, too quickly, leaving me behind, really scared me.

I ran my fingers along her chin, up her cheek, curving around her ear and through her hair. Will you be tired of me someday? Will you come out of the ground looking different and vanish into a crowd? I tried to ask in the moments I managed to catch her eyes. Will my body rot away in the earth while yours renews itself again and again? How long from now? What does it feel like for you? Do you understand how it makes me feel? How can I make you feel the same way?

"Is it okay," I managed to murmur once, holding her breasts and kissing along her neck as she pressed against me.

"It feels good," she said. "Relax." Her hands snaked around my lower back, holding my hips, then one slipped between my legs and I felt the familiar process: blood rushing, heat moving, muscles going slack or pulling into tight fists, glands from groin to mouth kicking into gear. I imagined rainwater running down the gutter and away.

The world went on indifferently. No betrayal of the arbitrary assumptions I had been operating on would cause the sky to fall or poetic comeuppance to single either one of us out, but this didn't trigger any existential despair in me, or any feeling of unbearable smallness. It was an exciting secret, passed between us in our smiles, despite everything. A section of my life felt increasingly surreal, not just that someone like this would love me, which had seemed impossible, but everything that had come along with it. Sometimes I wondered if I was imagining it all, that I was caring for two children who were left alone in an otherwise empty house.

Things continued like this: when I needed him to, Martin would drive me to Target, or the nicer convenience store that made decent sandwiches, or the one shitty bookstore still clinging to its place in a nearby mall, hawking identically uninteresting paperbacks. I kept searching for something to do with myself beyond performing my duties and waiting; but whatever it was I'd try, anything that would move me forward felt like it was being kept on a high shelf away from me. On Wednesday nights Mollie would come over to Martin's house as well, bringing along a bag of takeout, and we'd watch a movie together — a motley crew united in our defeat by obligation and/or love, not knowing what could be done. The arrangement started to feel familial, then it started to feel sinister.

Chapter Ten

I should have known something was coming when I began to feel like I had sealed off all leaks, made myself airtight to the investigations of my mother, the innocence of Jessica's children, a benign witness to Martin and Mollie piecing their relationship back together. I had almost worn in a track I could walk through without becoming a wrecker, as long as I stood in the middle of my submarine, comically running around with pans and duct tape.

Martin and I waited at the takeout counter for the Mexican place Mollie had brought up around lunchtime, initiating plans for that evening. She had suggested it, but hadn't sent a follow up confirming that she'd made the order, or when to pick it up. No big deal, Martin knew what she liked, and put it in himself. She hadn't responded to a message saying he'd done that either, and with a combination of duty and spite Martin had left his job to pick me up and retrieve the order. As our wait dragged on, Martin picked up his phone and read a message, suddenly looking agitated.

"Is that her?" I asked. Martin frowned, tilting the screen display with a rather substantial text bubble away from me.

"I have to go see my father," he said. He had always been like that; I imagined a little three-year-old Martin, with the same dour expression, saying 'my father', even though his father was the shitty, irresponsible image of a 'dad' par excellence. Martin went on, "He got fucked up as usual. We'll have to call off the thing tonight."

"Oh, so you're heading home?" I asked. The order in Martin's name was placed on the counter in a big, folded over paper bag, and I grabbed it.

"His house hasn't been my legal address for at least five years, so, no," he replied, wielding predictable and infuriating emphasis. He was almost frothing with barely withheld resentment, which in this case could be conveniently aimed towards me. When we fought before it was always his even reasonableness set against my hysteria. Now, maybe, I was less scared, and could feel almost like the reasonable one. I was already a failure, but he was the one pulsing with insecurity over what little autonomy he had scratched together.

"Really. Should I call Mollie then?" I asked.

"That was her," he said. He pulled open the car door like he wanted to hurt something, even himself, but this was the only action available to him.

"Well, you can still drop me off after, right?" I proposed this slowly, taking a deliberate tone I knew would bother him, as I put the takeout bag into the back seat and then went around to sit in the passenger side. Bullshitting some reason to tag along would be enough revenge. As he drove, staring at the road and refusing to make any conversation, I thought about how Martin had never outright refused my frankly irritating impositions, always needing a ride, even though it'd be good for him to feel low and wallow in a little self-pity, maybe even turn me down, rather than being the dignified one all the time.

I was glad it was a role from high school that he fell back into so well. Another thing that hadn't changed was that Martin still went out of his way for his dad, not out of any tenderness, but as a sort of distributed, minor revenge. In his mind, this put his father into an emotional debt to him so deep that not even genuine regret and contrition could get him out. From an outside perspective it was a ledger his father would obviously never acknowledge, the difference impossible to ever collect. But this was the strategy Martin had committed to, probably small, unhappy, ignored seven-year-old Martin, so it was just as impossible for him to change course. He was trapped between the dispositional poles of nobly bearing his father, treating it almost as a side job that would pay dividends someday, and open frustration at how pathetic it made him seem, for less and less each time. It gave him the characteristic malleability, like a bag of candies left to disintegrate in locked-car heat, underneath his hard resting bitch face.

Martin's old house was triangulated between my own neighbourhood and the denser area of town. The roads started looking familiar, even though I hadn't been through this area in years, and I remembered the places we'd pull into a side street to fuck around or just sit in Martin's old junker of a car, acquired almost immediately after he got his license, just weeks after we'd started dating. From my perspective, he seemed to never get tired of it. He wanted to drive me everywhere, and take himself to school and back every day. It gave me a few more minutes to sleep in. We rolled through an intersection and further down another long road with fields on one side and woods on the other. Then he took a left into a development of sparser, better finished houses. I recalled that both his parents were realtors.

When we arrived at the house, Martin went in, sulking in his own worries, strongly implying I should just sit in the car and wait. "I'll be quick," was the only thing he said, knowing it wouldn't be quick at all. I counted out fifteen minutes on the clock on my phone and looked at the last messages Mollie had sent me, from before the cookout, selfies and stupid jokes.

The windows around the natural wood door, divided up into stained glass patterns, offered a distorted line of sight into the house. There was no movement, and no sound that made its way out, either, not even another faint argument. I was impatient, but also felt a weird surge of anxiety, an ominous jolt that *something* had happened, so I got out of the car and walked up the cutely maintained cobblestone path to the front door.

I tried not to make a sound turning the handle, and braced myself for claws rapping down the hallway, maybe that horrible, low, reverberating bark, before I realised that Martin's father's dog must be long dead now, under the dirt in the yard, just hair and bones worked around by worms. The entryway of the house was quiet, mostly dark, but filled with the distant white noise of a sink running in the guest bathroom. The high foyer led straight back into the kitchen, marked by a hardwood plaque printed with 'Home Sweet Home' over the doorway.

I had to peer around the kitchen island to see Martin's father slumped over, leaned against a row of cabinets underneath a counter covered in mishmash décor approximating a cartoonish image of a mountain cabin. A deep red streak stretched from the side of his neck down his shoulder to his hand, which rested on the floor. The missing chunk of neck was spat on to the ground next to him like a cherry pit. Its fibrousness, how it seemed ripped out of something, stood out against the clean, cream-coloured tiles. He was still bleeding, though only slightly given the depth of the wound, and breathing like he was asleep. A cheap cell phone, the type I used to have to pay by message to text Martin after my mom and sisters were sleeping, rested in the crook of his hand, like someone had put it there in a confused helpful gesture.

I took a step back into the foyer, so that if he managed to open his eyes he wouldn't look up and see me. Seeing Mollie in the ground had startled me, but this was somehow less gruesome than what I had expected to find when Martin and Mollie didn't emerge from the house almost immediately. I couldn't work up any sentiment about seeing Martin's dad like that, it wasn't like I even had many memories of him from when we were dating.

The most vivid memory wasn't even a direct encounter. Martin and I had been making out on an unrolled foam mattress topper that had been tucked behind the too-narrow couch while watching a bootleg DVD of the *Evangelion* movie with laggy, garbled subtitles. Everything in the basement was recently refurbished, slick black plastic, leather and stainless steel detailing, and smelled strongly of new carpet. The enormous, oversaturated TV image felt too small all the way across the room, and the surround sound system relayed tinny sounds of smashing metal and guttural wails all around us.

Martin pulled away, like something he had been listening for finally occurred, and got up to go stand at the top of the stairs. Because the stairs were unfinished, I could see that he was bracing one arm against the door frame and holding the arm rail that was provisionally hung on the bare support beams in his fist. His nerves were jumping into me from across the room, like electricity, and I flattened myself down on the mattress topper, imagining I could blend in if I lay there like a wooden board. I couldn't tell what they were talking about across the room, over the sounds of the movie, only that Martin was speaking in an irritated, hushed way and his father was red in the face but not angry, trying to crane his neck around to see, well, me. His head weaved with curiosity like a child's at the zoo.

After he got bored and turned away, Martin returned to me with a, "Sorry." He didn't rewind any of the movie that he'd missed and spent the rest of the evening breathing evenly into my neck, spooning me from behind. When the movie ended neither of us moved to get up, and he asked me if I thought my parents would get divorced, since my dad was still, well, you know.

"I don't think my mom cares," I said. "If they do anything it'd be from my dad's end, because she just wants to guilt him back by waiting around."

"I mean, it's been a few months. So they're just separated, or whatever?"

I scoffed. "Yeah, 'just', whatever the fuck. If it makes so much of a difference to you. Don't worry, you've still officially got it worse."

"It's different," he said, not really denying that I had identified his intent in asking. At the time I envied his overly legible family dysfunction: a mother who had followed her career aspirations all the way to the city and into a new family with her widowed boss opposite the loser dad left behind whom he protected me from like a pearl. In the midst of all this, it was still shaking out what kind of familial damage I'd come away with.

While his mother was physically remote, except every other holiday when she doted on him, his father was almost as checked out, seeming to resent that he was the one who really did have more time for his son, all things considered, and primary custody let him stay in the same school district, too. The rare times he tried to talk to either of us, the conversation swirled around his particular complex, that, against everyone else, he was the last rugged, sensible individual, maybe the only normal guy left in a sea of others' inscrutable desires and needs, dictated by circumstances he considered humorously incomprehensible to him (outside of how they could be coerced towards particular suburban housing floor plans, of course). How could he not, whenever Martin glanced at him over the back of the couch, reporting sarcastically that yes, we were watching 'more foreign shit' to get him to leave, see more of his ex wife looking back at him than his own contribution?

So, I concluded I only vaguely recognised the man on the floor, and it was none of my business. He was like a deflated, diminished version of any extrapolations about him I'd made from glimpses of face, stature, dress and voice that I had picked up to Martin's chagrin. I tried to force my attention onto something else, and it fell on the sound of water, still burbling cheerfully in the guest bathroom sink. Through the crack of the door left open I could see that Mollie was there, fixing her makeup, like she was freshening up after a meal. She seemed to press the sides of her face back together, smoothing away a familiar seam that split over her mouth. When she lowered her hands for a moment, I saw a long, hairy-looking spine extending from what should have been the centre of her trachea. Her eyes darted to the side to catch me watching her reflection, and looked away, before she hurriedly prodded it back into her neck with a fingertip.

"Amy?" Martin had come down the stairs behind me. He was holding a fresh set of clothes, a roll of gauze and a box of band-aids. He was not happy to see me, to have the barrier he had set up breached years after it fell out of use. I stopped myself from looking back at the man on the floor.

"Sorry, I got worried."

"He's fine."

"Had a bit too much and made some mistakes," I said.

"Same as always." Martin walked past me and tossed the clothes and bandages on the kitchen island. He had retrieved the stuff from upstairs, maybe just to put some space between him and Mollie, but obviously the plan didn't involve offering any more help than that.

"Mollie's in the bathroom," I added.

"Right, great," he pulled the car keys from his pocket, walking back through the foyer, still bristling at whatever scene he had walked into or the explanation he had received for it. "Maybe we'll even have enough time for movie night."

"Martin, why is Amy here?" Mollie's voice echoed in the cavernous, tiled bathroom.

"We were picking up the food, since you wouldn't get back to me about anything." I could imagine her frown in the beat of silence that followed. "Forget it, anyways."

"She saw me… well, I guess it doesn't matter."

"Yeah, you're right, it doesn't matter," Martin said. "Just tell everyone, let anybody see every fucking bit of it. Who cares?"

I had a feeling Martin was going to do something spontaneous and ugly, or maybe I wanted to, so I grabbed the wrist of his hand that was holding the car keys and pulled him into a hug. It impressed me, like it was a surprisingly mature thing to do on my part. Looking over his shoulders, which were hunched, bringing his height closer to mine, I could see myself in a small, round mirror hung next to the front door. I moved my hands up and down his back, stroking the back of his blue work shirt, and watched myself do this, then turned my head to the side to conceal my face. My hair was growing out from the short style Josie had kept trimmed up for me in New York to no style at all. A bit longer and I would start looking more like Mollie. I felt a frustrated, hot exhale on my neck and pulled back.

"I'll be in the car," he said.

"Okay," Mollie replied. "I'll be done in a sec."

I followed Martin outside. In the car, I willed myself to reach over and pat his forearm, to make it seem like I was especially making an effort. He edged away.

"Martin, are you okay?" I asked.

"Great," he said venomously. "I was just thinking I needed your honeymoon-phase advice, or whatever."

"Oh come on," I said. "I wasn't even going to say anything."

"Jessica is an idiot to trust you, anyways," he went on. "What's stopping you from just going somewhere else and locking the door behind you when it gets hard?"

I felt my face contort like someone had slammed a door next to my ear. I pulled back, facing forward in my own seat again, but I wanted to scream at him, like we were having a blow-out argument on the phone again, a pair of stupid teenagers. Seeing him start acting like he was the principled one, the one who wanted to stick around, made my own fear of being trapped here feel like it was squeezing in on my chest, and it made me feel betrayed. I wanted to say, "What the fuck is wrong with you? You were supposed to hate it here too!"

But I didn't. Instead, "I was trying to calm you down, or something. You're so angry, as much as you say that you aren't, which means it's easy to take it out on me but act like you aren't doing anything." I hated the bodily sensation of it, but I began to appreciate why Martin let himself be angry so often; I became unusually fluent at expressing my own feelings when I could make them a complaint about him. He wouldn't look at me, practically resting his head on the steering wheel. I had been able to say it but it had made the immediate situation even worse. "You still walk around acting wounded, even though you were the one who got to humiliate me back in high school."

"Oh, it was 'humiliating' now? More than you expected fucking off to college and just dumping me to be?"

"I was going to try to make it work!"

"If you genuinely believe that, I feel like that's even stupider."

"Fuck off."

"You didn't even think about me again until you saw me in a fucking Target aisle."

This was not strictly true, but I couldn't muster a good argument against it. As the exit drew closer back then, I increasingly considered Martin 'adequate', almost certain I would find something better at college, nearly daydreaming about it. I felt myself going still and silent, my mind racing, the words not coming up. Maybe softened by his own self-pity, Martin seemed to feel at least a little bad for me too, when it turned out I wasn't going to fight back.

"Sorry. Listen, could you go around to the back?" He asked me, not looking up from the steering wheel.

"What," I said.

He steered a hard exhale into a laugh. "Well, you're not my fucking girlfriend."

It was true, but I felt spurned, on top of just having an old-fashioned argument. I got out and walked around to the dark back seat of the car, taking my seat next to the bag of food, which had gone cold and sludgy by now, feeling like a child.

Mollie entered the car a few seconds later, placing herself with dignified indifference in the shotgun seat.

"Alright?" Martin asked. She laughed. "Please don't come over here without telling me, okay. Seriously."

"Oh? He called me." Her voice was provocatively naive, pointing her usual carefree demeanour like the tip of a knife.

"Ignore him, then," Martin replied.

She seemed to fume at this, and was oblivious to my presence in the back seat.

"But it's not like you aren't on speaking terms with him."

"He's my father!"

"So what?" She laughed again, like a protective reflex against the intensity of the conversation. "You won't cut him off all the way because he helped with the house, so now he always bothers me when he has something for you, but you also want me to act like you've cut him off..."

"Just don't talk to him, don't come over here. Why are you making this so fucking difficult?"

They had both pitched up to the edge of raising their voice.

"It is so hypocritical to say I can't when you talk to

him about me. I know you do. I was just trying to be a nice, friendly girlfriend for you. A sweet little wife."

"Stop it."

"Do you know what he said to me this time?"

Martin had mentally rolled over, his voice flat and soft now.

"I don't want to know."

"Your father said to me, I know what you are. I know you can just wear the face of anyone who's left someone in the dust to get close to them. So, come on, why not?"

In the windshield I saw Martin grimacing and gripping the wheel, from an angle like I was floating slightly above him. I cleared my throat into the queasy silence.

"Oh my god." Mollie jumped. "I'm sorry, I thought you left or something—"

"I was waiting with Martin. Sorry."

"No, uh… sorry for yelling," she said quietly. She leaned her forehead against the passenger side window, leaving a round imprint of reapplied foundation. "I want to go home, please, Martin."

Martin started the car and drove out of the development. I watched Mollie's reflection, squinting attentively at the patterns of lights going by outside.

"We're not going towards town," she said after a few minutes.

"Yeah, I was going to drop Amy off first."

"Isn't that more out of the way?"

"Oh, sorry." Martin swung moodily into the next available turn and changed his route. So he still had some shred of hope that he'd be the hero here, contrasted with his father, that she'd be happy for a moment alone with him, or even follow him home. From Mollie's demeanour

I could come up with more or less lurid versions of what had happened. No matter how gruesome, it was all the same boring story, though.

Whatever Jess and Mollie were, if they had their own particular sense of sex or gender, they were, at the very least, not any form of dyadic human science was familiar with. It was probably a coincidence that Jess and Mollie both appeared to me as women, but I could speculate on certain benefits to this approach and it wouldn't surprise me if some of the most successful of them stuck with that form. When I tried to be a good girl, and then, even more briefly, a good woman, there was no better camouflage than being quiet, and in situations where you were expected to respond, to be agreeable. You could learn a lot from going along with things, but when either of these tactics painted you into an ugly corner — ice queen, pompous bitch, you knew what you were getting into, why're you so upset all of a sudden — following the line towards blaming yourself was instinctual, no matter how angry it made you feel. The whole drive I watched Mollie from an angle where she seemed to stare down her reflection in the dark window, wondering if there was something different she could have done.

Martin intuitively knew which of the looming, anonymous apartment buildings was hers, the tucked-away angle that was most convenient to drop her off by, which played out as a strangely tender gesture. I watched him watch Mollie key the door code in and disappear into the yellow light of the lobby, and looked away when he caught my own eyes in the rear view mirror.

"You can be honest with me how bad that looked," he said, once the density of town lights was receding behind us and we were on a dark, quiet road. In the low light he looked feeble and small, like the mass added on to his body since he was a sixteen-year-old track team back bencher had fallen off all at once. He looked back at me through the rear view mirror again, and I could tell he was asking for the moral support I used to reliably, emphatically muster, an exercise in acting that made me feel maniacal and wrong. I couldn't give it. I must have pulled a face like I smelled something. He wanted me to go easy on him, say something funny.

"Bad," I said, and then laughed to try and force some levity about it.

"Yeah," he said. I felt cowardly after my performance had gotten him to smile. We stopped at a red light, the intersection before the convenience store, and he looked over at me. "I want to think she's not doing it on purpose. She doesn't understand what upsets me, because, you know."

I stopped him. "Maybe the perspective that it's one or the other is what frustrates her. That she's stupid or that she's deliberately upsetting you, I mean." I folded my arms, sunk low in the seat, and fixed my gaze out the window. "Anyways, I don't want to be the person you complain about your girlfriend to."

"Yeah, fine." He continued driving around the curve and back to my house. The car's headlights briefly flashed on a signboard, placed perpendicular to the road between the yellow-orange chevron signs, double-wide and openly bloodthirstier than any Bush era advertisement. It dispersed the heavy atmosphere in the car with a grim, insane sense of amusement that lasted a split second. We looked right at each other, this time Martin turning back towards me for a second, and we were both laughing. I said, "Jesus Christ." Martin, "What the fuck."

I didn't think about it any more than that. My mental catalogue of reasons I needed to leave already felt full to bursting, overlong and made of limp, cheap paper like a Tupperware party brochure.

"Can we just talk for a bit?" Martin said, nearing my house.

Even though I had just steeled myself against any sentimentality in the sense that we had unfinished business, I glanced across at him, surprised. "Sure, of course," I said.

◆◆◆

Martin was exhausted, unable to fake his usual warm greeting, but my mom was happy to let him in, offering to get out drinks and snacks for the occasion.

"He's fine. We just need to talk," I said. Out on the back steps, the evening was getting cool and the sky was clear, with a precisely divided half-moon above. There had been warm nights spent like this before, an awareness that sat in the air between us.

I understood Martin's impulse to act like it was nothing the first time I had confronted him. If I acted like I forgot everything, I could get along with him too, in that nostalgic, idealised way, and lazily stargazing together could be almost pleasant. But barbs always emerged, pinching at tender, protected portions of skin, cutting closer to vital organs.

The circumstances surrounding our breakup had been the elephant in the room we were carefully navigating around. I knew, as soon as I had wrecked our awkward state of denial, that the uncertainty of how we'd have to relate to each other now was worse than going on pretending.

For almost two years we had managed to smoothly enact the wholesome public image of teenage courtship, while enjoying what rewards we could get in private. There was a sense of doneness, both in that this was what we were supposed to do, and that I had finished, we both had. No longer did we have to wrestle with the terror of being alone, what so many women wept and tore their hair about in the culture drought of mid-aughts film. An itch, scratched, receded under the skin again.

The mismatched expectations that had always been there, how we would, even in the sweaty potency of adolescent horniness, wince and pull back from the other, started to gain a definite shape.

I received an early acceptance and scholarship package for the college application I had put the most effort into. No excitement. I only read the letter to recognise that I had absorbed the expected portion of financial burden that would have otherwise fallen on my parents, had cannily invested my expected potential, and that the solitary pursuit of filling in a mass of forms at the kitchen table on silent autumn evenings had bore fruit.

"I'll tell your father next time he calls," my mother said. The trajectory smoothly continued.

Feeling restless, I decided to tell Martin on the drive home from school the next day.

"The scholarship for what?" had been his response. He had an implicit understanding that I was going to apply to college and likely get in, though he chose to play a bit dumb about it. Just like, it went without saying, I assumed he had no interest in the institution, but never brought it up as one of the significant areas where we diverged.

"College, the college I want to go to," I said.

"Really?"

"Yeah, I mean, it's not so far away, and you have a car."

"Ah," he said, like he was going to go on, but didn't.

"So, what, you're just going to stay here?"

"It's just more school, isn't it?" He was grimacing, acting preoccupied with the temperamental dashboard lights. "I want to be done already, you know? Get an actual job and be able to do shit."

"Here, though?" I asked.

"At first, I mean, you have to start somewhere. Not forever."

I pressed my lips together, shaking my head side to side, trying to be polite about how immediately doomed this plan seemed to me, sensing something unsettling like a subterranean fault.

Of course, to him it was obvious that I was trying to extricate myself from life here like a double agent about to be evacuated from a war zone. Despite this, I had been all passive smiles, which was, in hindsight, probably what pissed him off the most. He pulled away, even blew off driving me home one afternoon to take a girl from the track team to the mall for ice cream cones. When I lingered too long, perplexingly to her, in the background of Martin's life, she told me a few days later what was up, either out of mercy or annoyance: not that they were dating or anything, but it was kind of pathetic, like, *don't you get it?*

"I wish you had made her suck your dick or something," I ended up moaning into my cheap little Nokia when Martin had finally decided a call would be easier on me than a barrage of 20-cent texts. "It'd make it a lot easier to figure out what the fuck is going on with you."

"Fine, let's stop making it hard then."

It was over then, though we fought a bit more; I remember screaming at him, "It isn't even out of state, shithead!" Sitting on my desk chair, pushed flush against my bedroom door with the bad latch so the twins couldn't peek in, only just restraining myself from chucking the phone across the room. The betrayal felt total. But I would have been betrayed eventually, anyways. He was supposed to hate it here as much as me.

Because it happened so privately, there was no appeal in making some sort of retaliatory gesture, like going to prom on my own, which neither of us cared about in the first place. We had tried to get one over on each other, and tactically dissolving relations was probably the first adult decision either of us made in our lives. The silent consensus we reached was to pretend the other didn't exist. I would go away soon, reinvent myself, this would all have been a trial run. And I wouldn't stop him from getting whatever he wanted here.

Did it still hurt? Not really. It wasn't the bottom of the pit of shame, and more indignities and failures had been heaped on top of it, too. But it felt like a tender sore in my guts that I carried with me, which could act up sometimes. At worst, it reared its head with a predetermining power over how I approached my relationships, the insecurities, the power plays I'd default to, the things that made me unhappy or suspicious, the conflicts I'd defer, and in the end, it had brought me back here, hadn't it?

"Didn't you want to talk?" I asked.

"Sorry, I was just cooling off." He sighed, leaning back on his hands. The first fireflies sent out tentative yellow-green flashes in the grass. I had carefully reviewed my resentments and still didn't know how to start the conversation, so I watched Martin fidget, stand up, stretch his shoulders, feel at the pocket of his pants.

"Oh, here," he said suddenly, his voice low. He pulled his hand out of his pocket and it was curled around something, gesturing towards me. My fingers had to fold almost entirely alongside his to take it, and it was the pen I lent him at the bank, weeks ago. I just laughed. "What?"

"I honestly didn't expect you to give it back," I said.

He scoffed. "Jesus, just say you hate me."

"You think that's what I mean?" I rested my hand on my knee and flitted the pen back and forth with my fingers. Even though my face was turned stonily to the side, I could feel him looking at me.

"When you said it I realised that it kind of is my default mode — to feel justified being a shithead to you. So I don't blame you."

"Right," I said. "And I make myself out to be the joke, anyways."

He moved to sit down on the step next to me. The nearness of his body returning was like a slight vapour that made me feel warm from my sinuses out.

"I think we should apologise to each other," I said impulsively, into the silence. "And not act like it was just kid stuff or whatever."

"Ok," he said, waiting for me to go first.

"I'm sorry for how I treated you, even if it wasn't as clear-cut as lying about taking random girls out for ice cream."

"Yeah, well, sorry about that," he said. "I should have been honest with you too, before it all happened." Compared to my own statement it was shoddy and incomplete, but ambiguously satisfying to hear. We had climbed up to an approximately equal footing, or dragged each other down to it.

"Thanks," I said. I felt Martin's body shift so that his arm crossed near to the small of my back and his thigh was against mine. I tried to place myself in my body, recall what I wanted, like I was consulting a rolodex. By now I knew what was coming. He put his hand on my knee.

This was what I had wanted, or at least contemplated as an interesting possibility — interesting enough to pursue it. Martin was leaning his whole torso in towards me, then pressed his mouth half on my cheek and half on the corner of my lips, and I turned my head further away, to deny him but keep the side of my body flush with his. I felt him sigh and almost laugh against my skin, dangerously close to muttering 'come on'. The hand on my knee moved up and across my stomach, brushing up against one of my breasts, and Martin leaned in closer, lips more on my lips than not now. It felt gruesome, but also like a victory. The worst part of me wanted to see if he would push through, make a truly desperate move. Then the back porch light's timer clicked on, throwing us in a sudden spotlight. I carefully peeled his hand off of me.

"What?" He wasn't angry; he had already shifted to that gentle and attentive mood that came over him when I let him touch me. The bliss and fascination of open tenderness, giving and receiving in one, doubled when he fastidiously held himself off from it as long as possible. I was glad that somehow, that remained, though it dissipated quickly.

I felt myself go red, trying to explain myself and coming up blank. I had already written this scenario in my mind, dreamed it, experimentally longed over it, even. We could give in and fuck each other, perhaps finally in the privacy of an actual bed in an empty house. We'd meet, burning up with the soft-focus view of the past and unfinished business and how we'd held each other so stubbornly at arm's length. But seriously considering it, I could tell the act would feel underwhelming and mechanical before it was even done being consummated. It wasn't just that it would be a stupid, self-destructive act, ripping through our closest relationships, but ultimately, we had only gotten more ill-matched. We would never have the cohesion of needs and desires that suited us as well as it did when our horizons were so constrained, when we were so naive.

"This is ridiculous," I said, keeping my voice low, as if my mother had her ear pressed on the door behind us. "Whatever you're trying to do right now is just convenient." Just like I had always been, I thought, but didn't say it. "Maybe if you're not so much of a shithead you can make it work with Mollie."

"She really hates me now, and I can't even be mad at her about it. We just fuck each other up."

"Martin, I think we're better as friends," I said, with more than a little irony. "And you should really try to patch things up with her. She obviously still likes you, despite your best efforts, but I think it's important for her to have someone on her side, not even a boyfriend, or whatever."

It wasn't what he'd wanted to hear. He paused, fuming. "Well, you didn't have such a crisis of conscience before."

"I didn't know everything that was going on. I thought she was just some girl you were seeing, and then weren't. Come on. Forget this, go home, apologise, try being a family man," I said. "Like I'm going to really try to make things work with Jess, I think."

"Cool, yeah. If only it could be that easy, right?" He stood up and reached to open the back door.

"What, it can't be?" I asked. "I mean, not easy, but less difficult, since I'm in on it too now."

"For as long as it suits you," he said, with a tone like he was correcting me.

"Can you at least not say it right at the door?" He ignored this. I lowered my voice to a harsh whisper. "And what's that supposed to mean?"

"Your Jess fobs off the responsibility of telling you to us, what do you think happened before that? I'll tell you—"

"Martin," I cut in, worried he really was raising his voice so my mom could hear, but he went on.

"I had no clue, right? She comes over to my house, acting kind of out of it and clumsy, so I assume she got a little drunk or something. I tried getting her some water and just sitting with her in the kitchen, but all of a sudden she runs out to the backyard, starts digging at the ground with her hands, almost like an animal. And when she noticed I followed her, she played it off like a joke, like, oh, I just want to mess around in the dirt for a bit, and then taking off some of her clothes like, oh, you know, it's a kinky thing. I was freaking out of course, even with the fence it felt like everyone in the world was fucking watching, but I got the shovel out of the garage and played along, right, just to try and understand what's going on. I covered her legs and up to her waist, and it's obvious I'm not going to do more than that, and she just looks at me and starts groaning, like she's sobbing, but there's no tears or anything. She starts telling me everything, even as the rest of her body's going stiff and getting this weird skin on it and I have to believe her, even though it's obviously insane, and I feel like I'm going to smother her to death if I actually do it, you know? She put it off as long as possible, and who knows what would happen if she hadn't explained it to me before she's just totally gone under. That's how it went."

I was quiet for a long time. Martin seemed like he'd expected me to say something immediately, and when I didn't, he started to get antsy, with his hand still on the doorknob.

"You shouldn't have told me that," I said, at last.

"What, because you'll pull everything off so perfectly?"

"I feel like you only told me that to try and embarrass her, even though she isn't here and what happened earlier wasn't even her fault."

"Of course, whatever I try to tell you, I'm the bad guy."

"Wait," I said, too late. He'd already cracked the door and I imagined my distressed cry bouncing through the whole house. He only turned back to glance at me for a second before walking into the house.

"What's wrong?" My mother's voice was in my ears before I could tell where she was. In the kitchen I looked around and saw that she had been sitting in the living room, with one of the curtains on the window to the backyard half-opened. Martin was still walking through the kitchen, towards the front of the house, and I took a few steps after him, trying to come up with a decent cover.

"It's nothing. He just had a fight with his dad." From my vantage point, I could see Martin pause at the front door, making sure I caught his resentful look before slipping out and back down to his car. My mom didn't see, but still looked at me suspiciously.

"You need to be more thoughtful if you're going to bring people over," she said. "You know I don't like it when there's whispering and fighting around the house."

I had nothing to say. My stomach growled; the food I'd ordered hours ago was sitting on the back seat of Martin's car, irretrievable now. I made a big show of shrugging and sighing, her least favourite thing, and took a tub of leftover spaghetti from the fridge to reheat, practically throwing it into the microwave.

♦♦♦

And then, trying to sleep, I was pulled under again, like a nightmarish abduction hallucination. Repetition, fixation, no answers, just 100% conviction of the incomplete scenario playing out in my mind. If I had followed him out through the front door, into his car, back along the same old roads, no street lights on them in the dark, in some quiet bend with no direct line of sight he'd pull over to the side of the road and with an automatic symmetry we'd exit from our own side doors and circle around to the back seat.

Martin wouldn't want to take me home, and wouldn't express any curiosity over why I had rejected him at first, what had changed, before going for the fly of my jeans. His wrist would disappear under the waistband of the underwear I had on. The idea of warm fingers, not my own, against me made me sigh again, like a puncture emptying a tire.

He'd say: "You're so wet already." Then me: "Are you 12 or something? Don't fucking say that."

It would go like this: Martin would be mostly still fully clothed, and I'd be straddling him with my pants completely off, shirt hiked up over my bra. He'd be grumbling with propriety as I tried to arrive at the correct angle to consummate the act, but just like high school gym class, my best attempts would lob off the backboard of my pelvic bone or whiff under entirely.

"It's been a while since I've taken dick," I'd joke, compensating. When I glance at him after finally manoeuvring it in he'd look at me like he really does not want to know this.

Seeing Martin from above, my head bowed over him to avoid smacking the roof of the car, I'd have the urge to make a grab for his neck, not to choke him, but to just hold him down, like two dogs play fighting. Maybe I would do it, and he'd put his hand on mine and lift it away, looking annoyed and confused, repeating the action as I tried a few more times.

"Stop it. What are you doing?" Even in my imagination.

I'd fill up, not with him but with agitated embarrassment, like pouring water into a saucer that can hold more and more than you thought imaginable before it starts dripping over the edge, bracing my legs as he fucks up into me. We'd regret it even before either of us got off.

I was glad he was gone, driving away to his empty house on the other side of town, both alone with our enormous, stupid desires. I fell asleep with my fingers over my eyes like I was deep in thought or mortified with embarrassment, my palm compressed down the side of my face. *Jess, it's so fucked up. I don't want to be here any-*

more. I wished she and Mollie could lift both of us out and away. But even if they could, did we have any right to ask?

Chapter Eleven

Across the kitchen table, Jess looked like the centrepiece of a nightmare ad for familial harmony, bathed in the soft lighting of slightly outmoded home decor that suited her so well. Her bemused satisfaction while serving dinner, squaring out perfect chunks from a wide pyrex casserole dish, could lift me up off my feet and put me back down like an ocean wave. That day she had finally insisted that I stay for dinner, rather than asking, and I knew my role wasn't to resist her, not anymore. She would let me be the kind of person who ate home-cooked food sitting opposite a beautiful woman with kids around us on either side. It was like discovering a talent that I had no expectation of ever developing, without precedent in my physical capabilities. Like my whole life I couldn't whistle, and then one day I just did.

The feeling underneath something like this coming to me so easy was entirely uncanny. After dinner, I watched Jessica rinse off the plates, fill the casserole dish with warm water and an elegant loop of dish soap to loosen the hard bits of cheese and pasta that still clung to the sides. The kids were in the living room, Cecil absorbed in his tablet while a comedy show played.

"I don't know what I'll do when I have to get a real job. You won't need me soon, when they start school again," I said under my breath, pressing one of my hips against hers. She grinned, handing me a rinsed plate to put in the dishwasher.

"I could always think of something, if you were up for

it." She quickly pressed her mouth to my forehead, the most unambiguously romantic thing she'd done with the kids in an adjacent room, and went back to scrubbing. That spontaneous display of affection, the homeliness of it all, made it feel like her brief touch had pushed any visualisation of my own future that I had running as a background process out of my mind, leaving a steep drop into a black chasm instead.

As summer waned and the evenings began to shorten, we both started to feel like we were running out of time, gliding along like Bugs Bunny, only putting out the next five seconds of train track in front of ourselves. What we could do when the kids were back to being occupied with school and extracurricular activities was an appealing problem to joke about, but the bigger one to consider was what was to be done about the rest of my life?

More and more nights Jess would make a big show of saying goodnight to me and sending the children to bed. I would stand in the laundry room or recline in the passenger seat of the car in the garage, exercising my patience, and then she would quietly smuggle me up to her own bedroom once the sinks had run and stopped and both doors upstairs had closed.

If I could lie next to her, flat and silent in the dark, and the kids weren't stirring, I could spend nights without coming home at all. I put less effort into coming up with convincing explanations for my absences, to begrudging non-comment from my mother. Maybe she could tell, but was unequipped to confront me about it. Did the children know? Jess always clamped a hand over my mouth at every sound, even a sharp inhale, that exceeded a whisper. It was easy to classify Cecil as suspicious but naive and Susie as too young to care, but I knew looking back that it would be obvious. It was a narrow, strange streak in our lives that created the exact conditions that lifted something into memory above the forgotten everyday. Of course the kids will, in hindsight, know. Know what? That it had to end.

Later that night I was cocooned tight against Jess under the covers, damp all over my thighs, feeling limp and sombre. It was raining, a nighttime summer storm with fat hard drops hitting the roof audible in every room of the house, which seemed to put a muffling barrier of slight imperviousness around us. Jess stroked the side of my arm, lulling me into a strange mental emptiness where I felt like I could be especially honest as she asked me questions about myself.

"Do you think about having children?" was one she came up with, after a period of hesitation. I laughed, but tried to keep my voice low.

"Never. Absolutely not. I feel like getting pregnant would be one of the most freakish things my body could do to me. It would feel like a bad joke." Jess scrunched a side of her mouth up like she was thinking about what I said and wanted me to say more. My own feelings about how my body could, I guess, reproduce another human into the world were probably interesting to her, but usually I felt guilty about stating my position so bluntly to a fellow warm-blooded, breathing mammal. "Obviously I wouldn't be a good mother anyways," I went on.

"You're great with them, though. Cecil doesn't even complain about you." This made me smile, knowing him well enough by now to understand the compliment.

"Yeah, but I'm not their mother."

"I think kids can use a weird babysitter as well," she said, maybe a little self-effacingly, keeping me at arm's length from any more information on her own perceived relationship to motherhood. "I think they've been quiet for a while now, are you hungry?"

Sneaking downstairs, we split a bowl of dry kids' cereal wearing swapped bits of each others' pajamas. In one of my black shirts, the worn logo for some long-defunct magazine on the front, and with her hair down, Jess was charming and relaxed, and wouldn't have stuck out too much among any of the series of roommates I bounced between after college. It still felt novel to look at her and desire her as a near peer, in the moments we could slip out of our roles; it could make me shy again, like we were the last ones who managed to stay up at a slumber party. I tossed a piece of blue Trix into her mouth and she ate it happily, then leaned in to kiss me. When I ran my hand through her hair, trying to press myself against her, kiss her more deeply, she pulled back.

"Aren't you exhausted?" she asked. I stuck the empty bowl in the sink and we headed back to the bedroom. I walked behind her as always, in case one of the kids unexpectedly stirred. The sneaking around was fun, I thought, watching her softly climb up the stairs, a few steps ahead of me, but it also emphasised how I was still tangential to her life, not a full participant. Regardless of where she was in their overall life cycle, Mollie seemed more like me, still sorting out how she wanted to live in the first place. Jess fell into that conceptual abyss where I had so much trouble guessing anyone's age, late 20s to mid-30s, in human years, the sort of people I could be easily grouped with in one scenario, and then in an adjacent moment feel the same scale of gap open up as wide as the one between me and my fourth grade teacher.

"Why do you have them?" I asked, when we were

halfway up. The bedrooms, doors closed, stood at the top of the staircase, in her line of sight and mine. She turned and looked down at me, thinking a long time. This was probably the worst location to broach the topic, and the way I'd asked seemed designed to daunt her into a hurried denial — *what are you talking about?* — a foothold from which I could take a more explicit, antagonistic angle on her, if I had wanted. She didn't try to evade me, and I wouldn't have tried to corner her anyways.

In the moonlight and light pollution from the porch lights and passing cars that came through the front window, I was groping for her feelings through several layers of dark fabric. Enough of a change had passed over her face that I knew she intended to tell me now. It was silent; outside the storm had stopped, though long trails of rainwater still clung to the window panes.

In her bedroom, Jess put the radio on at a volume we could hide our voices under, for something harder and more risky than the whole mommy's-seeing-someone-new talk. We sat across from each other on the bed, and the program we had tuned in to — two grown men solemnly relating the known qualities of infant-alien crossbreeds — couldn't do away with my unease, or make their speculation seem comically normal by comparison. I tried to imagine what it would be like, to be confronted with the real thing, serving frozen yoghurt or holding down an office job with two kids in the suburbs, if you had been stewing in whack-job theorizations for so long.

Jess put a hand on my thigh, closed her eyes and didn't open them when she began to explain: there was also a process of remaking oneself, of total breakdown, not unlike being born from a pupa underground for the first time. Sometimes you run out of options, the deception runs thin or suddenly derails. If you're really skillful, you can convincingly reach the end of a natural human life. But, up until very late in their lifespan, anyone like Mollie or Jess could, with careful planning, pull open the emergency exit.

In, as far and deep and undisturbed as you can go, the body breaks down and your senses heighten. You take in the soil around you. Like a mycelial network can tune in to all the plants and trees around it, you hear the thrum of life. Radio waves, sound, the thumping vibrations of routine in the 21st century, a variety of formats and styles that can all be incorporated into a cohesive whole. This was how you became a convincing mimic. Held completely still on all sides by the press of dirt, their bodies went slack, wet like warm drool, and their minds opened up, like mine did, daydreaming and trapped by my little life, rehearsing the life to come. Consciousness floated back to the top of the pupating slurry when it was almost time, like a skin forming on hot milk. That was when the main attributes of a totally new outside appearance, not merely refreshed or adjusted, could be redetermined. It was not unwilled, but the process determining it happened at a deeper level of will than decisions like how to dress, how to respond to a text from your boss, how to comfort a child on the rim of a crying fit — it was a relief from the relentless minor challenges of waking life.

Like dreams had a tenuous relationship to organising consciousness, this dormant, remote sensing state was an adaptation to enable better success in acquiring DNA from other complex organisms that could be incorporated for biological resilience without sexual reproduction. While these bits of flesh and blood could be taken violently, or in self-defence, the ability to communicate across worlds and across species enabled cooperation, maybe even consensual handovers.

For a species whose reproduction was asexual and impersonal, splitting off an egg that would incubate a precise copy of themselves given enough time undisturbed, the relationship to any progeny would be, at most, unknowingly encountering them at some later point. Of course Cecil and Susie weren't hers, though she had been around them long enough that she understood the feeling that came from actually knowing and raising something now, she thought. By now past copies of herself had split off and staggered away into time-delayed alternate lives, likely expanding their own family trees, with or without children, partners, webs of love and violence she could only hope she would still understand.

"I was mostly honest, when we first met. That woman's husband really had died in a plane crash, and she was stuck with two kids on top of that." She looked at me and tucked a strand of hair that liked to fall across my face and poke into my eye back against my hairline. "You probably would have understood her."

I frowned, thinking I couldn't have much in common with this second-order Jessica. "How do you mean?" I asked.

"She felt trapped in her own life. I could feel her, never sleeping, turning on the TV or just sitting up in the dark." I shifted closer to Jess on the bed, unsure of what was coming but feeling like I wanted to press my face into her chest and cry anyways. "So while I was underground, it was kind of like a dream, right?" She asked me, like I would know better. She was prodding at my own experience of dreaming more than anything. "Like I wasn't quite making a conscious decision, but I was reaching in that direction. And at one point I realised I could help her. By then I knew all the things I'd have to do. When you're underground, it's like you're doing the things you tune into in a dream." Jessica's explanations often wound between the digressive and bluntly technical, her role of bubbly caregiver dropping off of her, stepped out of like shoes. I took it to mean she respected me, and wanted me to understand.

"So it was harder?" I asked, trying to follow. She smoothed my hair again, entertained by my guess.

"What are your dreams like? It was easier. I knew where everything was, everything that was done," (until you started rummaging around in my cabinets, my pat little schedule of going to work, caring for the kids then going to bed alone, was implied) "and I could reach out my hands and do it." Of course, if you cleared your mind you would just know what to do, which explained why I could never be like her — it was impossible to clear my mind.

What had happened was, one night Cecil and Susie's mother, the pilot's wife, the conceptual entity who had a social security number and birth certificate and credit card et cetera, which all pointed to the woman, Jessica Wain, looked out the back window over the lawn of her family home, a structure whose contents had fallen short of the promise that they would be sufficient and sustain themselves, and she saw her own face outside, streaked with dirt and rain. That was like a dream. And when that woman saw herself emerging from an unsettled corner of her lawn in the moonlight, it was obvious what this would enable her to do. It was winning the lottery, a miracle.

"She understood immediately," the Jess in front of me said.

"Okay but," I hesitated, wondering what was my right to ask. I felt the ambiguous relief that often followed any attempts I made to predict the truth of a matter. Jess' intervention was not made in the most unambiguously heroic circumstances I had imagined, but it didn't indicate any evil motive either. It was the peaceful, consensual exchange her supernatural mimicry had been adapted over millennia for, knit together in the cast-offs of a different star or spiral galaxy, and the result was seamlessly becoming a suitable substitute for a loving but smothered mother. I couldn't know what Jess had been before, maybe it would never be my business, but this was what she had reached out for into the dark and chosen. I felt like I had first-hand evidence, a Copernican level of scientific potency that could destroy the cliché sentiment that someone's humanity, their ability to care, was summed up in how closely they raised offspring. Jessica loved me, her attention held me, she had no idea how many or the nature or location of her own children, and the way she lived had resulted in a strange and enormous act of care for the two children I also cared for. These facts all coexisted peacefully.

So my body had naturally put her in a curious mood, but to me their approach to reproduction was far more noble than succumbing to family obligation, or worse, simply taking on these feelings and making yourself feel them as biological or social destiny. It wasn't deceitful, at least compared to the other possibilities I had feared, the more gruesome fictions of alien body-snatchers, easily drawn a line around, who fed on the equally discrete category of 'the living'. The way they changed moved with an indifference to morality or what was superficially natural. It could operate like alchemical exchange, attuning itself in terms of sympathy, or affinity. Martin's father had identified this when he confronted Mollie: they would only arrive as wanted, and someone had wanted her like that. After they emerged from the earth, though, anything could happen.

Jess waited, enjoying my consideration. She slid a bit closer to me on the bed, while still giving me space, not placing an arm around me yet.

"But what?" she said. I didn't have a single question in mind. I wasn't even sure of what I didn't know yet, but one occurred to me, and I impulsively went with it.

"When you did that," I asked, "how long were you here, underground?"

Jess acted like she had to think about it, buying time. "A while. Seven years or so."

I tried not to be distracted by the feeling that, as this conversation had gone on, my admiration for her became so enormous and inflamed that it was seeping out from inside me, pressing out from cracks like an overgrowth of slime mould. Lowering my eyes towards one of her shoulders, I did some quick mental calculations. My voice pitched up, recalling some vague statistic about cicada broods, counting backwards to when my dad left and then subtracting approximately two, "Seven years?"

"It was a full renovation," she said, softly.

All the things she had done to tease me, to force me into feverish patience, this was the one that finally twinged — the facts increasingly adding up to the conclusion that, as good as she was, she could have basically known the whole sad story I told her in the convenience store, but had acted like she had not.

"So you were just underground there the whole time,

listening in on our lives?" I could tell my face had become unflatteringly red, like I was a kid about to launch into a tantrum. From the way my tone went harsh, too harsh, in a way that surprised me, I knew Jess could tell where the conversation was going.

"I had a sense of you being there, sure. I didn't know how you felt about anything," she emphasised. "I didn't have any sort of plans or insight into anyone beyond that, I just thought you seemed like..."

"A screw up?" I suggested, defensively. In the back of my mind, an even uglier thought: if you took the form of what you wanted, why didn't you want to save *me*?

"Once I got to know you, I thought you'd understand." Jessica was trying to gracefully turn things around, and I sympathised. Of all the things for me to get stuck on, to resist and get mad about, this was nothing I had to search the stars or nonhuman intelligence for. Someone being gently dishonest because they pitied me or thought the truth would hurt my feelings was harder to grapple with than human-size carapaces or body doubles.

I frowned, "Were you still there underground while my father lived here?"

She looked away, unusually evasive. I pressed harder.

"If you knew all this about her, you must have known all the stuff with my father, when he left and stuff. Maybe even why, or where he went."

"Amy, I'm not psychic." She shut me down, standing up from the bed to turn off the radio and then get the lights. "I'm tired, ok? We can figure out some way to talk about it tomorrow."

Sulking, I thought about how just a few minutes ago I was standing in the kitchen, feeling like I was a refraction of my love for her from the inside out, like the light thrown out from a faceted stone. She was attainable, human, right there. Now she felt far away again, an abstraction on high, who might humour me but would never be my own. I got under the covers and rolled on to my side, my back to her back. Were we fighting? She didn't say anything else, and I ran back and forth over the conversation leading up to her silence until the sound of rain starting up again interrupted my thoughts and I fell asleep.

♦♦♦

I woke up as Jess got out of the shower and was dressing herself in front of the mirror.

"Good morning," she said, noticing that I had shifted in bed. It came out stilted and formal. Hearing her voice, I realised sleeping on the issue hadn't improved my mood. I watched her in the mirror, avoiding studying her face.

"Did you sleep okay?" I asked. She didn't answer, pulling at the shoulders and collar of the blouse she had put on. As she brushed the tips of her fingers down the front of the blouse, then turned her head slightly to the side to check her hair, I thought she might leave without a further word, which would really make me angry.

"Someone else did see me back then, before," she said suddenly. I felt exposed as I sat up in bed, trying to make some connection between what she said and what I knew that would make sense of what it meant. Light coming in from the sun seemed to glare at me, like I was staring into a spotlight.

Coming up with nothing, I just said, "What?"

She spoke in a quiet, deliberate kind of voice that pinned me to the spot. Past the first sentence, a fluttering dread grew in my stomach, I felt like I had to run to throw up, or piss.

"I tried to go underground on a Friday night, but by the next morning I had only gotten myself halfway underground. I was hardly able to lift my head, right in the middle of your tomato plants. It was the height of summer, the ground was hard, and I didn't look like I do now. Everything was already grown over, mid-change. But someone saw me, got the garden hose and wet the ground for me anyways." She looked over her shoulder at me and I could feel my face jerk into a scowl, even if I didn't really want it to. Her tone made it seem like she was doing me some sort of favour. "Isn't that what you wanted to know?"

"So what do you want me to say? That's hardly anything to go on," I said. My voice seemed to roil with disgust, against my will. She was quiet for a long time, smoothing out the edge of her lip liner with her pinky finger.

"I wish I could tell you more."

"So that's why he left?" This snapped her out of it. She went from having to will herself through a measured, deliberate admission that, I realised too late, never got any easier, to being angry because it was easy.

"I don't know if it was your father, Amy. I could have just as likely been about to ask if it was you."

"Bullshit!" I said. "You were what he found." I wanted to say that seeing her was what made him leave, but the thought itself seemed dangerous, like saying the word 'leave' would remind her she didn't have to put up with any of us. It was the fact that he'd chosen to leave, that something could convince him of that, could make me feel helpless again. My mind still whirred, wanting to say something cruel to her.

"You're disappointed," she said. "But I know just as much about it as you do. By the time I could read the surface again, he wasn't there." I looked across at her, tried to raise my chin and shake my head in the background of her reflection, if only a little. I thought about her eating those disgusting hamburgers in front of me, listening so kindly, like we were new acquaintances. "You know everything I know now."

I didn't though, I could never know everything. Beyond the things at the top of the list that I still didn't understand: how long of a life do you remember? When will I have to leave you next, and then for good? Has there been someone like me before? How long did you stay with them? There was also the permanent problem of unknowableness itself, not even between myself and an organism whose life exceeded human experience, but even among other humans. The intractable problem was that anyone could always surprise you, though how horrible if they couldn't again, ever.

"It's not even that I had trouble accepting everything else," I managed to say.

"I know. I'm sorry."

"But you'd keep that from me? Like I'm just some stupid bug crawling around in the dirt to you, something to pity?" Thinking over the sentence, weighing it out, considering saying it, I had known that it would hurt her, and I said it anyway, surprising myself. I watched her back and avoided the reflection of her eyes in the mirror. She refused to start an argument with me.

"Amy..."

"What."

"I love you, okay?"

It was difficult to hear and didn't make me happy, like it had once been so easy for her most benign praise to do. I rested my head in my hands and heard the rustle of her clothes, her footsteps going downstairs, the familiar sounds of hot water boiling in the kettle and the glass coffee pitcher being turned over and placed on the counter. I didn't go down to her. I waited until I heard her leave for work. When I went downstairs the coffee pot was still out, with just enough in it to fill a mug, the liquid sitting in the dregs at the bottom, stone cold.

Even as close as I could get to her, closer than seeing her as an alien or seeing her as a mother, Jess still represented another ideal to me — of being completely unentangled with my prior life. I had unearthed her myself, and she was like a glowing green vein of peridot brought here by an asteroid. Except, she had been on Earth long before that. She had been like the telephone operator of our lives, sitting in the centre of these dull suburban houses that would only occasionally acknowledge each other, knowing how they were all knotted together underneath and able to stick in one cable and yank out another.

Jess was like anyone else, neither one of us could completely partition ourselves off from the world no matter how much of a perfect, all-homemaking, all-copulating pair we could become. My instinct had been that knowing all her secrets would give me ownership and access that she wouldn't share with anyone else. What knowing her better had really done was opened up a series of possibilities, rather than shutting them out.

Looking into the low puddle of cold coffee, I realised I

was being a little immature. I cleaned the coffee pot, made my own coffee and waited for the sound of the kids getting up. I cleaned the coffee pot again, in anticipation of Jess coming home, so it could be shining and upended in the dish rack when she walked in and she wouldn't have to think about cleaning it in the morning. I got out my phone, dismissed some messages from my mom and opened up the strictly businesslike texts I had sent back and forth with Jess. I sat in the kitchen, warm coffee in the cow mug, the sounds of morning coming into full swing all around. I thought about trying to explain the whole gemstone and telephone operator metaphor to Jess, but it would take too long to type out, and sound stupid. This was a matter when, as soon as I came to a conclusion, I should act before I stopped myself. Sometimes the line between desire and fulfilment could be so direct, if you could catch it. I typed three messages, impulsively, fast.

I'm sorry

I still love you too

and I want to keep loving you

I turned the phone face down on the counter and looked at Cecil, who was eating scoops of cereal while placing rows of blocks across his tablet screen.

"Are you happy?" I asked. "Like how are you feeling lately, in general?"

He looked up at me, not pausing whatever he was doing. "Of course I'm not happy. I hate school and mom said we have to go shopping for supplies soon because it's only like three more weeks until it starts again. I still have half of the stupid homework they gave me over the summer to do."

"But other than that, are things good?"

He rolled his eyes.

"Seriously!" I said. "I'm curious. I can't let kids suffer under my watch."

"It's basically fine," he said, looking down at his tablet. "I don't know. Like, things are weird, but at least it's not the same stuff over and over."

"So?" I asked.

"So yeah, I only hate it sometimes. Is that fine?"

"That works," I said.

Cecil put his bowl in the sink and went back up to his room. I turned the phone right side up. Jess hadn't replied, but it didn't make me feel sick with anxiety the way it usually did to check my phone and see no messages after sending off something like that. Maybe I had accepted, in a fatalist way, that if what I said and how I acted had hurt her too much, I would still be her babysitter when she needed me, and I would keep her secret absolutely. It was how I pumped the brakes to try and avoid feeling too sorry for myself, accepting a foregone conclusion so that whatever happened would at least be tolerable, which never worked. All day I felt calm and highly aware of the time as I carefully balanced not busying myself too much with extra chores while still being attentive to the kids. It was like a workday, but one of the more tolerable ones, when time passed with an inevitability that was both comforting and ominous since there was just enough to do.

Still, I felt a prickling layer of sweat over my body when I heard Jess pulling the minivan into the garage. As usual, I got up from where the kids were and met her at the door. She embraced me, without even craning her neck over my shoulders to check behind me first.

"Amy," she said. "I worried about you all day."

"I'm fine," I said. I breathed in the close, papery smell of her body, the notes under the residual smells of her deodorant and soap and laundry detergent that I knew to look for now, which had just seemed like absence before. "And I meant what I sent you, but, you know, if you don't want to, anymore," I pulled back, feeling myself blushing. "I'll still watch the kids, and you can trust me about everything."

"I was worried about you leaving," she said. She was laughing in relief. I squeezed her hand before retreating back into the kitchen, as if nothing had happened between us, to start getting out things for dinner.

In bed that night we huddled under the covers together, keeping the lamp next to the bed on, looking into each other's faces, studying them. My eyes moved restlessly over each part, from her eyebrows and temples, chin, cheek, wrinkles at the corners of her eyes, like it was a large pond rippled by the strange movements of schools of fish. When I had interrogated her opinions and preferences on human foods, and it was her turn to ask me something, Jess spoke directly, also evaluating each twitch and wince of my face as she did.

"Okay, so, in science fiction," she said, narrowing her eyebrows but still smiling, "people write about aliens as a bad thing, typically, especially ones that are intelligent and social."

"Yeah," I tried to look away, under her amused scrutiny I felt embarrassed. "I apologise on behalf of all humanity for that."

"Sometimes it's not even under their control, that the way they live is antagonistic to humans' lifestyle, or even just to your matters of taste."

"You seem to have watched a lot of this stuff," I said.

"In my past lives I had more free time." She tossed her hair playfully and looked a little sad. "There are exceptions," she went on, shrugging. "I don't know. I guess I don't have a particular question to lead you into, sorry. I just thought you must feel some way about it now."

"Well, in general, I think it represents all kinds of the unknown, like other people, or a metaphor for foreign cultures or immigrants, like, that's bad obviously." I propped myself up on my elbow, taking an analytical posture. "But I think people can also relate to the general concept of alienation. Like feeling that you've just been dropped into a completely different place, where everyone else is part of this coherent thing but it makes no sense to you. Or that there could be something out there that also doesn't fit, or that totally screws up the way things fit together. So the stories always have two aspects, like that."

"It seems like a lot of them just find the idea of something being here menacing, regardless of what it's doing. The fact of hiding or impersonating a threat, even if it's benign." She ran a finger through my hair to draw my attention back to her, looking serious.

"Ok, so what would you do if the other Jessica came back? Like do you think it would be awkward for her to see someone wearing her face?" I asked.

"I think that counts as a serious question," Jess replied, but she spent a few seconds thinking about it anyways. "I don't know what I'd do, I'd have to leave, I guess. But I hope she won't be annoyed with how I've done things."

"Do you think she went off to go kill herself?"

"Amy!" Jess tried to keep her voice hushed, but I could tell it was something she had considered. "No, I hope… I really think she's still out there. Anyways, you've done two in a row."

"Sorry." I waited as she thought again.

"I guess a kind of serious thing is, I couldn't tell you where all of us are, any more than you could tell me where and how many people there are without looking it up. Does it scare you, that I don't know things like that?" It felt like everything was tied up in this question: how much I trusted her, how much she could trust me, her concern for my feelings but also how much I could be expected to feel for her.

"I don't think of it so much," I say. My eyes were flicking back and forth across her face, so close to mine. She moved to lie on her back, while I was still propped on my elbow, so she was vulnerable below me, under the covers. "I mean, you know, my general political principles are like, free movement, peace between nations, goodwill to all—" I trailed off. I was looking at a slightly crooked tooth underneath her lips that were pressed back into an amused grin. She saw that on Cecil's mother and didn't know or didn't bother to correct it; she had no vanity. I loved her. How could she be strange to me? I understood, even if I found it challenging, how she could be so relentlessly practical, almost mercenary. As much sympathy, curiosity and love she could muster, there was still an animal with the knowledge that it was not among its fellows inside her, a muscle that always had to be held taut in anticipation of rejection. But, I thought, isn't that the fate of the alienated in general, the same tension that was always thrumming through me? I could feel my throat constricting, the old, all-too-common misery.

"What's wrong?" She said.

I wanted to tell her that despite her love I was unhappy, unmoored. That I already knew I couldn't stay here. That I envied her, able to change her body and step in and out of a life, that her choice seemed selfless, and I believed she was a good person, the kind of person who would do things like that, but I couldn't understand why she had gotten herself stuck here. Instead I groaned, working myself down to sobbing silently, as she poked her head above the covers, looking around dismayed. I know, I know, I thought, curling around myself, groaning harder with the weight of self-loathing. A horrible thing for children to hear.

The chrysalis had shattered. I cried and cried. What was I now? Jess pulled back the covers and looked at me, really freaked out, like she thought I was having some sort of anaphylactic shock, like she had never seen anyone cry this hard before, or maybe only children. I guess I looked really bad.

"Amy, what's wrong?" She pushed herself up and spoke a bit more firmly. In the context we'd established, anything that could be heard by a child standing at the door came across as a shout. I winced away, covering my eyes with my hands. The more I struggled to catch my breath, the more my thoughts spun out and I forgot what about the things she had said had made me suddenly so miserable in the first place. It wasn't her. It wasn't even the kids. It was the sense of coherence, outside of my control, of being neatly slotted into a trap before I even knew I was doomed.

"I don't know what to do, I can't stay here," I said. "But I can't go, either."

"Here?" she asked.

"I feel stuck," I managed at last. I was calming down, just streaming tears rather than filling with mucus, my throat tightening. Jess started petting my hair nervously.

"I'm sorry," she said.

"It's not you, I don't know," I said. I lay on the bed, exposed, selecting my next words carefully. "It's like, the more involved I get with you and the kids, the more stuck I feel. Not *with* you, but just that life gets more constrained, and claustrophobic."

She hummed thoughtfully.

"That could always change. I don't want you to feel like you have to do anything on my behalf."

"But I want to," I said. This was half true. I desired it and was equally afraid of it.

"Eventually the kids won't rely on us, I won't need to be Jess, necessarily." She hesitated on the last part, and her voice went low again as she pulled the covers back up, lowering her body back into the bed, next to mine. Her tone seemed to imply that she was willing to help me how she already knew to, but I didn't want to be saved in a way that would inherently force us apart. Of course, I couldn't articulate this, and the thought just made me curl tighter on my side. I could envision that far-off woman almost jealously. Where did she go? When I thought about what Jess said, that the children won't need a parent forever, I still felt ripped off. She'd had a year, maybe two away now. Cecil's legal adulthood stood aloof and practically immobile, just under a decade away on the horizon.

"I wish she would come back," I said. "So we could go off on our own, you know, she should take responsibility." Jess went like a wall when I said this, not revealing her own feelings if she had any. Once again the different biological trajectories of our lives meant that her definition of patience was much more capacious than my own. I had no idea how she had exited her own previous lives when the time came. Was she afraid that I'd judge her? Could I? Hadn't my whole life been evading what obligations felt foisted on me that I didn't want to choose, to try and make a life that was bearable?

She moved to look more closely at me, considering my tears, which were still squeezing out and down the side of my face as I tried to stop myself from crying. When she really had to think about something, when it couldn't just be carried on her practised ease, the skillfulness of her mimicry, I again had the sense of her intelligence being enormous and probing, not like an aloof supercomputer operating at arm's length, but curious, wanting to touch and taste and swallow, like my own hunger. Around two weeks ago, she had three fingers in me up to the third knuckle, and they came back with a long, phlegmy strand of dark blood clinging to the side. I groaned in mortification, doubled by her unfamiliarity with this phenomenon, and my mouth started running — forget it, it'll ruin your sheets, it's not even worth it, sorry, I feel so gross now, I mean, it's fine, it's like normal blood not blood from hurting me — and she stared back at me, her clean hand still braced against the inside of my thigh. She said my name, to get my attention, to soothe me, or cut me off, and then experimentally ran her tongue up the side of her hand, beading the stringy mucus on the tip of her tongue.

"Try not to think that far ahead. It'll be time soon," she said at last. She didn't need to specify what. "Before the end of the summer, it'll definitely be my time." Jess sighed, resting her head on my shoulder. "The longer it goes, the more I feel like I'll make a mistake."

♦♦♦

The next morning, we sat in the kitchen very early for a quiet breakfast, having come to an agreement not knowing the exact time the terms of that agreement would arrive. My ears were attuned, even more than usual, to the sound of Jess slicing an apple into wedges and then eating it. It was a task that was impossible to do quietly, the flesh was light green and almost translucent, a structurally ideal matrix of sugar and water. It was delicious, and of course, I knew now, as a lover of simple organic materials at heart, she was enjoying it. The sound of the fruit in her mouth, maybe the concealed mandibles underneath working it down, dominated my attention. Normally this would be unpleasant bordering on painful. The almost physical irritation I felt at chewing sounds was a source of repeated low level annoyance in every other relationship I could remember, but in this case the sound struck me as fascinating, almost precious. Because she would be gone, of course, I thought, and the next little bite of apple she took was almost enough to make my eyes well up. I could jump forward in time, to when we were back together, and know it would annoy the shit out of me again, with the prospect of separating, of changing, totally out of mind until it would sneak up again. Peace so complete I could start a new list of small annoyances with her, like her gentle, rustling respiration in the night, close enough to breathing but not the same if you paid close enough attention, which jolted me into a panic when it lapsed into a temporary silence.

♦♦♦

How long would it be? (When it started and also when it stopped.) When would I be without her, and also how long would I have to bear it? In daylight, going about our prescribed roles, these seemed like gauche things to ask, tied to both her most private biological functions and the general sanction on asking an older woman her age. Well? If I loved a tree, would I cut it to count the rings? I waited for her to say more. I waited out days as we tried to wind down the rest of the summer like we weren't outrunning it. I tried to trust her, and waited.

Then one evening, when Jess led me up to the bedroom as usual, there was a thick envelope on the dresser at the end of the bed. Inside was a series of neatly stacked documents: Cecil and Susie's birth certificates, information on their doctor, a neat, untouched copy of a credit card issued to Jessica Wain, photocopies of a social security card, passport and drivers' licence under the same name, a stack of bills.

"It'll be a week," she said.

"Until?" I asked.

"No," she said quietly. "I'm sorry. I drew it out. I have to do it two nights from now. And it'll last a week."

Even though I knew it was coming, I froze, feeling sick and cold at this revelation. Concrete now, in the documents in front of me, was my own responsibility and complicity in the scale of disguise we now maintained together, and it was heftier than my college application packet.

"You're asking a lot," I said.

"That's why I'm giving you everything." She pulled me into a hug, and the envelope crinkled between us. I felt like an unwilling child being sent off to their first day at school. "I didn't want to ruin what we had left of the summer, but..."

"Why does it have to be so long?" I asked. "How much are you going to change?"

"Are you scared I'll change too much?"

I wanted to groan, miserably, yes. She understood as much from my grimace and went on.

"Because I put it off I've got to be more careful about getting it right, but you'll still recognise me, I promise." She held me a long time, and I tried to remember every aspect of her as I pressed my face to her chest. But, I had almost no visual memory. Even with her arms around me, it felt like she was already gone. If only she could reverse engineer me from my tears, if I could remain with her, in part, while she slept and rebuilt herself, just by expressing my fear and grief. Then I could live on in her metabolism, which strains of common cold she was vulnerable and resistant to, those pieces of me would be carried in her body, broken down into recombinatory bits that would disseminate until they were unrecognisable, all to prevent her from stultifying and falling apart. Life demanded a deeper cut for the commitment that came from biological incorporation.

These scientific digressions were secondary to actual understanding, which was right in front of me. If she, if all of them like her, had been wandering the Earth so long and managed to piece together a friendly appearance from shreds of organic material, how was she ever any different from me, who so often felt like a fake, an intruder in this life? What would it say about me? What did I stand to gain, in a practical sense but also more abstractly, morally, in terms of my sense of self, by drawing a line and saying, human, worthy, here, not human, not worthy, there? Martin had run the same arithmetic and the sum had come up with zero, maybe less. Maintaining this line offered no benefit. Which of its rewards didn't repulse me, or shame me? My alliance with the non-human, that I decided on in that moment, was as principled and pragmatic as when Jessica had drawn me to her bed, to satisfy her curiosity.

How could I explain my decision? I didn't want to blame my love for her, as nice a sentiment as loving someone was considered to be. She hadn't done something to me, but as a presence in my life had allowed me to open a door inside myself that I hadn't previously known about, on the other side was the me who loved her. I was proud of having done this with myself, what it had gotten me to do. No matter what would happen, I was glad to have become someone who loved her. I wanted to run my fingers along the vaulted ceilings of how this expanded my thought and feeling. Even if she had stepped into another person's appearance and life, the Jess pressed against me under the blankets was the fluid outcome of the circumstances of her life so far, and on that level I could relate to her. Even if she was biologically alien, sort of immortal. I kissed her at her temple, feeling the fine hairs that smelled sweet, like grocery store shampoo, and she smiled shyly at me, our course determined.

♦♦♦

On the intervening evening, I felt like we should be apart. Cecil looked at me desperately, clued in to some kind of uncomfortable change in the air, part of him knowing it wasn't really that his mom had to travel for work, but unable to further speculate. Leaving before dinner, as soon as Jess got home, had become the anomaly he squinted at now, hanging close at his mom's elbow as she unwrapped a boxed pizza. I wanted to reassure him, but knew in practice that would make the situation seem more serious than I was meant to be treating it.

As I walked back towards my house I texted Martin: *want to do something tonight?*

Then, quickly: *sorry things were weird at my mom's house btw*

He had started typing something just as I sent it. The grey blob paused, slipped out of view for a bit and then popped back up decisively.

Sure, can I bring Mollie along?

I raised my eyebrows, holding back from instinctively jabbing back something like: *if that's still an option*

of course! I ended up typing. He would pick me up at seven.

We went out to the hill with the radio towers on it, because that night was forecasted to be clear and the local news had been saying there were going to be intermittent meteor showers that week. The towers stood in a cleared space at the crest of a series of rounded hills that ran along the road leading to our old high school. From the top of the hill you could even see the rims of the nuclear silos upriver peeking over the trees.

I'd loved the radio towers. Whether I rode the bus or got picked up by Martin I would try to spot them as I went by. With the morning sun behind them they were black silhouettes, except on dark winter mornings when their trusses were hinted at by trails of red lights. They were glamorous structures, and strange, that reached up and away, becoming the image my mind called up, though slimier and in cotton-candy colours, when I read about the tendrils sprouting out from the ocean on Solaris. Now we were sitting under them, me and Mollie, on the cement pedestal of the largest. Martin settled slightly further down the slope with a pair of binoculars, leaving the girls to talk. I swayed my body in and out and across the barely audible strands of radio waves that converged in a canopy over us, just as real as the metal. I could tilt my ear and cut into a totally different type of buzz or crackle, turning my body into a receiving antenna, feeling the transmissions passing through my teeth.

"Have you gone through the whole thing with Jess yet?" Mollie asked, unusually direct, as if she was wondering how a personal hobby or adopting a pet was going.

"She's given me a heads-up," I replied, "but not yet."

Mollie frowned with concern. "She's pushing it," she said. "It's hard for her too. She probably wishes she didn't have to rope you into this."

"Is that how you feel?" I asked. It was getting dark and I looked over the waves of uncut grass, going blue, where Martin was still sulking around by himself.

"It's nice to have a rope," Mollie said. "Sometimes I think I need it." I didn't laugh with her. I didn't envy either of them, her or Jess, even though Jess had smoothly bluffed it all, reaching a level of success even I couldn't claim as a human. She had done the full interpretive labour required to meet me and every other human as an agreeable, legible projection, while Mollie still struggled with it sometimes, and let me see her frustration. I wonder if Martin understood enough to see it too.

"Listen, if Martin ever does anything fucked up, you shouldn't hang around him. Tell me, or I'm sure Jess would help you too."

"Amy!" She looked surprised, really laughing now.

"What, do you think he beats me, or something?"

I answered honestly, from my understanding of Martin.

"No," I said. "But he can be kind of an asshole, especially if he gets the idea you're looking down on him, for whatever reason. So I don't think you should be forced to rely on him, you know?"

"Yeah, thanks, I get it," she said. "It'd make it easier on him too, right?"

She was looking at me to evaluate my answer to this, so I held off a bit before answering. On the drive over, sitting in the passenger seat and flicking excitedly between radio stations, she had seemed more at ease with Martin, even though they would still sometimes go quiet around each other. They had come to some sort of agreement, or re-articulated it, and anyways, she was still trying to be a normal girl, though with less of the posed deference that felt like a barrier before. In moments when she both looked at me and let me see her, direct, alien, frustrated but desiring, sometimes happy — I was happy for her too. Her life as an underemployed yoghurt slinger, with an older and slightly pathetic boyfriend and a room of her own in a shared apartment, was interesting to her, for now; she held it close like how I squinted at the grey-green screen of a handheld game under the glare of a flashlight propped on my shoulder, childhood nights when I couldn't sleep.

The four of us had clustered in a particular way, even as internal connections shifted, dissolved, strengthened. I felt close to Mollie like this; the resentment I had felt for her, stepping in as the cruel living image of the version of myself I worried my mother and Martin had really wanted, became something I was ashamed to recall. I wanted to say I was glad I met her, and that I didn't mind her borrowing my face, consciously or unconsciously, but I blushed as I thought this, worried it would come across kind of gay.

"Yeah," I said. Martin, still standing far away, now turned to look up at the top of the radio towers with the binoculars, since nothing interesting had shown up in the sky yet, only a bit of the cloud cover we had tried to avoid. I left it unsaid that maybe things being easier would finally let him roll over and show his stomach. Despite trying to be friendly alongside Mollie, he still acted distant with me; we hadn't talked about anything that had happened. As he lowered his binoculars, I waved, and he started walking up the hill towards us.

"Say cheese." A few paces away, he got out his phone and the small red light of the photo timer was flashing, pointed at Mollie and I sitting at the base of the radio tower. I thought, as I always do, about how strained my smile looked to me in pictures, like a thick awful mask I had to hold up with the muscles of my face.

"I don't want to smile," I said.

"Then don't." The red light started to blink rapidly, and Mollie leaned in towards my shoulder, flashing her tongue between her middle and forefinger, both pointed up at either corner of her mouth. In the dim evening the rectangle of light from the phone hit us almost like a shock wave. Martin looked at the screen.

"Beautiful," he said.

I held out my hand. "Let me see." He handed the heavy paddle of a phone over to me, taking a few steps closer to where we sat. On the screen, Mollie and I were overexposed and pale looking, and the meshed structure of the radio tower looked pure black and stretched back into the shadow behind us. I zoomed in on our faces and, noticing I was taking kind of a long time with the phone, Mollie forced a slight laugh.

"I probably look so bad," she said.

She didn't. I adjusted the screen to look at our two faces side by side. For some reason, the low light, the harshness of the flash, our poses — our similarity seemed heightened by the image. "Beautiful," Martin had called it, with the sort of half derisive tone that let him access genuine appreciation sometimes. Yes, I thought. I think there's something beautiful about it too.

We spread a worn picnic blanket over the grass once it got dark. I lay on my back, between Mollie and Martin, and felt the stretch of ground under me. I thought about how, even if it wasn't strictly accurate, this length, felt along my whole body, was the longest span I could directly experience and understand. Any other distance was abstract, only graspable by some sort of comparison.

As the only one of us coming off a retail shift, Martin quickly fell asleep. He had been quiet for a while, but suddenly sucked in a giant, stone unconscious snort that made Mollie and I look at each other and laugh. I propped myself up on one elbow to look down at his stupid face, and felt Mollie's eyes on me — not pissed off or even suspicious. Then, when I lay back down on the blanket, she leaned her head in to rest near my shoulder, so our view of the sky would be more similar. Her proximity didn't make me anxious for once.

Spread out on the blanket under the cloud cover, Mollie told me how they died, though I didn't want to think about it. Up until the urge to bury yourself, the chill of torpor, it felt the same, apparently, except you didn't wake up. With the dark all around me I thought that maybe it was lucky, to drift off to sleep with only the idea of a new and improved you in your head when the lights went out, no gradual depletion, no fear, no sense that the end was coming. Martin would snore every few minutes, and we pointed when we maybe saw a tail streaking by in the gaps in the clouds, even if there was usually no way to confirm if it had really been there or was just a trick of the eye.

I wondered, then asked, did they believe anything in particular about it, like an afterlife, or at least a soul or consciousness that persisted? Mollie seemed to get a bit condescending at the idea, that no, it was such a distant thing, they had always been such solitary creatures, the peace of sleep had always been appealing enough.

I found myself agreeing to the same extent that she seemed slightly unconvinced by this conclusion. It was something it was possible to make peace with, but not enough on its own. Maybe that was a sort of convergent evolution.

Chapter Twelve

I didn't get to be a true gentleman when it came time with Jess; we ended up using the shovel she kept for her own use, in her garage.

"Just a week, right?" I confirmed, standing out in the backyard with her.

"Minor renovations," she joked, hugging her arms against herself in the dark. She didn't clarify anything else about what to expect, maybe she didn't even know.

The stalled excavation pit a few lots away, where I had taken Cecil and Susie to play on the high mounds of dirt, had been left alone for months with no sign of that changing over the coming week. At least I got to feel a little gallant, taking her by the hand, leading her across the dark, overgrown lawns like we were sneaking away from a party to be alone. I would have caught her as we lowered ourselves down into the pit if she hadn't laughed and shook her head at me before making the slight hop herself. She landed gracefully in her ballet flats, while I almost rolled my ankle despite my practical boots.

I put the duffel bag on the ground for her clothes and started digging a narrow ditch near one of the walls of the pit. She watched me, frowning, as I clumsily scooped packed chunks of the clay to the side.

"Are you sure you're alright? I usually dig it myself," she said.

"I'm not going to let you dig your own hole if I'm here," I replied, spending all my effort on not sounding winded as I worked. I stuck the shovel in the ground, embarrassed that I was probably only about halfway there. "What did you usually do, anyways?"

"I'd park the car in the long-term lot near the bus stop and then walk a mile down the road to the woods, and go as far in there as I could. Pull as much dirt on top of me as I could by myself, hope I was up before sunrise, you know."

I frowned, picking up the shovel again. It was painful to imagine her like that, the loneliness of her rigorous, perfect routine, inside the secret that had to be managed in solitude that was her whole life. I didn't turn around to look at her face. "That sounds really risky. Like, your car never got stolen? No one was ever hunting back there?"

"I guess I was lucky," she said. "Plus once you're down there, gunshots and boots are both pretty loud."

I glanced down at my own feet, letting my arms go slack and the shovel hang in front of me.

"Well, sorry if I keep you from having sweet dreams," I said.

She smiled, looking down to size herself up against the hole. "It's fine. I'll be happy to hear you walking away."

My palms began to feel raw, like the skin had already decided to break out in blisters, but at last what I'd dug seemed sufficient. Jess stepped out of her shoes, rolled her stockings down her legs, unzipped her skirt and let it fall. She moved without a sense of modesty, or even feeling slightly cold in the mild night, with the unselfconsciousness of an animal. I could tell a mild torpor, the strange mood I had found Mollie in, half-buried in Martin's backyard, was already taking effect. Jess began to look tired, a bit absent, but still not so far off from how she came home after work. She lifted her blouse over her head, mechanically undid her bra and pulled down her underwear. I took each item of clothing as she removed it, feeling the dwindling warmth against my hand before I dropped it into the bag. The almost unnaturally smooth shapes of her body underneath her clothes stood out against the rough, exposed soil. I wanted to press her against that wall and kiss her, but I felt shy and she seemed only half there. I took her hand and helped her down into the hole, reaching down to help stretch her legs out.

"Are you alright?" I asked, once she was lying flat in the ditch. It looked much shallower with her body inside.

"Yeah. Amy, it'll be okay."

I crouched down next to her, trying not to cry and wanting to lay my body on top of hers, let the earth take us both, sleep underground forever.

"I'm really freaked out," I said. I laid myself flat out on the dirt, reaching over the lightly packed ledge. She held my hand to her chest.

"You'll do it, you'll pull it off," she said, her gaze tilting up towards the moon. "I do feel a little lonely, though."

She was trying to keep me from leaving. As long as I had my skin against hers, it felt so possible that a horde of her fellow extraterrestrials could appear and take this whole town, the Targets and Longhorn Steakhouses, the dilapidated nuclear towers and gutted warehouses, the stupidity and boredom, all between their mandibles and crush it, pulp it, reform it into something else. A place where there were more of them than us.

I wasn't quite them, but I had never felt like 'us' either.

"Hey Jess, do you wanna," I trailed off, squeezing her arm gently. She was quiet, her eyes half-closed and my stomach sank, wondering if she was gone, or *gone*-gone, already. I slid off the ledge and climbed on top of her in the ditch, propping myself up on one arm and using the other to feel her forehead. Her body felt uncannily cool, like it hadn't been alive in the first place. Still, as I leaned in, stretching the warmth of my bare neck up towards her face, I heard a strange sound, like rustling leaves, or hands working a head of lettuce apart. Her face began to split, opening vertically from the centre of her lips down to her chin. There was that sharp smell again. I could turn my face and sink my teeth into the strips of parted flesh, like salad bar slices of pale mushrooms. My breath caught in my throat, but I lowered myself closer.

"What?" Her eyes blinked a few times, responding as if my voice was only reaching her as an echo down a long tunnel, despite her own sounding so close, like it was being whispered through a tissue-paper screen. She looked up at me, as if she was expecting me to screw up my face in disgust. Even with her chin and neck splitting open she was more beautiful to me than ever.

"I was thinking you could, you know. Take some of me. For the road."

Her body shuddered underneath me, hesitating, but knowing from my offer that it would connect a circuit of shared desire between us. Instead of how it had violently shot out of Mollie — a last resort, grasping for some form of self-defence — I watched as the spine gradually slid out from where Jess' neck had been, covered in dripping, dewy bristles and coming to a thin, hollow tip. Where I had fumbled before, I felt unambiguous, immense carnal desire on her part, now. For once she was begging for me.

I lowered myself onto the point, my whole body tensing. The drops of venom from the hairs made my skin go numb and my mind hazy and loose before the spine pressed in. There was only a gentle push, and then something of my own flesh giving way. Jess winced with effort as her hand shot towards the centre of my back, easing me against her as my elbow started to wobble. It didn't feel like the spine was going in deeper, but that it was splitting inside me, becoming the veins and muscle and nerve, and at the base of the spine, something as gentle as a cat's tongue dipping into a saucer of milk played in the stream of my heartbeat. I lay on top of her, our bodies flattened together and slightly mismatched. I worried about leaving scuffs on her with my boots.

I tried to screw my eyes open for a last look at Jess' face as it was. As she fed at my neck her eyes rolled back, not in pleasure or as a petulant teenager, more like the learned gesture for trying to hold in tears so that you don't ruin your makeup. I remembered that I never found out if she actually produced tears, and felt like an asshole for not knowing, and for leaving her here, even though it was what we had agreed on — our desperate play at a new way to live.

She pulled back from my neck, the stinger sliding out with only an inanimate tugging sensation, no pain. I touched my fingers to the side of my neck, which felt fleshy and indented, like someone had stuck their thumb into me and I was an overripe peach. My stomach pitched forward in my gut, I didn't recognise the wound as my own at first. I rolled on to my side and tried to sit myself up on the side of the hole.

"There. Part of me with you," I said, struggling to push myself up. Jessica was mostly inside of herself, still and respiring shallowly, a dribble of my blood running down her neck and between her breasts. "While I'm gone and taking care of the kids. And even after that, no matter what happens."

"It'll make me better," she said. "You're alright?"

"Yeah, I have a great immune system. I have the metabolism of a train furnace. I have to eat a ton and never exercise just to get chubby like this." I was babbling, puffing myself up, trying to get her to smile, to take a load off her mind before I had to bury her. Shakily, I had pulled myself almost upright.

She wiped her bloody neck and mandibles with the back of her hand as the spine receded and took the slurry of my biological matter into her body. Up close, I could see fine golden hairs between the glossy black curves of her jaws catching light in the dark, gone orange from blood speckles that sprayed from and ran down the stinger, collecting in seams where shell and skin met. She looked, almost longingly, at the reddish-black streak that ran from the back of her wrist up to the root of her middle finger, then let it rest on the ground. I flexed my knees hard and stood at the edge of the ditch, feeling lightheaded, but the panic of my blood pumping, freshly hot from my body sensing the intrusion and strange venom, kept me on my feet. Jess seemed to be listening for my small, rapid breaths.

"There's a handkerchief in my skirt pocket," she said. "Don't press too hard. It'll clot fast." And then she was asleep. I stood over her, black drops of my own blood falling on to the dirt to the side of her half-assembled face. Half what she presented to me, half what was underneath, though one being false or the other being real didn't seem to matter — it was all her.

I went over to the bag of her clothes and checked the slit pocket of the skirt. The handkerchief was neatly folded, but in my hand it spread out like a languid ghost. I thought of my father, always offering me the rumpled one from his pocket when I was obnoxiously sniffing boogers back up into my face. And then I grew up. I touched the cloth to my neck and held it there until I stopped feeling new streaks of blood running along my collarbone, soaking the collar of my shirt.

I wondered if Martin felt like this when they'd started out. Now he could use the shovel to throw the dirt back onto Mollie's body, everything except her face, but had he once looked down at her and wanted to scoop and mound every last bit of dirt with his bare hands? It moved me that way. I must have been caked with blood and hard clay, hobbling around in a squat, pushing the dirt onto her gently. It seemed like it would have been easy when I started, but my hands were so small. Eventually I did it, my knees and ankles creaking with exhaustion, and I wanted to fall asleep on top of the small mound of soil her body displaced.

I couldn't. This was only the start, and it had been more work than I had imagined. In the moment I had talked myself up, though I knew she could see through me, even with the torporous state setting in. In certain ways I could be grown up and brave but my heart was the same, the kid that when shadows started to close in — God or Mayan prophecies or math tests or the terrorists or the new millennium or black holes or nukes or your mom or your own sense of wrongness in the world — just wanted it all to stop.

I imagined myself like an unplugged appliance in these moments, fantasising about the ability to switch off completely. The first time I tried to explain it, my mother told me to get in the car and drove me past the hospital, punishment and threat in one. "Do you really want to kill yourself?" She was ready to shut me away until the problem was solved, even though she had misunderstood it. Later, significantly toned down but presented to a therapist whose scrutiny also felt like a sort of imprisonment I was begging for parole from, my explanation evoked a concerned frown, a sharp check from the pen, passing me a card printed with a phone number underneath. I noted with irony the phrase "It's good to talk." She repeated a dry, practised statement, "You know, if you are serious about this, I do have to report it."

That was the end of trying to talk about it. To call that feeling suicidal didn't even crack the lid of it. The more my life opened up, the happier I was, the more this longing for a void, for deep, subterranean sleep was provoked by the thought of it all vanishing, of screwing up or getting trapped in some old, childish fear that ate up my mind. But Jessica could understand. I could see the tenderness in her own eyes at the inflexibility of mine and every human life, that she would give a part of herself to step in and alter this inevitability, even on a temporary basis. She would have let me sleep on top of her, there, under the earth, head rested in her blood and venom-dripped breast, if it wouldn't have suffocated me, my poor defenceless body that couldn't even go without breath. It was a tragedy to her that we couldn't do that for each other, that she couldn't alleviate this pain of continuousness, but there was so much left that we could do. I let myself cry again in the privacy I had leaning against the loose dirt wall of the foundation pit, since it would probably be my last chance to, for a while. Then, with the clarity that comes up after a heavy, wrenching sob, I pushed myself forward.

I grabbed the duffel bag of Jessica's clothes, picked the shovel up in my stinging palms, climbed up the slope out of the pit and paced along the edges of the lots, cutting through the high grass back to Jess' house. It felt like every distant orange light, left on in the neat lines of houses, had some pinprick of consciousness tucked inside it, watching me. My vision blurred with dizziness and tears, and didn't sense, among the unfriendly windows, the red lights gathering on the horizon, until I was surrounded by an unnatural glow.

They were closer now, and I could get a better sense of the character of the light and heat they gave off. It felt old as hell, dry and roasting, like a slowly depleting red giant. Ancient, both outside and bigger than human time, or even my more paranoid estimations of Jess' or Mollie's lifespan. I knew now why seeing them so close, low on the horizon, had scared the shit out of Cecil — a vision he received as both personal and cosmically momentous, something he wanted to keep preciously and terrifyingly private.

The lights watched me from all sides like a conspiracy, mutely waiting for my questions, though I knew they wouldn't answer. What were the lights? A hallucination on my part or some sort of genuine manifestation of supernatural or explainable qualities, or a symbol, or—

I threw the bag down on the wet grass, standing still, considering, as if I could just ask this of them. What had happened to Cecil's father? Maybe it was nothing, he had 'just disappeared'. Cecil's fantasy about it was a red herring. But his absence was also relevant, the precondition for all of this.

Under the dry heat of the red light my skin felt persecuted and hot. And my own father? Same as the above? I thought about the way dad would cynically repeat the most common dismissals of the unknown, 'swamp gas', in his ironic tone, and here it was now, the inexplicable, in front of me. I couldn't dismiss any of this. He would want me to look directly at whatever situation I ended up in, even without understanding.

I had taken it out on Jess before I could really think about it, how the pain at my father seeming to blow past me and out of my life, and the degree to which I understood his impulse, even envied the stubborn way he managed to get away with it, had always been butting heads inside of me. What he saw must have jolted through him, an intuitive understanding that unfurled in the mind like a reflex: *These aliens, no, the alien in general, was a medium that briefly, conditionally, allowed impossible things to happen.* Impossible to stop as an orgasm or sneeze, it could jump beyond the limitations of twins or kin, generating connections that had their own internal logic while retaining some randomness. More like lovers, maybe, but lovers distributed out all over, in the way that you could fall in love with anyone, and how that could change everything. Now I was confronted with this understanding too, in manic, over-exerted reality, tinged with a dose of alien narcotic. I had to consider that I knew I was following his exact path now; I was never going to stay.

The heat radiating through my skin eased, they had retreated, now no more than tail lights. I hoisted the bag back over my shoulder, forcing myself on.

♦♦♦

Back inside the house, I snuck up to Jess' room, ignoring the slight stirring I heard as I passed Cecil's room. I closed the door behind me and turned the feeble locking mechanism, then tossed the bag on the bed and looked at myself in the mirror on top of her dresser. My clothes were wrecked with dirt and blood, and the entire side of my neck was tender and bruised under the puncture hole. I thought, if I went home like this, my mom would finally absolutely flip. Watching myself in the mirror, I peeled the clothes off and kicked them under the bed.

In the bathroom, I turned the shower on high and hot. The houses on this street were so built to spec it was something I could do blind. The smell of drying blood sloughing off my skin was also familiar, disgusting as ever, but eventually the water going down my calves went from reddish brown to pink to clear. I ran a handful of Jess' shampoo through my hair, almost choking up again at the smell of her. I felt afraid to scrub at my body, and just let the hot water beat on it until it felt like there couldn't be anything else left, only surface.

Experimentally, with my tender, pink fingers, I touched the side of my neck again. It stung and at the same time felt insulated by several numbed out layers of flesh. I looked at my palms, where small white blisters were beginning to form, and swept a finger between my legs, like I was testing the ability of my body to feel and respond to its environment, like I had lost faith in this feedback loop. Even though my fingers came back clinging to each other with slime, I felt sated and distant from how this would usually make me feel. I put my hand under the shower head for a few seconds and then stepped out, padding across the tile floor to the towel rack to pat myself dry with one of Jess' fluffy, thick towels, and stood in front of the mirror again. The side of my neck looked purple, like someone had throttled it several times. I winced and looked in a side drawer for gauze or a bandage to put over the worst of it, and found the end of a meagre roll, just enough.

Tucking the ends in, I studied myself. I looked tired and distressed, and found myself unable to change my face. Nothing I could think of at this point served that sort of superficial, external display of placid happiness.

I took Jess' clothes out of the bag. The skirt wouldn't fit me, but surely I could find some sweatpants somewhere in her dresser. Burying my face in the blouse, I could still smell her, not a rich, human smell, but something weightless and faraway, like clean, unlined paper, leaves, crisp air, pollen. My nose was wrinkling, I could feel snot kicking up. I shoved the clothes back in the bag and under the bed, and dug around in the dresser until I was able to find a pair of pajama pants and a sweatshirt that only smelled of detergent. Then I looked at the envelope of cash, credit cards and documents she had left on the end of the bed. Only a week.

The doorknob jerked ineffectively as someone outside tried it. I jumped, then took a few seconds to work my breathing back down. It was tempting to ignore it, see if whichever child it was would just give up, but I thought, Jess wouldn't do that, would she? I sat on the edge of the bed, too anxious to move. Soft footsteps went away after a moment, and I relaxed, until I heard the back door open and close, matter-of-factly, as if it wasn't nearly one in the morning. I pushed myself up, fumbling with the lock release on the doorknob and almost lost my footing on the steps, the socks I'd found slipping out from under me.

There was no time to look for shoes, so the socks clung to my feet, getting damp from dew and collecting grass clippings as I ran out over the lawn and after Cecil's slight, wandering shadow. He moved with a dazed quality, the light seemed warm and surreal. One side of my head throbbed with a headache.

When Cecil reached the edge of the dug-out basement, he hopped down, as he had already done so many times over the summer, but this time it made me yelp after him in anxiety. As soon as the sound escaped my mouth, he disappeared over the edge of the pit, indifferent to whether I had said anything at all. I reached the edge and looked down. He had landed on his feet on a sloping ramp that led down to the bottom of the pit, looking up from just below my feet.

"Hey!" I shouted down to him and extended my hand. He looked at me, seeming unsure of where he was and why I was reaching down. I could see the mound Jess slept under, down the ramp and towards a far corner of the pit, and extended my hand more urgently, knowing I couldn't bear to let him look at it, though for his sake or mine I wasn't sure. "Come on, let me help you up."

Taking his small hand, marked with a few scrapes and smears of dirt, to hoist him out of the pit, I realised our strange connection was the nature of being an alien. Regardless of whether I had children or not, there would be children like me, unmoored from a quaint hometown or comfortable ease with biological kin. Despite the world we would find each other.

"What's going on, where's my mom," he said flatly when I strained to place him safely on the grass. I put my hands on his shoulders, studying his drowsy face as I patted him up and down to check for any injuries, testing that he responded with awareness to touch.

"Why are you here?"

"Mom's away on the work stuff, remember? I'm staying here. I heard the door open. Are you alright? Were you sleepwalking?"

"Oh yeah," he said. "I heard a noise. What happened to your neck?"

I tried to avoid the question by indulging speculation on the prior statement.

"Really? What did it sound like?"

"Like a hum, or something. So I thought I had to look outside, in case..." He trailed off, feeling embarrassed to talk about his lights on the horizon again.

"Well, I was just running the shower, so it might have been that," I said, offering him cover. He looked at me with a degree of confusion that made me worried he wouldn't believe anything I'd say, after something as benign as that. "What?" I said.

"Why were you taking a shower at night?"

I shrugged. "I like to shower at night. When you're an adult you can make weird choices like that, if you feel like it."

"Seems like a waste," he said. Of time, of showering, of the capability to choose, not specified. He turned, looking back towards the house, and I walked with him, still holding on to his hand.

"Hey, are you worried," I asked, as we crossed an empty lot. "About your mom being away, or anything like that."

He paused, standing barefoot in the grass, stopping to yawn.

"I don't know. It's probably something important. And it's not that long."

"Yeah," I said. "That's a good attitude."

When we got back into the house, he rubbed his feet on the mat next to the back door until most of the grass clippings and muck clinging to them came off. I peeled off my own socks, dirty and soaked, leaving them in the laundry room. We walked to the top of the stairs together, Cecil nodded and turned down the hallway towards his own room, leaving me alone to return to Jessica's.

I flopped onto the bed, feeling like I had gotten away with something. I had miraculously navigated between the rocks of failure on one side and suspicious competence on the other. Despite this, I also had a suffocating feeling that if we stayed in the house it would only get harder to maintain the facade that Jess was away for work, that everything else should otherwise proceed as normal. I looked at the envelope on the far end of the bed again, thinking. The way we had discussed the plan never assumed I would stay in the house the whole time. Jess had said to me, "I'm giving you everything," and she had. With that had to come some degree of freedom.

I let my arms hang over the edge of the bed and pulled my jeans out from where I had hidden them, fishing my phone out of my pocket. I looked up the site of a nearby bus company, studying the destination list until birds started singing outside and the window panes let in grey sheets of light. Around 4 AM I'd made my decision, but I lay there awake with my mind still tracing the routes and nodes. I waited until 6:30 AM to call Martin. He sounded like he had just woken up and spoke softly.

"Hey," he said. "You alright?"

"Yeah," I hung on the line, waiting a long time either to order my thoughts or for him to go on. Eventually I said, "I had to bury Jess last night."

"Oh. I had a feeling," he replied.

"Can you swing by in, like, two hours? We just need to go somewhere."

He went quiet, and I could hear him shifting his weight around on a creaking bed frame.

"Sure, I should still be able to get in to work on time, if it's not that far."

"Thank you, it's just twenty minutes away," I said. I hung up and went down the stairs to make myself coffee in the glass pitcher, which rang gently in my hands when I set it upright on the counter. I took the full mug and stood outside, leaning against the siding of the house, peering down the street, waiting for my mother's car to pull out of the driveway. I finished the coffee, took the mug back inside and slipped into my own house.

It wasn't hard to pack a bag, since my own suitcases were still scattered on the floor of my bedroom. The process was always fast when I was driven: count days, count shirts, count underwear, take everything out of the bathroom, plus a cable for the phone. I dressed myself in my old clothes and dragged my own bag along with a spare on tiny, rickety wheels down the side of the road, back to Jess' house. Then I used the same system to throw the kids' clothes in the other bag while they gradually stirred awake.

"Okay, let's get breakfast," I said. "And pick out some stuff to bring along on the bus."

"School bus?" Susie asked.

"No, we're going on a trip. You'll see," I said. Cecil

watched me closely as Susie happily went about stuffing toys into a small tote.

♦♦♦

When Martin picked me up from Jess' house, it was less the arbitrary hour or the sudden request that bothered him, but what I was wearing.

"This has to be a joke," he said.

The outfit I had assembled for travelling consisted of one of my good impression blouses, neat wool slacks that were already too warm and one of Jess' silk scarves, jauntily tied around my neck. My hair was held into a fashion I concluded was as close as I could get to something a young mother would ask for deliberately, using a handful of the dull gold bobby pins I had purchased from Target weeks ago. I was holding two bags and the kids were with me, looking bored and sleepy. I loaded them into the back seat while Martin stacked the bags in the trunk. Cecil clutched his tablet, headphones already over his ears, while Susie soon had the heavy unresponsiveness of the unconscious. I wound around to the front seat, getting in next to Martin.

"Seriously, thanks for this," I said.

"It's whatever," he replied. "Or, like, last chance to back out."

"What do you mean?" I asked, looking back at the kids. Cecil was frowning, letting the tablet sit on top of his thin knees. Susie leaned against the door as if she had been chucked into the car from the opposite direction.

"It seems more complicated than just staying in the house." Martin had, accidentally, gotten to the root of the issue. It was anxiety-inducing and possibly foolish to travel, but it felt haunted, like a trap, to stay. I felt chased out of it. "How long did she tell you it was this time?"

"A week. And she took out some cash, so I thought we could use a change of scenery," I said. Martin laughed.

"I can't believe you're responsible for two children. It almost feels like I should call the cops."

"Come on, I'm not that awful."

"Sure, maybe," he conceded. I looked again at the kids in the back seat as he started driving. Cecil quickly broke eye contact with me and flicked on his tablet.

"Do you need gas money, by the way. Or, like, just for your time?" Martin considered this when I brought it up.

"It'd be nice," he said after a few moments. "But I also feel like I owe you. The stuff with Mollie, you know."

I tilted my chin up, curiously. I couldn't tell whether this meant a sort of embarrassed apology for what I had seen, or a way of thanking me for shutting down his impulsive behaviour. I was glad I could still rely on him, even if I couldn't think of him as mine, in that way, anymore. My feelings were not quite like a dog returning to its vomit, even though I had been carefully prepared by childhood faith to feel that way. I didn't regret anything, afterwards, when it hadn't worked out. I'd done it all because I wanted to. There had been a time when sex between us had been somehow generative, but the desperation to grab and hold that, fumbling around for change that had fallen under the car seats, would only prove that we couldn't recover it. We would have to do the harder thing now — learn to be friends without jealousy or resentment.

"Things going better, then?" I asked.

"It's still complicated," he said.

"Yeah, how can it not be, as you'd say."

He looked in the reverse mirror at the back seat to make sure Susie was asleep and Cecil had his headphones on before continuing.

"What kind of deal did you strike with Jess, though? Money? I didn't think you wanted to stay here long."

I glanced at him, driving. The roads were mostly empty and he was acting nonchalant, but I could tell that he was closely watching my response.

"I think our situations aren't so different." After I said this, with a teasing tone as rich as I could manage, I looked at Martin, trying to catch his eye, all of my effort put into conveying the crude implications so that I wouldn't have to say them out loud.

"Really?" He lowered his voice. "I thought you just looked at her like an insane person. You really can't control your face. I didn't think it was like *that*."

"Well, surprise," I said. Martin stopped at an intersection, but paused to look at me for a long time before pressing on the gas again.

"You can look like you're in love with anyone, given the right circumstances, but in the wrong ones you can't fake a single thing."

I still looked at him, sometimes, and only behind his back, like that, but I said, "That's right," and glanced up into the rear view mirror to study myself.

Martin seemed to go quiet, getting unhappier as we drew closer to the bus stop. I thought about asking what was bothering him, but it didn't seem like my place. I wouldn't blame him if my imposition was most of what was wrong.

"You told me how Mollie told you," I said, after a

while. "But not how it made you feel. Did you pity her?"

"Do you pity Jess?" He asked back.

I was silent. Of course I didn't.

"I dunno. I respected her. I felt really sad for her, being pushed around by the world like that, having no one place to stay." He looked thoughtful, choosing his next words slowly, trailing off. "I thought, if I could give that to her, then..."

I swallowed a lump rising in my throat, feeling lonely again. Martin hadn't offered me that, but it was equally true that I never would have taken it. I wasn't jealous. Jess represented an alternate type of freedom, idealised at first, but now obviously beholden to its own practical limitations and problems. She was inside the earth now, coming up with her own resolution that could cut through our dilemma, or at least make it bearable. I had to trust.

The traffic closer to town began to clog the streets as the daily commute from the suburbs began. We got held up at a four-way stop, where cars from all other directions greedily careened through out of turn. They were only going where they went almost every day of their waking lives, surely, but repetition had made them willing marks for, then numb, to the risks and bad wagers they had made part of their routine. I felt the frustration coming off Martin like a vapour filling the car. For a second I forgot about the kids in the back, worrying about Jessica, my own home life (in which I would soon have a degree of explaining to do that I was not at all prepared for), and instead I was myself before all this began. How often have I been in the passenger seat while Martin drove? I had the same feeling now as I did then: I wished he could be less angry. Not just because he could be an asshole to me when he was, though that was part of it, but because it felt like his anger was shot through with something like physical pain. It put blinders on him the same way that a migraine or a toothache or period cramps are all you can think about when they happen.

He held off on laying on the horn for the benefit of the kids, instead saying bluntly, to no one in particular, "So this is it?"

"I'm coming back," I said, after a moment. "It's just a few days." He glanced at me, like he hadn't expected me to respond and looked back to the road to pull through the intersection. The cars were going consistently now, evenly spaced. Everyone could take a breath.

"Yeah, isn't that what you said in high school?" Martin said. "Even I heard you didn't even come home for Christmas freshman year. Your mom was so pissed."

"I'm obviously not going to disappear if I have two kids with me," I said.

"Right," he said, like he was dismissing the comment rather than being convinced by it. "This is so like you, though. Why can't you just stay put?"

I let myself slump down in the seat. "I don't know. It freaks me out, to just be waiting around."

"You were always like that, body here, brain somewhere else. Or at least thinking about it."

I wanted to say that he had opened the capability to think about life that way, in me. Of course, he hadn't been the only one, but the first, the formative one. Instead I said, "I don't think that makes us so different." I shifted in the seat, already feeling tired from my long night and lulled by the gentle sound of the car running. Martin looked out over the steering wheel, then pulled his mouth into a slight frown, angling the car towards the right exit.

"It feels like an accident. Like why did we ever get together in the first place?" He replied. "Sometimes I look at you or think of what you're up to and feel like it was a fluke, we should have stayed two people who didn't know each other."

"Do you really think that?" I asked. It made me feel miserable, more than being rejected or even unceremoniously dumped, for him to consider undoing everything between us in the first place. I would have just looked across the field during gym class one day, at the track kids practising, made eye contact with one and contorted my face into a comical, self-deprecating grimace, and that would have been the beginning and end of it. Or not even that? But he had said it experimentally, like he wanted to see how it would make me feel before he decided if he believed it. I hoped my face, whatever it was doing, could achieve the same sort of instant transmission it had at one point.

"I don't know. No, it's just something that occurred to me a few times." He fiddled with the indicator. We were really close to the bus stop.

"I thought about it a lot," I said. "And I'm glad we at least talk to each other again."

"And I drive you around everywhere, still."

"Yeah, still." I said.

Through the car window, I looked out at the woods and my eyes would try, as they always did, to focus on the gaps in the trees that opened up to the side of the road as we rushed past. Ever since I was a kid, I always held out for the possibility that, in the receding undergrowth, I'd see a rustling bush, the passing shadow of a bigfoot or hoopsnake. When I recognised where we were I wanted to sob, but waited as Martin pulled the car closer to the side of the road, where a sidewalk led up to the bus station, and then stepped out of the passenger door without another word. While I was helping the kids out of the back seat, Martin put on the parking brake, got out and unloaded the bags from the trunk. He did it automatically, even though the car wasn't in an actual parking lane, just on the shoulder of the road, like he had to. It felt like an unusually tender gesture on his part.

"Good luck, Mrs. Mom," he said, handing me one of the bags.

"Oh yeah right, I'm still just a babysitter," I said. "I'll call you when I'm back."

♦♦♦

The bus we boarded for Ocean City would drop us off at a non-beach-front hotel done up like a faded Patrick Nagel drawing, all thick layers of old paint, magentas and deep greens that had gone dull teal and dusty pink. The online listing showed an exhausted blue parrot in the lobby and a pool. There was a dinosaur themed mini golf place on the same street, a boardwalk cluttered with vulgar T-shirts and every type of fried food further down, and infinite souvenir warehouses. Where easier to occupy two children? I was aware that it was the most basic, clueless move, and a déclassé one at that, but going to a city that had an art museum, I worried, would make me too sad.

When we trundled onto the tour bus, the retirees aboard hardly looked up, and I was naturalised as the slightly irresponsible, but ultimately unremarkable guardian of the two children, carrying bags too big, finding our seats too slowly. The seats went in pairs, so I sat with Susie on one side, who for once was largely occupied with watching the countryside and highway strip malls go by at the window, and monitored Cecil, who kept his head down next to an older woman, staring at his tablet but only half of the time doing anything with it.

For the first half hour, I sat staring at my phone screen in my lap; my mother had given me a bit of a longer leash, pointedly not grilling me about my whereabouts if I wasn't home, but this absence would need to be explained, and better if I was the one to initiate it. Still, I didn't know what to say, and instead counted cows and horses with Susie most of the way.

We arrived in the evening. Filing out of the bus, everyone collected their bags and walked to their destination along the linear clutch of hotels, each with neon signs and names like Dunes Manor, Princess and Carousel. The air smelled like sea salt, with emerging undertones of sewage, but was blasted away with yellow artificial light, gritty carpet and chlorine as soon as we entered the hotel. We lugged our bags to the front desk and the teenage boy in a cheap-looking suit jacket running the check-in openly stared at my breasts, which felt unguarded under the flimsy, clinging fabric of the top.

Check-in was conducted with almost monosyllabic, purely functional statements, but I started feeling cold, almost shaking with nerves as I came up on using Jess' credit card. Not my Jess, it belonged to third-hand Jess, the credit card of a woman who had hit the road, suddenly, like I had, to consider a different life. Had she taken out a huge chunk of cash too, when she left? I had most of the money my Jess had taken out of the bank in one of the bags as an emergency measure, but felt protective and embarrassed about it, like a cat would curl around an injury. I wondered where the other Jess was now, when exactly the switch took place, had the children noticed anything, could they realise something so improbable, were things kind of normal to them now?

Not *now*-now, I knew, checking into the hotel and taking on a greater significance in their lives as a sort of impostor. This was profoundly not-the-usual. Cecil grimaced, still not sold on the appeal of a beach vacation and Susie flopped herself over one of the bags. While I glanced away, the card transaction went through and the kid slid us a plastic key card.

"Okay, is there, like, a continental breakfast?" I asked, expecting more.

"Nope," he said, looking kind of put off. Another expense.

We found the room, down a far hallway with a small window, two twin beds and a cot. Susie immediately hopped onto the cot, causing it to shake and let out a whining creak.

"Can we get some food already," Cecil said.

"Yeah, give me a sec, then we'll go."

I unzipped my own bag and grabbed some of the clothes I had packed that were more typical: black t-shirt, black jeans, though the cringeworthy slip-on earth mother sandals I had worn to get here would have to suffice for footwear. I changed in the bathroom, after shooing Susie, who was testing the faucets, out. In the mirror I slid the bobby pins out of my hair, which had gotten really shaggy, and looked at myself. I could pass for an older sister like this, maybe. I tentatively undid Jess' scarf and pressed the gauze underneath to the side. It was hard with brown, crusted coagulant, but the wound underneath had healed at a speed that seemed superhuman. If I patted some of Jess' foundation over it, it could probably pass as a bad hickey. I did, resurfacing memories of how makeup always seemed to sit awkwardly on top of my face, like a scummy oil slick on a pond, and then stepped out of the bathroom to check the kids' reactions.

"Ew, your neck," Cecil observed.

We ate at an Italian restaurant that seemed to cook everything in the same tomato sauce and served sludgy iced tea. The waitress was startlingly young, like the clerk at the hotel who'd stared at my tits. Unlike him she had the simultaneous naïveté and jadedness that pervaded holiday towns; boredom with the knowledge that the food is clearly bad but the feeling that nothing she could do would change it, even where to start would be a mystery. In a pact of recognition, which reminded me that getting away from my own predicament was only conditional, temporary, I told her the food was great when she asked and left a big tip.

I made myself think: it's fine. It even started to feel like I was turning the evening around as I furnished Susie and Cecil each with a funnel cake of their own and we walked the boardwalk in the twilight, carefully steering away from drunk groups of teenagers and crabby looking retired couples alike. We reached a point where a wooden ramp led down to a quiet stretch of beach, and, kicking off my shoes, I said, "Come on."

Cecil was trying to walk over the sand in his sneakers, though Susie got the right idea, copying me. She ran up to the edge of the water, just as it began to pull away, and screeched at a washed up clump of seaweed.

"Don't go in," I warned. "Or, just dip your toes in. Don't run far."

"Okay!" Susie crouched to poke a finger into the damp sand and Cecil waddled to a standstill next to me, still wearing his sneakers and looking sour.

"It's the ocean," I said.

"I know what it is," he said. "What's going on?"

I thought of what Martin said to me in the car, how sure he'd seemed that I wouldn't come back. Or maybe, that I'd come back so different that even our distant, clumsy points of reference for each other wouldn't mean anything anymore. When I'd quickly made up my mind and told the kids to pack, I was, of course, only considering getting out of town for the week that Jessica would be underground. The house behind me seemed haunted, or maybe too emptied out, too lonely. I didn't think seriously about what Martin had said. Now, standing at a crass, commercialised strip of ocean, it did begin to feel like a rehearsal of an eventual, glorious escape. How far could we go? What could we get away with? I'd lie in bed next to Jess, warm the length of her new, soft body with mine, and whisper the answers I'd managed to find.

"I just thought we could go somewhere," I said. "No particular reason not to."

Cecil shrugged, still rooted in his sneakers. Oh well, I thought. A whole week to try to get him to have some fun. I looked out over the ocean, squinting to make out the fuzzy horizon in the low light. A tripod and an old camcorder, if I could find one in the beach town shops, wouldn't take too much out of the stack of cash in my bag. I wanted it, not just to scan the misty horizon for some austere, magnificent long shot. I wanted to capture Susie kicking clumps of seaweed too, with Cecil moping off to the side, banal home videos, because I knew Jessica would want to see. I wanted to see for her, in the dark underground, but for the other Jess as well; your children can move over the earth, walking along a small stretch of coastline, safe, fed and not bothered by anything.

I was trying to break myself of my magical thinking, so I let myself imagine returning to a house repeated in the mould of my own family home, but inhabited by something different, something always changing. Jess would be there, beaming and new again. She would open her jaws and I would fall into her lovely night-black mandibles with the fine golden hairs. But it felt too neat to be true. Enough time spent underground, with my blood on her lips, and we could become something bigger than cavernous foyers, than two car garages, than refurbished basements and skylights. At the edge of the ocean, even though it was sentimental, I knew I could sink my hands, arms up to my elbows and all over me, into a universe that would expand beyond the known and my narrow radius of predictions.

A small red light dipped in and out of view, probably a ship in the dim distance, but I imagined it as an aloof observer monitoring the situation.

What do you think, Jess? I don't know if I like that fantasy very much, of hiding out in some big, boxy house with you. I wanted to be something that could only be vomited out of that predetermined little life where I grew up, because when I was inside it, it was me who felt claustrophobic and queasy. Can you hear me all the way out here? Can we remake ourselves in such a way? I think you are as much of Earth as I am. The alien is the antagonist of the veil of coherence modestly placed over throbbing life, throbbing like the hole torn out of my neck. Jess, my Jess, and that Jess, can you hear this far? Have you ever been buried near the ocean? If I had found your body in a pile of wood frass and dead skin I would still embrace it. No matter what comes out of the dirt, I will love it. Clean beautiful life disgusts me. I want this whole world to blow chunks.

REFERENCES

[1] Kraus, Chris. *Where Art Belongs.* (Semiotext(e), 2011), p. 155-156

ACKNOWLEDGEMENTS

Thank you to Stephen, who lived with me through every stage of this novel's development, and to Caeth, Candle, Dino, Freya, Kate, Mariken, Nat, Rumpel, Sean, Tom and Vi for their feedback and encouragement.

ABOUT THE AUTHOR

Em Reed is a writer originally from Central Pennsylvania and currently based in Glasgow, whose essays have previously appeared in *Murdered Futures: A Cronenberg Fanzine*, *The Serving Library Annual* and *Real Life*. This is their first novel. Their website is **emreed.net**

THE CREDITS

Creating a book is a massive team effort. Knight Errant and Em Reed would like to thank everyone who worked behind the scenes to make *More Bugs* happen.

Managing Director and Editor

Nathaniel Kunitsky

Publishing Assistant

Friday Schoemaker

Creative Director

Lenka Murová

Project Assistant

Angelica Curzi

Cover Art Illustrator

Lily Blakely www.lilybla.co.uk

OTHER WORK BY THE PRESS

F, M or Other: Quarrels with the Gender Binary

Queering the Map of Glasgow

Vicky Romeo Plus Joolz by Ely Percy

Love, Pan-Fried by Gray Crosbie

Tamlin by Aven Wildsmith

The False Sister by Briar Ripley Page

Andrion by Alex Penland

The Child of Hameln by Max Turner

ABOUT THE PRESS

Knight Errant Press is a queer micro press based in Falkirk, Scotland, established in 2017.

We have a focus on LGBTQIA+ intersectional storytelling and creators, and work within most genres and formats.

Showcasing new and emerging writers' careers is our ambition, and we strive to find 2 or 3 works a year to bring to the world.

You can find out more about us at www.knighterrantpress.com